I0652803

LADY OF THE HARBOR

A Jack Stenhouse Mystery

ALSO BY FRANK A. RUFFOLO

Gabriel's Chalice

Tres Archangelis

Trihedral of Chaos

Jack Stenhouse Mysteries

Stuck in Traffick

Blue Falcon

10048

Xanthe Terra

Distruzione della Roccia

LADY OF THE HARBOR

A Jack Stenhouse Mystery

FRANK A. RUFFOLO

This is a work of fiction. Names, characters, and incidents are either products of the author's imagination or are used fictitiously. Certain events, locales, and business establishments are mentioned, but the characters and situations are imaginary.

LADY OF THE HARBOR, A Jack Stenhouse Mystery, by Frank A. Ruffolo

www.frankaruffolo.com

Printed in the United States of America

First Edition, April 2022

ISBN: 979-8-9860720-1-2 (printed version only)

LADY OF THE HARBOR

A Jack Stenhouse Mystery

CHAPTER ONE

Winter in the Big Apple can be daunting, really daunting at seven in the morning, even for James Whitaker, a twenty-year veteran of the National Park Service.

James has been at his job long enough to know that even though the swirling snow and fifteen-degree outside temperature are bad, it won't be much better once he enters the Lady of the Harbor. Through experience, he knows the steel girders and large copper plates inside the Statue of Liberty will protect him from the snow, but they'll do nothing against the cold. On the contrary, they'll welcome it.

The weather has no effect on the massive structure. For more than a century, Lady Liberty has stood silent guard over New York Harbor in all kinds of weather. However, James isn't made of copper and steel. He's flesh and blood, and he's cold.

Before entering the statue, James pulls his cap down low and tightens the scarf around his neck. He dreads the long climb ahead, but it's something he needs to do. Every day, a part of his job is to check the statue inside and out to make sure it's ready to welcome the stream of tourists that will visit his island. So he trudges forward.

James has made this climb so many times before that it's ingrained in his muscle memory. He no longer has to think about what he's doing; he inspects the metal undercarriage like he always does, while the rhythmic clanging of his steel-tipped boots smacks the metal steps as he goes. This familiar noise rumbling through Miss Liberty's bowels always makes him smile. For some reason, it reminds him of a bowl of bad chili.

When James reaches the statue's arm, an area closed to the public, he prepares himself for the rush of cold air he knows will greet him. Pulling at his scarf, he raises it over his nose and mouth, then opens the gateway to winter's fury.

While the sun plays peek-a-boo with the clouds, James gazes out at the iconic Manhattan skyline, even though he's seen it a thousand times. Thankfully, the snow squall is starting to abate, and the wind is beginning to ebb.

Alone at the top, James mumbles to himself through the layers of cloth over his mouth. "All right, time to get to work. How're you doing today, my lady?"

James gets ready to check the famous lamp, then gasps in shock. Lying under the torch is a frozen body.

The wizened park ranger looks at the body in shock for a long moment. When he recovers, his first thoughts are, *How the hell?* And *What the fuck?* Then, with his fingers fighting the cold, he retrieves a hand-held radio from his belt.

"Hey, Charlie!" he shouts into the dying wind. "We got a problem!"

CHAPTER TWO

In a dark Manhattan bedroom, Jack Stenhouse helps his wife, Didi, out of bed. She can't move well on her own anymore since she's more than nine months pregnant. "When is this going to end, Jack?" she asks plaintively. "We're already one week past due."

Jack kisses his wife's forehead, while keeping similar thoughts to himself. "You're doing great, babe," he says, trying to stay upbeat. "Keep the faith. That kid can't stay in there forever."

Jack is already dressed for work. Today, he's wearing a sports jacket over a gray turtleneck, black slacks, and his ever-present Tony Lama boots. Leaving Didi to herself, he goes into the kitchen, where he clatters around noisily.

After a while, he returns to the bedroom, announcing, "Coffee's made. You know you don't have to go to work today; Sonia can handle the store. Besides, your mom is coming in later."

Didi responds through the bathroom door, "I know, and Sonia's younger sister said she'd help for a while. I guess I can call her and tell her I won't be in."

Jack heads back to the kitchen as his cell phone rings. "Stenhouse," he answers. "Oh, damn! Okay, I'm on the way."

Jack peeks into the bathroom to find Didi staring at her belly in the mirror. "I gotta go, duty calls. Call me when your mom gets in. You know, your belly is bigger than your boobs."

Overnight, old man winter has once again made his mark on Manhattan. The roads are deplorable, so Jack's fifteen-minute drive to the tip of the island takes almost an hour.

At almost 8:30, he finally climbs out of his red 1968 Plymouth Road Runner, and shivers in the 29-degree weather. As he walks across Battery Park, he buttons up his black peacoat and puts on his mirrored shades, wondering if the sanitation department plowed his street yet.

"Mornin'," greet sergeants Burley and Gomez under leafless tree limbs, with a not-so-hot cup of coffee for Jack. "How's Didi today?"

"She looks like she's ready to explode," Jack replies, gratefully grabbing the magic liquid from Sergeant Gomez. "Where's Giancarlo?"

While the officers walk over to a harbor police patrol boat at the ferry pier, Sergeant Burley says, "She's stuck on Riverside. She said she'll be here in an hour, but who knows. I told her to meet us out there. The medical examiner and the CSI crew are already at the scene."

Aboard the patrol boat, Gomez comments, "All I heard was that park rangers found a dead body. Do either of you know where they found it?"

Jack's eyes always water in chilly air, so while he pulls his leather gloves from his peacoat pocket, he blinks to clear them. "Yeah," he says, wiping his eyes and looking out at Miss Liberty across the harbor. "It was on the torch deck."

While the boat skims across the water, Gomez and Burley stare at Jack, then at the Lady of the Harbor. In unison, they exclaim, "How the fuck did that happen?"

Jack replies with a shrug of his shoulders, then finishes the rest of his coffee.

Still at home, Didi drinks her morning coffee while she sits at the kitchen counter and absently rubs her belly. Unlike many others, Jack and Didi decided early in the pregnancy that they want to be surprised about the baby's sex; they don't want to know if they're having a boy or girl. Nonetheless, Didi is curious. And as she rubs, the baby kicks and seems to push her hand away. *Ha, it must be a boy*, she decides, making this the umpteenth time that she's changed her mind.

Just then, a sudden tsunami of pain envelopes her, and she wonders, *Is this it? Is it time? Or is it just another false alarm?* Didi clenches her fist against the pain and waits for it to fade.

When it's gone, she takes a deep breath and stares at her watch. "Mom should have landed at LaGuardia by now," she mumbles.

At Liberty Island, Jack follows Gomez and Burley up the intestinal tract of Miss Liberty while his Tony Lamas smack the metal steps. At the landing that splits the stairway from the head to the torch, he stops and eases himself down onto a bench. "Gotta rest for a minute," he tells the others.

When Jack catches his breath, they continue upward, and Sergeant John Burley opens the door to the outside. "Shit! It's freezing up here!" he complains loudly when the wintry air hits his face like a blow torch.

"Better cover your face," Gomez calls out, "or Jack Frost's gonna take a bite out of your nose!"

With his scarf raised, Hector Gomez walks over to the M.E., followed by Jack and John Burley.

"How the hell did it get up here?" Hector asks reflexively, looking down at the harbor more than one hundred feet below. Then, looking up, he asks, "Could they have dropped it from the air?"

"Hmm. If they did," replies John, "they'd have to make a perfect hit. There's not very much room up here."

Jack smirks, "It may have been an unlucky shot. I'm sure whoever did this didn't want it to land here."

Jack puts his gloved hands in his pockets, then walks over to Doctor Sally Gibson, a young medical examiner recently out of residency, who looks too pretty to be involved with dead bodies. "So, doc, what's up?" he quips to the brown-haired, blue-eyed forensic pathologist.

"We have a female in her late twenties, blue eyes and dyed red hair. She's partially frozen and covered with snow, so she must have been here overnight. I can't determine the exact time of death yet. There's some head trauma and a broken neck, but that could be from a fall. It's hard to imagine that anyone carried her all the way up here, so she may have been dropped from the air. I don't know if she was dead before the fall or if she died because of it. As you can see, she's only wearing slacks and a sweater, no overcoat or shoes, so they may have flown off on her way down. From the condition of the body, I think the fall may have been from about 1500 feet or so. Oh, and there's no ID."

Jack stares at the dead woman. "I guess we need to see if any security cameras show overnight activity. Let's go, guys. There's nothing more to look at here. I'll have Giancarlo accompany the body to the morgue."

As Jack and his team turn to leave, Doctor Gibson calls out, "Detective Stenhouse, she has a tattoo on her ankle. It's the logo for Hofstra University's athletic programs. There are two stylized lions, and it says, 'Hofstra Pride.'"

Jack turns back, and takes a picture of the victim. "Guess we need to cross-reference college records and yearbooks. Maybe we'll get lucky there."

Sergeants Burley and Gomez also take photos, then they all begin the long descent down the arm.

At the halfway mark, they come upon Giancarlo making her way up the stairs. "Geez, it's a long walk," she huffs. "Sorry, Jack. An SUV flipped over on Riverside Drive."

"No problem; shit happens," Jack replies. Then he takes off his gloves and looks back up the stairwell. "We got a young lady up there, thrown out of a plane, we think. She's adorning the deck under the torch. Stay with the M.E. and go with her to observe the autopsy. We got videotapes and college records to review."

Allison heads up the stairs, while the guys head down. At one of the rest stops, they encounter Ranger Whitaker.

"I know you have security cameras all over this island," says Jack, "so we need to view the tapes. The M.E. should be done soon, but Forensics will be here for a while. They need to comb the base of the statue and the rest of the island. They should be able to release the crime scene before you open for the day."

James looks relieved. "Thanks, Detective. We have a small office near the gift shop where we can look at the over-night videos. We may not have anything worthwhile to see, but we do have hot coffee."

As the harbor awakens on another crisp winter morn-ing, the men head down the stairs, all of them yearning for that hot cup of Joe. Just outside the gift shop, Jack stops Hec-tor and John. "You two should head back to the First to check college records and yearbooks for our victim. If the pictures you took aren't good, call me, and I'll send you the one I took. Remember to check the missing person reports and to cross-check her photo with the DMV database. I'll stay here to review the security tapes. See you back at the First."

The sergeants get their coffee, then leave to return to the city, while Jack remains in the gift shop and sips his own cup of hot brown liquid, frowning at the taste.

Jack is now sitting in a small computer room, looking at a screen while mulling over how old the coffee must be and how the hell that body could have ended up under the torch.

Unfortunately, all the shots are from the base and the surrounding island; there are no videos from that area of the statue. So Jack leaves the computer room and joins the crew of officers combing the grounds.

When the forensic team brings the victim out of the grand lady, Jack abandons his search and watches Allison board one of the patrol boats bound for Manhattan. Looking skyward, he mumbles, "Damn, hundreds of planes fly over this city every day, including commercial airliners. Any one of them could have dropped that woman here."

Jack walks to the dock, then hears a voice cry out, "Detective! We found a shoe near the water!"

Turning, Jack sees a police officer holding up a black pump. "Bag it and send it to Forensics!" he tells him. "They can check it for matching DNA! I'm outta here!" Running the rest of the way, Jack calls out to the patrol boat that's about to leave with Giancarlo. "Hey, hold up! I'm coming with ya!"

On the boat, Allison asks Jack about his wife. "How's Didi

holding up? She must be getting anxious."

Jack shakes his head. "Ya think?"

It's now almost 10 a.m., and Jack is back at Homicide. Though he knows he should be tackling a growing mound of paperwork, thoughts of his wife and her bulging belly keep popping into his mind. So he clicks on her contact photo. "Hey babe, how are you feeling? Your mom there yet?"

"She should be here soon. She called earlier and said she booked an Uber. Jack, I had some contractions this morning, but they're gone now. I think it's getting close. I know we've already spent hours at the hospital, walking up and down the hallway, but I think today might be the day."

Jack is excited but doesn't want to show it in case it's another false alarm. "Just call me whenever you need me," he replies as calmly as he can, "and I'll be right there. But if you're okay, I gotta go now."

"Yeah, I'm all right."

"Okay, love ya! Kiss your mom for me."

Jack grabs a cup of coffee from the office coffee maker, then heads to the whiteboard near his desk. The board is blank now, but it's been used so many times before that past cases still appear as faint whispers in faded letters.

"Hey, Jack," calls Sergeant Gomez, "I got a hit on our vic's photo in a college yearbook. She's Catherine Stevens, 28, from Queens Village, a business marketing major. Burley is connecting with DMV to get an address."

Jack writes the woman's name on the board with a blue marker. "Good work, Gomez. Check her Twitter, Facebook, and the rest. Maybe we can get some insight into what happened."

CHAPTER THREE

At the medical examiner's office, Allison Giancarlo watches while Doctor Gibson probes Catherine's internal organs. "See anything interesting?"

"Well, it looks like our victim was about four weeks pregnant; she may not even have known it yet. I haven't seen any cause of death other than the impact on the torch deck. I'll get back with you after I get results from the bloodwork."

While Allison drives back to New York City's First Police Precinct, Jack sits at his desk, mumbling about the more than forty airports in the tri-state area. He knows that a small plane or chopper could have taken off from any one of them, so there could be hundreds of suspects to work through.

While he ponders the enormity of his task, Sergeant John Burley calls out with more information that may narrow things down a bit. "I got a current address; it's on the Lower East Side. Hey, Jack, this is near your place on Suffolk Street."

"There are a couple of things on Facebook that may help," adds Gomez. "Her profile says she was working at Stoneman Kelling Ad Agency on Madison Avenue, so we can check into that. She also recently posted a selfie that shows her with two friends at the Statue of Liberty, and she tagged them both. One of them is named Jane Heatherton, and the other is Elizabeth Pino."

Jack stands and cricks his neck. "Fuckin' A. That's good info, Gomez. Take Burley with you when you pay a visit to those Facebook friends. I'll check out her apartment and go to the ad agency with Allison when she gets here."

"Ugh," says a woman's voice at the entrance to the Homicide Division. "Guess I'm going right back out again."

The men turn to see Allison Giancarlo walking into the detectives' workspace area.

Jack asks, "Did you find out anything from the M.E.?"

"No, nothing yet. There's no sure cause of death, except for the sudden stop at the deck. The autopsy was still going on when I left, so the doc will keep us posted. Oh, but the vic was pregnant. It was early, so it's possible she didn't know. Doc says gestation was about four weeks."

"Okay, listen," says Jack. "We're all going out again, so Ally, you got time to hit the head. We'll meet back here later to compare notes."

When Didi's mother, Sharon, arrives at her daughter's apartment, the first thing she says is, "That Uber driver is so cute! If I weren't here for your baby, I'd ask him to go out! I haven't been on a date in ages!"

"That's disgusting, Mom!" exclaims Didi, ushering her mother into the apartment. "He looked like he just got his license!"

"The younger, the better," winks Sharon. "Now, let's catch up. How're you feeling, honey? Got any more pains?"

"Yeah, I had some contractions just before you got here."

"You think they're more Braxton Hicks?"

"I hope not. I'm so ready to see this kid face to face!"

Sharon runs a hand over her daughter's head to smooth down some stray hairs. "Won't be long now," she says soothingly. "But you may want to enjoy this time, while it's still just you and Jack. When the baby comes, your lives won't ever be the same again."

Didi's mother, a fabulous-looking woman in her late fifties, is an out-of-work actress who can pass for Didi's sister, and she's proud of it. The main difference between mother and daughter is that Sharon is shorter than Didi and has blonde hair, instead of Didi's reddish-brown.

When Didi was a young girl, she remembers asking her mother why her hair was brown and not blonde like hers, but Sharon never answered her. Instead, she'd always laugh and change the subject.

"So, Mom," asks Didi over coffee, "when are you going to sell that large house in Maryland? Dad's been gone for years. It'd be nice if you moved closer to your grandchild."

Sharon sips her drink and looks at her daughter thoughtfully. "You may be right," she says. "This may be the time to make a change. I'll definitely need to be near my grandson."

Didi nearly chokes on her coffee. "Why do you say it's a boy? We don't know what it is!"

"Call it intuition," replies Sharon with a smile. "So, anyway, what are you making for lunch?"

At a small private airport in Essex County, New Jersey, a phone rings at Tri-Wing Services.

"Yes, we have an MD 500 available for this evening," responds the clerk. "Three hours? Okay. Hold on; let me take down some information."

Jack turns left on Stanton Street, then right onto Suffolk, where he slows down to look for building number 120. When he finds it, he's not surprised that there are no parking spots nearby.

"Gotta make my own way in this city," he says, more to himself than to Allison. Then Jack being Jack, he pulls his Road Runner up onto the sidewalk in front of the entrance and parks it there. "Damn, I could walk home from here," he laughs.

While he and Allison climb out of the car, a police cruiser pulls up, and the officer inside points to the Road Runner. But Jack merely shows his badge and waves, causing the cop behind the wheel to shake his head and drive off.

"You're impossible," comments Allison. "I'd never do that."

"Don't cops have any privileges around here?" Jack quips.

"Maybe, but I don't like taking advantage of them."

"You wanna catch the bad guys or not? Call our position in, will ya? I'm gonna put a blue light on the dash."

Allison gives their location to Dispatch, then she and Jack walk up to the victim's building, where a panel with eight buttons beside the entrance door shows residents' last names in faded letters under yellowing plastic.

Going down the list, they find the button for Catherine Stevens, and another labeled superintendent, so Jack presses the one for the super.

While they wait for the building manager to answer, they peer through the door into a dark foyer with one bare bulb glaring from the ceiling. With a concrete floor and dark gray walls, the small area looks like a tomb.

"Not a very inviting place, is it?" Allison observes.

They continue to wait, but no one comes to the door, so Jack blows out a breath in frustration. "Fuck," he says. "If this guy don't show up soon, I'll just start pressing every button till someone lets us in."

"Let me try the door," suggests Allison, jiggling the handle. "You never know at some of these buildings." Then the door opens, and she looks surprised. "So much for security," she mutters.

As the pair walks into the building, a short Oriental woman confronts them in the narrow hallway. "What you want?" she asks. "Who are you?"

Jack and Allison push aside the flaps of their coats to display their badges.

"The security of this building isn't working very well," says Jack, pulling a photo of Catherine Stevens from his pocket. "Do you recognize this woman?"

"My husband out getting parts to fix door," lies the gray-haired lady, looking down at the picture. "This person live in 3A. Why you ask?"

"Ma'am, we ask the questions here. Who are you?"

"I am Mrs. Chen. My husband manage this building."

"All right, Mrs. Chen. This woman was found dead this morning. We're detectives from the First Precinct. I'm Detective Stenhouse, and this is Detective Giancarlo."

"Huh. Too bad she dead. I guess you want to see her place. Well, follow me."

The pair follow Mrs. Chen up a metal stairway, and when their footsteps echo in the stairwell, it reminds them of earlier in the day. Not as loud as inside the statue, but haunting, nevertheless.

On the third floor, beige walls and asphalt tile floors frame apartments marked by metal doors, while yellowed ceiling lights try to illuminate their way.

When they reach 3A, Mrs. Chen opens the door with a large set of keys she takes from her pocket. "After you done, you lock up from inside and let me know, so I can bolt door with my key."

As Allison passes the woman, she says, "Our CSU team will be here shortly. Please send them up."

Inside the apartment, Jack and Allison don blue nitrile gloves and place protective booties on their shoes, while they listen to Mrs. Chen complaining in her native language as she retreats down the hallway.

Catherine Stevens' apartment is small, and not very impressive. It's a one-bedroom unit decorated with modern, simplistic furnishings made of leather and glass. The living room doesn't contain much beyond the basics of a couple of chairs, a sofa and a TV.

Jack looks around the living area and the kitchen while Allison heads into the bedroom and bathroom. "Hey, there are a couple of photos in here," says Allison. "One is the victim with two women, and the other shows her with a possible boyfriend."

Jack walks in and takes pictures of both photos. "I'll send these to Hector so he can question her Facebook friends about who they are. Does anything else strike you?"

"No. Everything looks normal."

"Nothing's speaking to me, either, but the CSU techs will be here soon. Hey, what about this?" he asks, pointing to a blinking answering machine on a table next to the bed. "She has messages."

"Oops, guess I missed that," says Allison as she hits a button to access the recorded messages.

While the detectives listen, they hear concerned queries from the Stoneman Kelling agency, and various friends. All of them sound like standard calls, except for one. "Cathy," says a tense recorded voice. "Why haven't you called? I'm worried. Where are you? Call me as soon as you get this," the voice says, leaving a number.

Jack quickly adds the number to his contact list and calls it. When he hears, "Senator Richard Callahan's office, may I help you?" he hangs up quickly and stares at his phone.

"What is it?" asks Allison.

"Catherine must have known some influential people. That message was from our Senator, Richard Callahan."

Allison widens her eyes, then thinks for a while. "The senator's Manhattan office is way uptown near the Cloisters, and his house is in Nyack. Maybe he had a 'special' relationship with one of his constituents."

Jack makes another call. "Hector, when you question our vic's friends, ask them if Catherine knew Senator Richard Callahan; he left a message on her machine. I'll call his office after we go to the ad agency, to see if I can speak with him myself."

Jack ends the call, then both of them turn when they hear the forensic technicians entering the apartment. "Let's go," he says.

At the door, Jack balances himself with a hand on Giancarlo's shoulder while he removes his booties. "Hope the fuck the senator's in town, or we'll be heading to Nyack or DC, and I sure hope it's not DC. That's a place I don't want to see again anytime soon."

CHAPTER FOUR

According to DMV records, Jane Heatherton and Elizabeth Pino share the same address, so while Sergeants Burley and Gomez drive to the women's location, they marvel at their luck.

"Maybe this is a sign that the rest of this case will go smoothly," remarks John Burley optimistically. "If we can catch them both at home, it'll save us a heck of a lot of time."

"Here's hoping," replies Gomez, crossing his fingers for luck while he steps on the brake at a red light. "Our last case involved so much legwork that I'll be happy if we can avoid even a little of that this time."

At Washington Square Park, Hector swings the car onto the street they need. The women's social media posts indicate that they're both NYU law students, which makes sense since their address is near the school.

When they reach their destination, Hector takes a trick from Stenhouse's playbook. He pulls his unmarked police POS sedan up on the sidewalk, then turns on the grill's flashing blue light and the spinning blue light on the dash, to glares and one-fingered salutes from nearby pedestrians. Hector doesn't care, though. This is the fastest way for them to get to where they're going.

Burley sees the stir they're causing in the neighborhood and is just as indifferent. "They should be happy we're doing our jobs," he remarks dryly.

But when the men step onto the sidewalk, a meter maid stops her covered scooter in the street across from them. "You guys gonna be long?" she asks.

"Hey, how ya doin'?" answers Hector. "We're investigating a homicide. Should only take an hour or so."

The meter maid replies with a nod, then puts her foot on the pedal and putts down the street to check other vehicles.

In front of the building, John shows his badge to the doorman. "How ya doin'?" he asks congenially. "I'm Sergeant Burley, and this is my partner, Sergeant Gomez. We're here to question two of your residents, Jane Heatherton and Elizabeth Pino. Do you know if they're home?"

The doorman doesn't respond. Instead of answering, he sniffs the air and looks past the men into Washington Square Park as if the detectives were simply something stuck to the bottom of his shoe.

Infuriated by the man's dismissive behavior, Hector stands nose-to-nose with him and says, "Look, slick. Sergeant Burley just asked you a question, and he was pretty nice about it. If you ignore us, we can cuff you and put you in the back of our car while we do what we came for. We're going inside no matter what you say, so I advise you to answer the sergeant graciously and open the door like you're paid to do."

The doorman sighs, not because he's intimidated, but because he's annoyed. "Miss Pino is at her morning class at NYU," he reveals reluctantly, "but Miss Heatherton should still be upstairs." Then he turns and holds the door open.

As the sergeants pass, Gomez puts his foot on the man's shoe to purposefully ruin its bright shine. "Oops, sorry, bud," he says sarcastically. "Guess you're gonna hafta get that Kiwi out again."

The detectives are surprised when they enter the lobby. The way the place is decorated, it doesn't seem to be a building that houses students on a budget. It's much too ornate — every surface is covered by granite, marble, or brass, with all of it shining to perfection.

"Whoooee," whistles Hector. "How can law students afford to live here?"

"Maybe daddy's paying their way," replies John wryly.

As the men approach the elevator, the door slides open, and exiting residents walk past the strangers. "You gentleman going up?" asks an elevator operator sitting on a stool inside the car.

Once again, John and Hector are surprised. Most modern buildings no longer employ people to man the elevators, so they're not used to seeing this throwback to a bygone era.

"Sheesh," murmurs John. "I've only seen this in old movies, but it seems to fit this building. Look at how fancy that elevator car is!"

As the detectives enter, the elderly operator says, "Morning, gentlemen. Where can I take you today?"

"Good morning," replies Hector. "We're going to the third floor."

When a crisp, "Yes, sir," fills the elevator, Hector asks, "How many hours a day do you sit on that stool ferrying people up and down?"

The man laughs. "It ain't bad. When my shift's over, I fold the stool up against the wall and leave them all to manage it themselves."

The men fall into silence as the car rises, until it settles with a "ding."

"Here ya go, gents," calls the man, tipping an imaginary hat. "Have a nice day."

"That was interesting," says John as the sergeants exit onto their floor. "I'm gonna remember that."

On the way to Apartment 313, the men pass over expensive-looking carpeting that muffles the sounds of their shoes. "Wonder how much these units go for?" John mutters.

At 313, Hector reaches out to ring the bell. While they wait, the sound of footsteps on the other side stops, and they see a brief light shining through the security peephole.

"Can I help you?" asks a muffled voice.

Hector raises his ID so the resident can see it from the spy hole. "Miss Heatherton? We're from the First Precinct. We need to speak with you about Catherine Stevens."

As light once again shines through the hole in the door, they hear multiple bolts being unlocked from the inside. Then the door swings open, and an attractive woman steps back to let the men in. "You caught me by surprise," she says, not the least embarrassed that she's only wearing a skimpy, red lace teddy. "Let me put on a robe. I'll be right back."

As the woman struts off, John and Hector glance at each other with silly grins.

On Madison Avenue, the four hundred horses of Jack's Road Runner rumble through an underground parking garage at the high-rise that shelters the Stoneman Kelling Agency. Near the entrance, Jack spots a space reserved for emergency vehicles, and parks his car there. Then he and Allison walk up to the parking attendant.

"You can't leave your car there," says the young attendant quickly. "It's for official use only."

"I know, but this should make us official," responds Jack, displaying his badge.

"Oh, okay, that'll do it," replies the young attendant. "By the way, I like your style," he grins, looking at the red Road Runner.

"Thanks," smiles Jack, relishing the compliment for his baby. "What floor is the ad agency on?"

"It's on the fifteenth," replies the youth. "Mind if I take a look at your car between customers?"

"Be my guest," Jack says, "but no fingerprints. I just had it detailed."

After a quick elevator ride, the pair enters the Stoneman Kelling Agency, which occupies the entire fifteenth and sixteenth floors.

"Nice!" mouths Allison, looking around the expansive reception area stylishly decorated with a bubbling fountain and water flowing over a stone wall into an artificial pool.

At the reception desk, a striking redhead looks up and smiles. "May I help you?" she asks, standing to greet them while she removes a black headset from her five-hundred-dollar hairdo.

Jack grins at the pretty young thing with long legs under a black mini skirt, and Allison knows that he's staring. To move things along, she clears her throat and presents her badge and ID to the receptionist. "Good morning," she says. "We're here to speak with the person in charge. It's about one of your employees."

"Oh," says the redhead, somewhat taken aback by New York's Finest requesting an audience at her place of business. "Whom shall I say is here?" she asks in a business-like manner.

"My name is Detective Giancarlo, and this is my partner, Detective Stenhouse."

The redhead's tone changes abruptly when she realizes that Jack is checking her out. "Sure thing," she replies with a wink for him. "I'll let Ms. Stoneman know you're here."

While the woman contacts her boss, Allison jabs Jack in the ribs. "Hey, you're gonna be a daddy soon," she whispers.

"If she's gonna show her talents, I'm definitely gonna look," replies Jack without lowering his voice.

After the young redhead ends her call, she shamelessly checks Jack out and makes sure he sees her taking in all his good parts. Then she hands him a note. "Follow me. Ms. Stoneman will meet you in our conference room."

Allison frowns at the note in Jack's hand, but Jack doesn't notice. He's too busy grinning at the receptionist's leather-covered ass.

The agency's work area is typical of most commercial high-rise buildings: glass-fronted offices face floor-to-ceiling windows that provide employees with a grand view of the Manhattan skyline.

"Must be hard getting any work done with views like this," Jack quips. Then he opens the note and grins wider. "Hey, I still got it," he whispers to Allison. "It's her phone number."

At the apartment near NYU Law School, John and Hector make themselves comfortable on a long sectional sofa while they wait for Jane to return. When she does, she's wearing a short silk robe and pink bunny slippers.

"Sorry, I like to be comfortable at home. So what's this about?" she asks, seating herself nervously on an oversized matching chair. "Did I do something wrong?"

Hector looks at John and then at Jane, a blonde who looks to be in her mid-twenties. Silently, he wonders again how two students can afford an apartment in this building, but he keeps that thought to himself. Instead, he takes out a digital recorder and places it on a glass cocktail table. "Miss Heatherton," he says, "you haven't done anything wrong. Sergeant Gomez and I need to ask you some questions about your friend, Catherine Stevens. This is an official investigation, so we'd like to record this interview. Do you agree to be recorded?"

"Um, yes, I guess so. What's wrong with Catherine?"

"Unfortunately, we have bad news. Um, your friend was found dead this morning."

"What?!" exclaims Jane, while fear and horror wash over her face like a crashing wave. "What do you mean, dead?" she shouts, as tears flow from her eyes. "We just saw her not too long ago! What happened? Oh, Alan will be devastated!"

"We're sorry for your loss," says Hector. "But you can help us find out what happened by answering our questions. When did you see her last?"

Jane wipes her face, then blows her nose with a tissue from her robe. "It was last week. Cathy took a sick day, and we went to the Statue of Liberty."

"Who is 'we'?" asks Burley.

"Oh, my roommate, Elizabeth. She went with us."

"Where is Elizabeth now? We need to interview her as well."

"She's at school; she has a class today. We're law students."

John nods, then says, "Miss Heatherton, Catherine's body was found at the Statue of Liberty. Do you know if she had any enemies, an ex, maybe, or a coworker who didn't like her? Do you know of anyone who wanted to harm her?"

"No, that's crazy! No one would harm Catherine! She's a sweetheart!"

"How did she know Senator Richard Callahan?"

Jane gasps and stares at the sergeants, then looks down at the floor. "Wow, how do you know that? I know you're cops and all, but..."

"Miss Heatherton?"

"Yes. Cathy got involved with the senator when they hired her to help with his campaign."

"What did she do there?"

"I'm not sure, but I tried to convince her that it was a bad idea to hook up with him. Um, you know, the press and stuff. Wait, do you think he had something to do with this?"

John shows Jane a screengrab of the photo Catherine took at the Statue of Liberty. "Who is the other person in this photo?"

"That's Elizabeth."

"Elizabeth Pino?"

"Yes."

"Was there anyone else with the three of you when this photo was taken?"

Jane shakes her head no, but avoids eye contact as she does.

"When will Elizabeth be home?"

Jane blows her nose again. "Her class ends in about an hour. She should be right back after... No, wait. She's going to meet some friends after class. You can try to catch her at the main lecture hall."

Hector leans toward Jane. "You mentioned someone named Alan. Who is he?"

Jane blows her nose again. "Alan Cummings was Cathy's boyfriend. They met a while back, at Hofstra University. He's going to be devastated!"

"Why did you say Alan 'was' Catherine's boyfriend?" Hector asks. "Did they break up?"

Jane sits back and tries to close her robe, but doesn't do a very good job of it. "He found out about her affair and cut it off."

"Do you know how we can get in touch with him?"

"All I know is that he works for the Mets in season ticket sales."

"Thanks for your help," says Hector, handing Jane his business card. "If you think of anything that might be relevant, please give me a call. We'll go to the lecture hall now to speak with Miss Pino. Thank you for your time."

Before Hector rises from the sofa, he asks one more question. "How can students afford to live in an apartment like this? I know it's near the school, but it looks pretty extravagant, with school expenses and such."

Jane drops her tissue into her pocket. "My daddy pays for it. He made a fortune in oil fracking."

When the Stoneman Kelling receptionist leaves Jack and Allison to wait for the agency partner, she winks at Jack again, then gives him a little wave. Pleased by the attention, Jack responds with a toothy grin that makes Allison roll her eyes in exasperation.

"What would Didi think?" she asks when the two cops are alone in the company's conference room.

"She won't care. It's just harmless flirting."

Allison gives her partner a resigned sigh. "I don't understand you two."

Just then, a stylishly dressed woman enters the room wearing an above-the-knee pinstriped skirt with a white blouse and a matching jacket. Allison cringes when she sees her, knowing that Jack is making sure to get an eyeful of her tight-fitting blouse.

"Good morning," says the woman crisply. "I'm Vivian Stoneman, a partner at this agency. How may I assist NYPD today?"

"Thanks for meeting us," says Allison, hoping to quickly

steer Jack's mind out of the gutter. "We were just commenting on your décor," she adds, in case the woman overheard any of their prior conversation. "We've never seen marble covering an entire wall before, and the slate top of this conference table looks expensive. Business must be good!"

"Couldn't be better," responds Vivian Stoneman confidently. "But I'm sure you're not here to discuss our decorating choices."

"No, we're not here for that," says Jack, eyeing Allison suspiciously. "Ms. Stoneman, my name is Detective Jack Stenhouse, and this is Detective Allison Giancarlo. We're here to discuss one of your employees, a Miss Catherine Stevens."

"Oh, you want to talk to Cathy? She's not here."

"Do you know where she is?"

"No, she took some vacation time last week and was supposed to return today, but she hasn't shown up. Our HR director left messages, but we haven't heard from her."

Allison looks kindly at the woman, then says, "Ms. Stoneman, I'm sorry to tell you that Catherine won't be returning your calls. Sadly, her body was found at the Statue of Liberty early this morning; that's why we're here. We're investigating her death."

As that news hits Vivian, her carefully made-up, tanned face turns pale. "Oh, god," she frets. "Cathy's dead? How could that be? She was a jewel!"

When tears begin to flow down the partner's face, her mascara leaves black trails, so Allison pulls some tissues out of her pocket.

"Thanks," says Vivian, grateful for the help. "I must look like a wreck. Did Cathy have a heart attack or something, or… Oh, no, you don't think someone killed her, do you?"

"That's what we're looking into," responds Jack. "Did Miss Stevens have any problems that you know of? Are there any disgruntled clients?"

Vivian sniffles. "Everyone here liked Cathy, and the clients loved her. She was one of our top employees."

"Did she have any particular office friendships? Is there anyone who might know something about her personal life?"

"I don't think there's anyone here who was more friendly than the others," says Vivian. "We all work so closely together that we're like a big family, you know? And many of us hang out together outside of work."

"What about Senator Callahan?" asks Jack. "Any connection there?"

At the mention of the senator's name, Vivian takes a noticeable breath, which forces Jack to pay more than a little attention to the buttons on her blouse that are holding on for dear life.

"The senator was one of Cathy's clients. She handled some events for his re-election campaign."

"Okay, can you get us a list of her clients?" asks Giancarlo.

"Um, this is getting a little tricky now," replies Vivian sternly. "You're venturing into privileged information. There are privacy rules that—"

"Look," says Jack, cutting the woman short when she seems to be hesitating. "We're investigating a suspicious death, and we have no time for corporate BS. We're here for information that will help us get to the bottom of what happened to one of your employees. So if you won't cooperate, we won't be able to be nice about this anymore. We'll have to return with a search warrant, and I'm sure you wouldn't want that. I don't think your clientele will react well when they hear that your office is involved in a suspicious death."

With her mouth set in a Mona Lisa smile that reveals nothing, Vivian holds her hands up in surrender. "I had to try," she replies. "I'll be back in a few minutes with what you need. Meanwhile, can I have my receptionist bring you some coffee or sparkling water?"

Burley can't stop thinking about Jane's response to his last question. "Her daddy has money?" he scoffs as they walk out of the lobby. "I bet she meant to say her sugar daddy's paying her off."

Hector calls Stenhouse on the way to the car. "Jack, we're heading to NYU to interview Elizabeth Pino. She wasn't home when we talked to Heatherton."

"Any info from your talk?" he asks. "We're still at the ad agency."

"Yeah. Seems that Stevens was doing the senator while she had a boyfriend, and he wasn't pleased about it. I got an itchy feeling about this group. Heatherton, Pino, Cummings, and the senator may all be connected somehow."

"Okay, keep digging. We're heading over to Callahan's office now. Did you get the boyfriend's name?"

"Yeah, it's Alan Cummings. He works in ticket sales for the Mets."

"Good. We'll check Cummings, too. Listen, you guys have to decide which one of you will contact Miss Stevens' parents. It's a dirty job, but someone has to do it. And the other one needs to get background info on Cummings and call me with it. I'll send you her parents' info when we get it from her personnel records."

When Burley hangs up with Jack, he asks Gomez, "Did you catch Heatherton's reaction to the picture?"

"Yeah. She's hiding something."

Jack ends the call with Burley as Vivian Stoneman re-enters the conference room.

"This is Cathy's background information and emergency contacts," she says, handing a manila folder to Jack. "Should we call her parents? They live in Boca Raton, Florida."

Jack takes the file. "No," he replies. "We'll take care of getting in touch with the family. They'd want to hear from official sources."

"Yes, I guess you're right," nods Vivian.

When Allison and Jack get ready to leave, Ms. Stoneman pulls Jack back to hand him a business card. "Call me," she says softly.

Jack joins his partner at the elevator, where he sees her rolling her eyes at him.

"Damn, I still got it," he says, as Allison pushes him into the elevator. "I know what you said, but I got two phone numbers today!" he adds, waving a note and a business card in the air.

"Yeah?" responds Allison as the doors close. "And what're you gonna do with them, daddy?"

Jack just looks at her and winks, prompting Allison to roll her eyes again.

CHAPTER FIVE

It may be winter in New York City, but the weather is pleasant as Jack and Allison head to the local office of Senator Richard Callahan, near Fort Tryon Park. The morning snow has all but melted away, making the drive north a little more pleasant than it would have been otherwise.

On the way there, Allison is pleased to learn that the Senate is on another break, so the senator is in New York. His office tells her that he's expected to make a stop there around noon-ish, so Jack continues to point his muscle car north.

When they arrive at the senator's address, there are no parking spots, but Jack isn't worried, he just parks next to an expired meter.

Allison is used to Jack's inventiveness, so when a meter maid comes toward them on her blue and white three-wheeled trike, she waves her badge, and the parking enforcement officer nods and putts on by.

The place Jack leaves the car is about two blocks from the senator's office, but the officers don't mind the walk. It's almost fifty degrees today and the air is crisp and dry.

The detectives have no trouble knowing which office is Callahan's. His local headquarters is in a small space that was probably a store of some kind, with photographs of Washington, DC now fixed to the windows facing the street.

Inside the office, the rows of metal desks and chairs are occupied by two persons, both of whom look up reluctantly from their cell phones when they enter.

"Looks busy," remarks Jack sarcastically, as a young girl in her late teens or early twenties approaches them in Reeboks, skinny jeans, and a tight T-shirt.

"Don't say it," warns Allison, knowing that Jack is checking out the young woman.

"Hey, there," says Jack, displaying his badge. "We're from the First Precinct, and we'd like to speak to Senator Callahan. Is he here?"

The young woman stares wide-eyed at the badge, which Jack takes pains to keep looking shiny. "Oh, I'm the one who took your call," she says. "Senator Callahan left his house a little while ago, so he should be here shortly. Please have a seat in his office. Would you like some refreshments? Soda, bottled water?"

"No, we're fine," says Jack. "We'll just wait for the senator."

When the young woman thinks Allison isn't looking, she tosses her hair back and winks at Jack. "Okay, follow me, please," she tells them.

While they walk to an office in the rear, Allison leans in and whispers, "If that girl gives you her phone number, I'll just spit."

The young woman settles the cops into the senator's

office, then tells them she'll be right back. When she returns, she hands a note to Allison and leaves again.

Allison is surprised; this kind of thing only happens to Jack. So she reads the note quickly, with her mouth hanging open in silent shock. The only notations on the paper are a phone number, a smiley face, and a red heart. "What the..." she stammers.

Jack sees the look on Allison's face, so he grabs the note, and roars with laughter. "Hahahaha! Oh, my god! That's hysterical," Jack chortles as tears run down his face. "Hahaha! Wait till your hubby finds out! Hahaha!"

Jack can't stop laughing. The timing of this incident right after Allison's criticisms of his randiness is just too delicious to ignore.

But Allison isn't amused. She scowls at Jack and rubs her middle finger against the side of her nose, warning, "Stop it right now, you juvenile! It's not that funny!"

The room the detectives are sitting in is stark, but luxurious. While the floor outside this office is cheap linoleum and the walls are just painted sheetrock, in here, there is a plush area rug with paneled walls, cushioned leather chairs, and an oversized oak desk topped by an American flag and photos of the senator, including autographed ones of him with the last three presidents.

When Jack finally calms down, he rises from his chair and picks up one of the pictures on the senator's desk. "This must be his family," he says, showing it to Giancarlo.

Jack returns the photo to its place and wipes his eyes. "You have to admit, Ally," he says with a contented sigh, "that was just too funny."

Outside the office door, three persons are now in the outer work area: the two Millennials, who are still staring at their cell phones, and a slightly older female who is talking on a desk phone.

As Jack returns to his seat, Senator Callahan walks into the building. He stops at each person to say a few words, then enters his office.

"Good morning," says the senator. "One of the girls told me you're waiting for me. How may I help you?"

Senator Richard Callahan is well-known by his constituents, but not for his politics. His chiseled good looks and his fit, six-foot-tall, 170-pound frame are favorite targets of the media. They display his photo in their publications and programs as often as possible because they know their ratings will soar whenever he appears. And the senator is happy for the attention. For a man in his early fifties, his brown eyes, greying brown hair, and deep tan keep the people coming, so he's happy to fuel the media fires.

The senator is also something of a clotheshorse, which only adds to his mystique. Today, he's wearing an expensive golf shirt tucked into tight-fitting jeans, with boat shoes and no socks, and he's holding a stylish leather jacket.

Senator Callahan shakes the detectives' hands, then drapes the jacket over the back of his chair and sits down.

"What can I do for you?" he asks pleasantly.

Jack stares at him with a look that goes through the self-assured man like a fifty-caliber round. "Senator Callahan," he declares, "we're here to investigate a possible homicide."

Surprised, the senator blinks rapidly. "A homicide?" he asks, swallowing quickly to alleviate a suddenly dry mouth. "What would I have to do with a homicide? Who's dead?"

"It's Catherine Stevens," declares Jack without further elaboration. He wants to see what kind of reaction he gets, and he doesn't have to wait long.

Almost immediately, shock, fear, and grief pass over Richard's face in rapid succession. Then he lowers his head and cradles it in trembling hands. "What the hell happened?"

"We don't know yet," states Jack. "Her body was found at the Statue of Liberty this morning."

"Oh, my god," Richard moans. "Catherine is dead? Are you sure it's her?"

Jack fires back a reply as direct as an Abrams battle tank. "Senator, we know that Catherine worked for your reelection campaign and that you left her a rather emotional message at her home number. So the obvious question is, where were you last night?"

"Where was I? You don't think... I mean, I wouldn't...! Look, I wasn't even here yesterday! I was in DC at a fundraiser with the vice president, and I didn't get home until this morning!"

Allison isn't impressed. "It wouldn't be the first time a politician had an affair with a campaign worker, would it?" she asks. "And by the way, did you know she was pregnant?"

In the NYU hallway, John and Hector look for Elizabeth Pino among the many students exiting the lecture class.

As they look through the crowd, Gomez remarks, "Look at them all! They're so busy staring down at their cell phones that they don't even know we're here. We could be stark naked, and they wouldn't know it at all!"

Soon, Burley points out a short woman in her late twenties wearing a padded coat to protect her from the New York winter.

"Is that her?" he asks.

"Yeah, I think so."

John makes a beeline for the woman to catch her before she's too far away. "Elizabeth Pino?" he asks to gain her attention. When she turns around, he says, "I'm Sergeant Burley. My partner and I would like to ask you a few questions."

John waits for the typical reaction to his introduction as a cop, but Elizabeth doesn't miss a beat. Without a hint of surprise, she looks at him and asks calmly, "Where's your ID?"

Elizabeth takes her time inspecting both detectives' IDs. When she's satisfied they're who they say they are, she hands their identification back and points down the hallway. "We can talk in the student lounge."

At a small sitting area, the three settle onto a sofa and

chairs, then Elizabeth asks, "So what's this about?"

Gomez leans forward. "Your friend, Catherine Stevens, was murdered yesterday," he states succinctly. "A park ranger found her body at the Statue of Liberty." Then, just like Stenhouse, he waits for a reaction.

Instantly, Elizabeth's mouth falls open, and tears flow over her olive skin. "My god, I was with her at the Statue of Liberty just last week!"

Gomez takes a deep breath. "Miss Pino, do you know anything about Catherine's relationship with Alan Cummings and Senator Callahan?"

Trying to calm down, Elizabeth pinches her nose and rubs her eyes. "I know she was having an affair with the senator and that Alan wasn't happy about it," she says, her voice cracking with grief. "They had a huge fight, so she asked Jane and me to take a girl's day off and go to the Statue of Liberty with her."

"Why did she want to go there?"

"I don't know. Just to get away, I guess."

Elizabeth pauses, then gasps. "Oh, my god! Alan was a soldier! He was in Afghanistan, and he could get really angry sometimes!"

"Do you know what branch of the service he was in?" asks Burley.

"No, I just know he flew helicopters."

While Elizabeth cries, Sergeant Burley tries to comfort

her while students around them whisper and point their phones at them.

Jack and Allison are still at the senator's office.

"Cathy helped me promote my campaign," he explains. "I met her at the advertising agency I hired for my reelection. She had good ideas, and we became close. I didn't, and wouldn't, harm her in any way."

"Did you know she was pregnant?" asks Jack.

Richard moans slightly. "No."

"Well, we'll find out who the father is when we get genetic material from her unborn child. I assume you'll provide a sample for us?"

"Yes, of course," Callahan replies.

"Good. Now, is there anyone Catherine Stevens had a problem with, an old boyfriend, or someone on your staff?"

"There weren't any problems with anyone who works for me; it was just business. But I know that she was seeing someone before we met — a guy named Alan; I met him once at a cocktail party. You know, when this gets out... I mean, my family! Shit!" Richard stops to look at the photo on his desk. "Look," he says sadly, "I know I'm screwed, but I'll cooperate with your investigation. If there's anything you need, just let me know."

"There is one thing, Senator," says Allison. "Can you get us a list of your office staff and volunteers? We'll need to take statements from each of them."

"Ah, no problem," says Callahan, rising to stand on unsteady feet. "I'll have someone get that for you right away. Now, is there anything else you need from me? I'd like to meet with my chief of staff."

"Nothing else for now."

Richard nods and sighs deeply. "One of the girls will bring you that info," he says softly, then leaves without another word to either of them.

When the senator is gone, Allison turns to Jack with a look of confidence. "I have a strong feeling that he didn't do it," she tells him.

"Me, too," agrees Jack. "Next up is Alan Cummings. And I should call Gomez while we have some down time."

Sergeant Gomez walks some distance away to take Jack's call. "Hey, what's up?" he asks.

"Senator Callahan confirmed that a guy named Alan Cummings was Catherine's boyfriend, so press Pino about their relationship. We're heading to Citi Field after we get some records from Callahan's staff."

"Okay, but we just talked to Pino about Cummings. She

told us he was a helicopter pilot in Afghanistan and that Stevens fought with him over her affair with Callahan."

Jack pauses to digest that bit of information. "Well, fuck," he says. "Guess we need to bring him in. See if you can get anything else out of her, then go back to the First."

Hector ends the call, then rejoins his partner. "Sorry," he says to Elizabeth, who is still upset. "I need to ask you a few more questions about Alan Cummings. "How do you know he's a helicopter pilot?"

"Oh. Cathy told us, and he took us on a flight around Manhattan. Cathy and Jane liked it, but I thought it was kinda scary."

"And he fought with Catherine?"

"Yeah. He wasn't a happy camper when he found out she was seeing Callahan. He really blew his top. Cathy couldn't figure out how he knew."

Hector shows Elizabeth a photo on his phone. "When Catherine took this photo, was there anyone else there who didn't get into the picture?"

Instead of answering, Elizabeth looks down at a Mickey Mouse watch. "Oh, no!" she gasps. "I'm gonna be late! Look, I can't talk anymore, and there's nothing else I have to say, anyway."

"All right," says Gomez, while Elizabeth quickly gathers her things. "Here's my card. Thanks for your cooperation, Miss Pino. And we're sorry for your loss."

"Before you go," says Burley, glancing sideways at Hector. "We talked to your roommate this morning. That's a pretty nice building you two live in. Tell me, how can law students afford the monthly rent? It must be pretty steep."

Pino suddenly flushes and pretends to search for something in her purse. "Jane comes from money," she mumbles. "Her...father... Look, I really have to go now."

As Elizabeth hurries away, the cops watch until they can no longer see her in the ebb and flow of students moving from one place to another. Then they set off for their car.

As they walk, Burley suddenly jabs Gomez with his elbow. "What's up with you?" he asks suspiciously. "You sounded like robocop back there, and with Heatherton, too. 'We're sorry for your loss?' he mimics. "What the hell was that?"

"Fuck you," replies Gomez angrily. "I was just trying to be nice."

"Why? Heatherton and Pino are hiding something. You know they're persons of interest in a murder case, right?"

"So? That don't mean I hafta be an ass."

CHAPTER SIX

Ever since Jack moved to the City that Never Sleeps, the way people drive the clogged thoroughfares has amazed him. He needs no prompting to tell anyone who'll listen that if he didn't know any better, he'd think New York drivers were always late for something. Even though Jack has seen plenty of crazy things on the streets of his native Florida, he insists that it wouldn't take much for anyone, even a Franciscan monk, to lose their cool on the Big Apple's roadways.

Lately, though, he's become tired of hearing Allison's irritated complaints about other drivers. So before he points his car to Queens, he resolves to do his best to tune her out. Unfortunately, it took them much longer than expected to reach City Field, so Allison was particularly expressive on the long drive.

"Thanks for listening to my tirades about people's driving habits," Allison comments as they head to the stadium's main entrance. "I feel better after getting all that off my chest."

Jack expected his partner to say something because he knows it was unusual for him to let her go on and on. Even so, he can't help being snarky about it. "I thought you'd be pleased," he replies with an impish grin, "but I'm not sure how long I can keep it up. It's not easy being nice, you know. Sound familiar, Detective?"

Just as he hoped, Allison rolls her eyes in exasperation,

making Jack happy that he got a rise out of his partner. However, he makes sure to change the subject before she can get in her own gibe. "The Mets ticket office is in the lower level," he tells her in his best business-like voice.

Allison gives Jack a nasty look. "I've been here a few times," she retorts sarcastically. "But you can lead the way, Detective. You're happier to be here than I am."

Allison unbuttons her coat as they walk to the main entrance. "Whew, it's getting hot," she remarks, removing her scarf. "The weather guy said a warm front's gonna pass through, and then we're gonna get more snow."

"Hmm?" Jack replies. He's no longer listening because in his mind, his soon-to-be-born child is all grown up and stepping up to home plate in the packed stadium.

No one is at the ticket window when the pair arrives there. "Doesn't look like anyone's working today," remarks Allison, looking around.

Jack pokes his head through the window. "Anyone here?" he shouts.

Seconds later, a young woman walks up. "How can I help you?" she asks.

"We're Detectives Stenhouse and Giancarlo," replies Jack, flashing his badge. "We need to speak with Alan Cummings. Is he here?"

The young woman seems to be mesmerized by Jack's steel-grey eyes. "Sure thing, Detective," she replies with a sweet smile. "Can I tell Alan what this is about?"

"Just tell him that two detectives from the First want to talk to him."

The young woman brushes her long hair out of her eyes, then turns around to walk into the office behind her. As she goes, she makes sure to exaggerate her hip movements, hoping that Jack will enjoy the view, and of course, he does.

Looking on, Allison is more irritated by Jack's reaction than the young woman's deliberate attempt to display her wares. With a loud sigh, she smacks Jack on the back of his head. But this only makes him laugh.

A few minutes later, a man in his early thirties walks into the open rotunda area in front of the ticket office. He's a typical-looking jarhead — square-jawed, with a short-cropped haircut, and he wears his custom-tailored shirt and suit quite well. "I'm Alan Cummings," he announces. "What can I do for you?"

Now, it's Allison's turn to stare at all the good parts, which Jack notices right away. Clearing his throat loudly, he says, "Mr. Cummings, my name is Stenhouse, and this is Giancarlo. We're detectives from the First Precinct, here to investigate a homicide."

Alan opens his eyes wide, suddenly nervous. "What does that have to do with me?"

"Were you dating a woman named Catherine Stevens?"

"Uh, yes, Catherine and I were going out. Why?"

"Mr. Cummings, I'm sorry to inform you that a park ranger found Catherine's body at the Statue of Liberty this morning."

The detectives watch as several different emotions pass over Alan's face. Then he shakes his head in silence. "God, no!" he finally blurts out. "What the hell? What the hell happened?"

Jack narrows his eyes. "That's what we're going to find out," he states firmly. "Now, we need to ask you some questions, so please come with us to the station."

"Are you arresting me?" Alan shouts, looking around anxiously for a way to escape this problem. "I mean, I didn't do anything! What's going on?"

"It's just routine," Allison explains. "We need to ask you more questions, and it's best to do that at the station. Will you come with us willingly?"

"I guess I don't have a choice, do I?" he says dejectedly. "But I need my coat. Can you wait while I get it?"

Allison shakes her head and walks over to the ticket window. "Can you get Mr. Cummings' coat, please?" she asks the young woman who has been watching them with amazement.

"Mr. Cummings," says Jack, "you're not under arrest. But you are a person of interest."

Alan cricks his neck and pulls out his iPhone. "I'm not going to be questioned without my lawyer. I'll tell him to meet us there. Where are we going again?"

"It's Downtown, the First Precinct headquarters on Ericsson Place."

While Alan makes the call, Jack and Allison look at each other and at Alan. They're silently sizing up the situation to see if Alan will cooperate or not.

When the young ticket agent returns, she passes Alan's Armani wool and cashmere coat to him through the ticket window.

"Okay," Alan says. "Let's get this over with."

While Jack and Allison transport Alan through the heart of the city, Lena Callahan, Senator Callahan's ex-wife, is taking a selfie in front of the Tyrannosaurus Rex skeleton at the Museum of Natural History.

Lena makes sure the photo shows her in the best possible light, then she posts it to her social media account. When that's done, she enters another area to view more dinosaurs.

The redhead has no idea she's being followed. She's too focused on jostling with a group of school kids so she can read the information cards to notice that the same person is behind her at every turn.

At the police station, Jack and Allison are preparing to do some "reading" of their own. They're sitting opposite Alan Cummings and his lawyer in one of the station's interrogation rooms, getting ready to question their subject.

"All right. Let's start with your name," begins Jack.

"You know my name," says Alan stiffly. "Why do I have to—" he says, stopping when his attorney pokes him in the ribs. "Yeah, okay," he responds sullenly. "My name is Alan Cummings."

"Mr. Cummings," resumes Jack, "my partner and I are investigating the death of a woman named Catherine Stevens, with whom we believe you are acquainted. Tell us how you know Miss Stevens."

Alan sighs. "I've been dating Catherine for a few years now, and I was even planning to ask her to marry me. So I'm a little upset right now, you know? I even bought a ring and was trying to figure out the best way to propose."

Jack narrows his eyes at Alan. "How long have you known Catherine?"

"We've known each other a long time. We met at college."

"So, you were planning to ask her to marry you? Didn't you two have a big fight recently?"

Alan's face turns pale. "Yeah, we did. How do you know about that?"

"Tell us what you did after work yesterday, Alan."

"Uh, I went food shopping. Then I watched TV and went to bed."

"What time was that?"

"I guess it was about eleven. That's when I usually go to bed."

Allison asks, "Was anyone with you?"

"No, I was alone."

"All night?"

"Yes."

"So there's no one who can confirm that you were home last night?"

Alan glances at his lawyer, then says, "No, I guess not."

"Alan," says Jack, "we know you're a pilot. You fly helicopters, isn't that right?"

"Yeah," he responds, "I flew a lot of choppers in Afghanistan, and I still do some flying now and then."

Alan turns to his lawyer with a confused look. "What does that have to do with Catherine's death?" he asks. But the attorney just shrugs.

Jack continues. "Did you know that Catherine was having an affair?"

Alan looks surprised at the question. "You know about that, too? Okay, yeah, I found out about the affair. That's what the fight was about."

At that, Alan's lawyer leans in to whisper something into his client's ear, but Alan dismisses him. "It's all right," he says. "All her friends knew we fought about it."

Jack decides to wrap things up with a question that will get to the heart of the matter. "Alan Cummings, did you kill

Catherine Stevens?" he asks bluntly. "Did you push her out of a helicopter?"

The attorney cautions his client again, but Alan is too upset to listen. "I didn't kill her!" he retorts angrily. "I went to the organic market near my apartment and then stayed home the rest of the night!"

Jack cricks his neck wearily. "Tell us about your lover's spat."

Alan shakes his head sadly. "She was having an affair, and it wasn't with just anyone, by the way. It was with our good-for-nothing senator, for cryin' out loud! Can you believe that shit? She said she broke it off and was sorry, but we yelled at each other for hours, and I ended up storming out."

"When was that?" asks Allison.

"It was a week or so ago, and we haven't seen each other since. But yesterday morning, she called and wanted to apologize again. She said she wanted to get back together. We were supposed to meet for dinner tomorrow night."

Jack looks skeptical. "Sounds like a pretty story," he says cynically. "How long did it take you to make all of that up?"

"What?!" exclaims Alan. "What the fuck is this? I didn't make up—"

"Do you have a temper, Mr. Cummings?"

"Detective," the attorney interrupts, "do you have any facts to back that up, or are you just speculating?"

"Look, Mr. Cummings," says Jack, "I have to be honest

with you. This doesn't look good. You're a pilot, and it sounds like you have a pretty good reason to want to kill your girlfriend."

"Whoa, wait just a minute!" protests Alan. "I didn't kill her, I wanted to marry her! And what does my being a pilot have to do with any of this?"

"I'll answer that," says Allison, looking at Jack. "Your girlfriend was found on the narrow platform under the Statue of Liberty's torch, bub. The only way she could have gotten there is if someone dropped her from above. So, yeah, you're definitely a person of interest in this case."

"And if we find anything that links you to her murder," adds Jack, "you'll be charged with her death and booked into jail. Now, this may sound cliché, but don't leave town. *Capeesh*?"

The attorney pats Alan's arm reassuringly. "Don't worry," he tells his client, "they're just fishing." Then he turns to Jack. "Nothing you just said points directly to my client, so I don't expect you to have any further contact with him. We'll help with the investigation, but you'll need to go through my office. And now, Detectives, our conversation is finished."

Allison turns to Stenhouse while Alan and the attorney leave in a huff. "Hector just texted me," she says. "He and John are checking airports and air services in the tri-state area to see if any helicopters were rented recently. But that's gonna take a while. And we have no forensics on Cummings to match up with him if we find that he rented one."

Jack stands. "None yet, anyway. Check with that organic market. See if anyone remembers him being there last night. Or maybe there's a credit card transaction we could—"

Jack's thought is interrupted by his ringing cell phone. "Oh, crap, it's Didi," he says when he sees the caller ID. "I completely forgot that her mother's in town."

Jack clicks on the call. "Hi, babe, sorry... What? Oh, crap! I'm on my way!"

"Everything all right?" asks Allison.

"Her water broke! Shit's about to get real!"

CHAPTER SEVEN

Needing to get home quickly, Jack careens through traffic and calls on NYPD's finest for help. When a patrol car joins him, he drafts the car like a NASCAR pro, using the squad car's authority to scream to his apartment on the Lower East Side.

When they both pull into the underground parking garage, they screech to a halt near Didi and her mother, who are waiting impatiently near the elevator door in the dark facility.

Jack waves to his escort, then without a word, runs to his wife and guides her into the car. Then he runs around to the driver's side and gets in.

"You forgetting someone?" laughs Didi.

"Oh, geez," Jack mumbles. Stepping back out, he grins sheepishly at Sharon, who's still waiting by the elevator with Didi's bright red overnight bag, and one hand on her hip.

"Sorry," Jack mumbles, taking hold of the bag. Prodding his mother-in-law forward, he points her to the back seat, then jumps into the car while Didi rubs her belly and moans.

As they pass through an intersection, Jack reaches over and gives the baby bulge a loving pat.

"Ohh, Jack!" moans Didi when another wave of contractions hits. "Hurry up! Our baby wants to come out!"

Not in my car! thinks Jack inwardly. But outwardly, he says soothingly, "We'll be there soon, hon. How you doin' back there, Sharon?"

"Just keep your eyes on the road, Jack. We have to get there in one piece. I called the doctor's office before we left, and they said he'll meet us in the emergency room. He just finished another delivery, so he's already there. Must have been a full moon last night."

The winter sun has already set when the Road Runner arrives at the ER of Presbyterian Hospital's downtown location.

"Oh, there's a nurse waiting for us," says Didi, grateful for the wheelchair the woman is holding.

Didi settles into the chair as Jack stands aside, watching his wife like a hawk.

"Mr. Stenhouse," says the nurse, "your wife is pre-admitted, but there's still some paperwork that needs to be finalized. When that's done, they'll let you right in. As you know from your 'practice runs,' the labor rooms are just off the ER. Now, Mrs. Stenhouse, do you want this lovely young lady to come in with you?"

Didi smiles, "Yes, that's my mom. She had me when she was twelve."

"Oh, geez, that's not true," laughs Sharon. "I was in my early twenties."

While the nurse brings Didi into the hospital, an MD 500 helicopter hovers one thousand feet above Margaret Corbin Drive in Fort Tryon Park, about a mile and a half north of the hospital. Suddenly, it pitches right, and a body slips out the side door and spirals into the air. When it clears the landing skids, the chopper turns west and quickly leaves the area.

Five hours of hard labor later, Didi is finally ten centimeters dilated. "Your baby is ready," declares Doctor Gabriel Stratt, standing at Didi's bedside. "You two are about to become parents."

Jack and Didi grab each other's hands with nervous anticipation. "This is it," Jack whispers into Didi's ear. "No turning back now!"

While the nurses prepare for the delivery, a shrill ring suddenly fills the room.

"Oh, fuck, not now!" Jack groans, fishing his phone from his pocket.

"You better not answer that!" shouts Didi as a strong contraction washes over her.

Jack looks apologetically at his wife but steps away. He

knows he'll catch it from her later, but he's on a case, so he needs to let his partners know what's going on.

"Yeah?" he says into the phone, ignoring the frowns of hospital staff. "Oh, fuck... Look, you guys are gonna hafta check it out yourselves; I'm a little busy right now. Yeah, baby's coming! I'll call you when I can, okay?"

Allison is checking a report from the Thirty-fourth Precinct when Gomez and Burley enter the Homicide Department.

"Where's Jack?" asks Gomez, noticing his empty desk.

"Didi's in labor."

"All right!" exclaim the men, giving each other high-fives.

"Listen," says Allison. "I got a report from Richter at the Thirty-fourth. He thought we might be interested in one of their cases."

"Why? Can't they handle it themselves?" Burley wisecracks.

"Just listen, John. About an hour ago, they found Senator Callahan's ex-wife's body at Fort Tryon Park, same M.O. as Catherine Stevens — she was dropped there from above. Detective Richter said he would share his info with us if we give him what we have on Stevens."

"I still have that clerk downstairs checking on plane and chopper rentals," says Burley. "There are hundreds, and she hasn't seen Cummings' name yet. The guys at the Thirty-fourth will probably check rentals, too, so we should compare lists with them. But both victims have connections to Senator Callahan, so what's up with that?"

Allison adds Lena Callahan's name to the whiteboard at Jack's desk. "I'm going to see if one of us can accompany Richter; he wants to interview the senator. Jack and I have already talked to him, so it should be one of you," she says, looking at Burley and Gomez.

In the hospital delivery room, Jack looks uncomfortable standing next to Doctor Stratt.

"Don't get too graphic," he tells his mother-in-law, who's recording everything.

"I want to be sure to capture the birth of my grandchild," she retorts. "You can edit out the parts you don't want later."

"Aieeee," shrieks Didi. "Jaaack!"

Jack rushes to the head of the bed, concerned that something is wrong with his wife. "What is it, hon?" he asks, worriedly grabbing Didi's hand.

"I love you to bits," she shouts through clenched teeth, "but... Owwwww! Sonovabitch! I'm gonna cut your freakin' balls off! Owwww!"

Doctor Stratt isn't disturbed by his patient's curses. "You're doing great," he tells her calmly. "One last push; we're almost there."

"Ooooh, umph!" the mother-to-be groans, bearing down hard. "I don't know if I can!"

Jack watches speechlessly as Didi pushes their child out of the place he has pushed into so many times before. *This is absolutely amazing!* he reflects in wonder and awe. *It sure is a miracle!*

When the baby is fully born, the doctor cradles the newborn as the child cries lustily. There's no need for the customary slap on the butt because this baby's lungs are filling the delivery room with a very welcome squeal.

"Congratulations!" says the doctor. "It's a boy!"

Leaning over, the nurse clears the baby's mouth and throat with a small suction device. Then she wraps him in cloth and places him on Didi's chest.

"We have a son!" beams Jack through a stream of tears rolling down his face.

While the new parents cuddle their baby, Sharon tries to keep the camera on them, even though she can't see much through her own tears.

Jack kisses his little son on the head, then does the same to his wife, as the baby stares at his mother.

"What a beautiful family you make!" Sharon cries.

The doctor gives the threesome a moment, then brings

them back to the task at hand. "Mr. Stenhouse, would you like to cut the cord?" he asks, pointing at the instrument.

"Um, yeah, I guess so," responds Jack, gingerly taking the pair of sterile scissors offered by the nurse.

"Go ahead, just cut it right there," the doctor instructs.

When the baby is free, the nurse retrieves the scissors from Jack's shaking hand and lays it on a tray. "I'll just take him for a moment," she says, gathering the baby up from Didi's arms. "I have to get his weight and perform some checks."

Reluctant to let the baby go, the new mother watches like a hawk as the nurse whisks her son away.

"Didi!" calls Doctor Stratt to regain his patient's attention. "I need you to give me one last push for the placenta. It'll be quick."

Outside the delivery room, Detective Allison Giancarlo and Sergeant Hector Gomez take seats in the waiting area.

"Where's Burley?" asks Allison. "He left the station way before us."

"Sylvia's back in town, so he's picking her up at the hotel. Do you believe they're still a couple?"

Allison giggles. "A couple of what?" she asks comically.

"Har, har," retorts Gomez, just as Jack walks into the waiting room, beaming from ear-to-ear.

Jumping up from their seats, they ask expectantly, "So?"

"It's a boy!" the new father exclaims while his friends embrace him happily.

"Everyone good?" asks Allison.

"Yeah, they're both great! The kid's a bruiser... Ten pounds!" he says proudly.

"Holy cow!" winces Allison, knowing what that meant for Didi.

A moment later, John arrives with Sylvia. "What's the good news?" the couple asks.

Jack smiles, "I have a son!"

"Ah, that's great!" says John. "What did you name him?"

"His name is Mark, after Didi's late father. Come on, everyone! Let's go to the nursery!"

CHAPTER EIGHT

The next day, the Big Apple has a new Stenhouse to reckon with. While Mark is too young to be unleashed on the world, Jack will take a short break from police work, and Sharon will stay with them to help her daughter transition into motherhood.

While Jack is out, Detective Giancarlo takes temporary control of the case. To get her bearings, she stares hard at the whiteboard near Jack's desk as if it could give her some insight or unknown knowledge about the information they've gathered so far.

"Mornin'," greets Allison as Sergeants Burley and Gomez saunter into the work area. "Detective Richter is going to interview Senator Callahan today at his house in Nyack, and I decided to accompany him. Did you get anything from the list of chopper rentals?"

Burley drapes his overcoat over the back of his chair, then takes a sip of coffee. "Three choppers were rented that night," he says, looking at his notes. "Two in Jersey and one on Long Island. Either one of them could have been used to transport Catherine Stevens to the statue, but Alan Cummings didn't rent them. In fact, he didn't rent any aircraft that night."

Allison rests her chin on her hands. "Darn. It couldn't be easy, could it? Check out the rentals for a few days before as well. I think Cummings is involved somehow."

Gomez looks at her curiously. "He has an alibi. Why do you think he's involved?"

"My bullshit-o-meter is off the charts," Allison says. "Something's not right, and I'm gonna find out what it is." Then she rises from her chair. "All right, boys," she adds. "I'm heading out to meet Richter now. Check Mrs. Callahan's social media posts like we did with Stevens, and contact Cummings again to yank his chain. See if something slips out."

While Allison heads for her car, Senator Callahan holds an emergency meeting with his chief of staff in his Nyack kitchen.

"Max, we're in the middle of a shit storm," he says. "First Catherine, then Lena, and the press is circling my house like zombies. I need to make a statement."

Maxwell Cauley, a young man with a law degree from Harvard and an attitude to match, sips his dairy-free, sugar-free, macchiato. "I'll take care of the zombies, just prepare yourself for your interview with the police. Stay calm and admit to nothing, but remember to show extreme remorse and surprise. This will all blow over. I got this; I'm going out there right now to smooth the waters. Just keep your eyes on 1600 Pennsylvania Avenue."

Later, Allison is happy that she's not the one who has to drive to Senator Callahan's house. It's not far, only about an hour north of the city, but the route will take them over the Tappan Zee Bridge, and she's not a fan of heights.

Uh, oh, she says to herself when the bridge comes into view. *Just breathe, you'll be fine.* As the steel girders go by, it sounds to Allison like they're dancing to the rhythmic song "Duke of Earl," which helps with her anxiety. But she needs to keep her mind occupied, so she thinks about Jack holding his newborn son, and tries to imagine how far Senator Callahan will go to dodge the questions that she and the detective intend to ask him.

When Kurt Richter finally exits the bridge onto Route 9W, Allison breathes a sigh of relief.

"We should be there soon," he says. "It's only a few miles from here."

"You've been there before?"

"No, never had the pleasure."

"Well, I have a feeling that today isn't going to be very pleasurable," Allison responds with a sideways glance at her fellow detective.

Allison and Kurt Richter don't usually have much contact with each other, but when they do, the man always reminds her of Jack. Though Richter is older, probably in his fifties, with a slight potbelly and no hair, there's something about him that seems familiar.

"Hey, what's going on up there?" asks Allison, looking out of the windshield.

"Looks like the press is here," Richter groans.

Ahead of them is a confusing mass of media vans and satellite trucks parked on the street outside of Senator Callahan's estate, with private security guards directing other vehicles away from the area.

"We're NYPD," declares Richter to a burly man in an official-looking uniform who approaches his unmarked vehicle. "We're here to interview the senator."

"Okay, park it up there," says the man.

The place the guard points to is a tree-lined driveway leading up to the senator's two-story house, located on a scenic bend of the Hudson River.

As Richter eases his car up the driveway, he takes sweeping glances of the well-cared-for landscaping. "Guess it's good to be king," he jokes. "You wanna take bets on whether he owns this place himself, or if the taxpayers are paying for it?"

Allison frowns at the thought of public funds being used for private luxuries. "If we're paying for this place, we better get a private tour," she replies dourly.

The officer stops his car in an attractive slate and concrete courtyard in front of an eight-car paddock with a brick façade. "Okay, now what?" he asks when they get out and there's no house in sight.

"Let's go through here," suggests Allison, peeking into a stone archway next to the garage. "There's a garden in there, and there's a house beyond that."

As the pair walks through the formal garden, Allison whistles in surprise at its beauty. "This place is gorgeous," she says, admiring the various plants and flowers. "It must take a fortune to keep up. But you know what they say, 'The bigger they are, the harder they fall.' Have you heard that he wants to run for President? Wonder how he's gonna explain the opulence of this place when the voters find out about it!"

When the detectives reach the house, the senator's housekeeper is waiting for them at the door. "Please come in," she says welcomingly. "Senator Callahan is waiting for you in his study. It's down the center hall, just past the library. I'll bring you all some coffee."

The detectives nod, then follow the housekeeper's directions, all the while marveling at the home's decor and vast cathedral ceilings exuding the scent of lemon oil and money.

Senator Callahan greets them outside his study. "You're prompt," he says to them both. "I like that." Then he extends his hand to Kurt and shakes it firmly. "You must be Detective Richter." Releasing Kurt's hand, he turns to Allison. "Detective Giancarlo, it's a pleasure to see you again. I didn't expect that we would talk again so soon. Please come in. This room is a little nicer than my office in Manhattan, wouldn't you say?"

The senator directs them to a cluster of tufted leather chairs and glass-topped tables in a well-appointed room.

When the detectives are seated, Kurt says, "I invited Detective Giancarlo to this interview because you seem to have a connection to both of our cases. And the manner of both deaths is similar."

"I see," replies Callahan. "Would either of you like a drink? Some water, perhaps? My housekeeper will be bringing us coffee, but you can have something else if you prefer."

"No, thank you," responds Richter, looking at Giancarlo for confirmation. "We're fine. If you don't mind, I'd like to begin."

"Oh. Yes, please do."

"Now, Senator, I know that you and Lena Callahan have been divorced for a while, but can you tell me if there is anyone who may have wanted to do her harm? The circumstances under which we found her body were quite unusual."

"I don't know of anyone who didn't like Lena. Of course, she and I didn't get along at the end, but she wasn't someone who made enemies."

"Did she know Catherine's boyfriend, Alan Cummings?"

Senator Callahan shakes his head. "No, I don't believe so, but Lena and I have been divorced for almost a year, and I haven't been involved in her life for longer than that. We began living apart years ago. Look, I'd like to help you as much as possible, but I don't have any information that would link these tragedies together, other than I knew them both. And now, I have two people to mourn."

Giancarlo can't help giving the senator a disparaging sneer. "Yeah," she says mockingly, "such a shame. Two people you had sexual relationships with are now dead. What a coincidence."

The senator gasps at Allison's cutting remark but remains silent, so Allison continues the theme. "Maybe you paid someone to do away with the people who could damage your political ambitions."

Finally, Callahan goes on the defensive. While beads of sweat form on his brow, he shouts, "That was uncalled for, Detective!" and points accusingly at Allison. "And I'm highly offended by the suggestion that I had anything at all to do with these women's deaths! Yes, I knew them both, but I'm not a killer!"

Callahan sighs and runs his fingers through his greying hair. Then, in a more reasonable tone of voice, he says, "Now, I think we're done here. I have to prepare for a public statement and get back to Washington, so if you need me again, please get in touch with my lawyer or my chief of staff. I'll have my housekeeper see you out."

Senator Callahan opens the door to his study just as the housekeeper walks up with coffee. "Sorry, Imelda," he says, "they're leaving now."

The housekeeper places a silver tray on a small table in the hallway, mumbling her displeasure in Spanish. "Follow me, please," she says to Richter and Giancarlo.

On the way back through the garden, Allison replays the senator's brief remarks in her mind. "He knows something," she says confidently.

Richter agrees. "Yeah, there's a connection to him somewhere."

Allison ponders various scenarios as they drive back to the city. "My team is interviewing Cummings again later today," she tells Richter. "I'll let you know what happens with that conversation, and we can compare notes. Funny that both women were pushed out of an aircraft."

John Burley and Hector Gomez have an appointment to talk to Cummings at his apartment in the Soho district, a high-end community in Lower Manhattan. The sergeants announce themselves on the building's lobby intercom, then board an industrial-looking freight elevator to Alan's fifth-floor apartment.

On the way up, Burley comments, "Jack has one of these elevators, too. I wonder if Alan's place is like his."

Gomez chuckles. "Yeah, like a Fiat's the same as a Ferrari. Jack's apartment is about 1300 square feet, and I bet Alan's place is five times that. This building is about four times the size of Jack's. The rent here would probably choke a horse."

When the elevator stops, Burley grabs the car's leather strap and pulls it down to open the door lengthwise.

"Come in, sergeants," echoes a lone voice beyond the hallway of this 6500-square-foot loft apartment. "Join me in the kitchen for coffee."

The policemen walk toward the voice, treading over expensive Oriental rugs and polished hardwood floors, past furnishings that make the place look like a showroom.

"Season ticket sales must be damn good," Gomez whispers. "Wonder if they need more salesmen."

Burley laughs. "You couldn't sell heaters to Eskimos."

In a slate and stainless-steel kitchen, Alan Cummings pours three cups of coffee, making sure to keep the bag out so the officers can see it.

"I hope you like it," Alan says, innocently pointing to the coffee cups. "Try it before we go into the study to talk."

Burley and Gomez shrug at each other curiously, but they each take a sip while Alan watches expectantly.

"It's okay," pronounces Gomez after swallowing a healthy amount. "Tastes a little nutty."

"This coffee costs $100 a bag," reveals Alan while he proudly holds up the bag of Kopi Luwak coffee."

Burley looks incredulous. "Why on earth is it so expensive?"

Alan smiles at them mischievously. "They call it poop coffee."

"What?!" ask the sergeants, spitting into their cups.

"It's okay," laughs Alan. "It's called that because it's made from beans taken from the poop of civets, a cat-like creature that lives in Indonesia. The civets eat the coffee cherries, then poop out the beans. It's a delicacy."

"You gotta be kidding!" exclaims John.

"Nope. Bring your cups with you. My attorney's waiting for us in the study."

Inside Alan's man cave, his millennial lawyer closes a folder and looks up from a grouping of chairs. "I said you had to go through me," he says smugly, "so now's the time. Speak up, officers."

The three men take seats, then Gomez looks directly at Alan. "Mr. Cummings, the body of Mrs. Lena Callahan was found this morning in Fort Tryon Park, and her death was similar to that of Catherine Stevens. So we need to ask, what were you doing last night?"

The familiar question startles Cummings just as he was swallowing a mouthful of his precious drink. While coffee squirts out of his nose, he coughs loudly and grabs an expensive cloth napkin. "Mrs. Callahan is dead?" he sputters. "That's... That's horrible!"

"Yes, it must be quite a shock," responds John. "But please answer the question. Where were you last night?"

Alan wipes his eyes and blows his nose. "I was home alone," he says, clearing his throat repeatedly. "Do you think I had something to do with her death, too?"

"Mr. Cummings, you are featured quite prominently in Mrs. Callahan's social media posts," says Hector. "It seems that you two were rather close. Did anything change recently?"

"Let me simplify that," interjects John. "Did you have an argument with Mrs. Callahan, too?"

Cummings widens his eyes and confers quietly with his lawyer. Then he stands and paces around the room. "I'm not going to say anything else," he declares firmly, while the lawyer in the light blue skinny-fit suit also stands.

"I asked you to go through my office, but you did not, and you made this appointment without me," he tells the sergeants. "If you have evidence against my client, present it now and arrest him. If not, please leave."

But Burley isn't done yet. "By the way," he calls out, "how many season ticket packages did you sell to afford this place?"

Alan stops short in his tracks and turns to stare at the police officers.

"We'll be back, slick," states Hector, "with or without your lawyer present. Don't leave town, capeesh?"

Back on the first floor, the officers step out of the elevator as a delivery man edges past them carrying a package. Gomez holds the door open for him while he places a call to Allison Giancarlo.

"Hey," he says, following John to their car. "Cummings had his lawyer there. When the questions got thorny, he clammed up and did his 'talk to my lawyer' routine again."

"Figures," says Allison.

In the car, Gomez offers a thought aloud to his partner. "It's so obvious the guy's dirty. There's no way that selling baseball tickets provides enough income to pay for that apartment."

CHAPTER NINE

"GODDAMMIT!" The loud expletive explodes from the bedroom while Didi rests on the living room sofa and Sharon works in the kitchen. Concerned, the women rush to check on the new father and son.

As they walk into the bedroom, they find Jack hovering over the changing table. "What happened?" Didi asks in a voice somewhere between puzzled and amused.

Jack doesn't reply; he just wipes down the table with a bunch of tissues. But his face and t-shirt are wet, and so are Mark and the changing table.

Didi bursts into laughter. The sight of her intrepid husband brought low by a newborn is too funny for her to hold back. "You were just christened by your son!" she laughs. "It already happened to me several times. Welcome to fatherhood!"

"Yeah, ha ha," chuckles Jack. "He's more like me than you know."

For a long moment, Sharon stands in the background, watching Jack fumble with the cleanup. Then she clucks her tongue and pushes him aside. "I got this, hotshot," she declares firmly. "Go get lunch. It's ready for you in the kitchen."

When Burley and Gomez walk into the Homicide Department, Lieutenant Conrad is shouting from his office. "We gotta dead body on Wooster Street!" he yells, waving a piece of notepaper in the air. "Eyewitnesses say he fell from a building!"

Gomez and Burley stare at each other with their jaws on the floor. "We just came from Wooster!" Gomez declares. "That's where Alan Cummings lives!"

"You two must have really irritated him," says Allison tartly. "He called the department right after you left, and I was the lucky one who answered the phone. He reamed my ass! I'll be happy to go back there with you now."

The unforgiving New York streets stretch the seven-minute ride to the scene of the death into almost forty-five. So when the trio arrives, the ordinarily quiet neighborhood is already framed in yellow tape, and police are swarming the area.

"There's Gibson," says Allison.

To approach the M.E., the team from the First Precinct lifts a line of yellow tape over their heads and ducks. Then Burley blurts out, "Holy crap, that's Cummings! What the fuck?"

Doctor Gibson turns to face the homicide officers. "You know him?" she asks.

Gomez shakes his head in disbelief. "Yeah, we just interviewed him about an hour ago. He was a person of interest in two separate homicides."

Gibson shrugs. "Well, the guy either hurled himself through a closed window, or he was helped through it," she says, pointing upwards. "There's a broken window on the fifth floor. I sent the crime scene unit up there."

Allison rolls her eyes and sighs. "Jack's a lucky guy," she says wryly. "He's missing out on all this fun. Come on, let's check out the apartment."

Doctor Gibson calls out to the officers' retreating backs, "I'll let you know what I get from the autopsy!"

At home, Jack looks at his wife while he gulps down a Guinness and eats the grilled cheese sandwich that Sharon prepared. *Dee looks better now than she did before she got pregnant,*" he thinks happily. *The little guy must have added at least one more D to her trademarks.*

While Jack eats, Didi rests on the sofa next to her mother. "You sure you don't want me to take him?" she asks Sharon. "Don't you need a break?"

"No way," Sharon replies. "He's comfortable, and I love how he nestles into the crook of my neck. Besides, you'll have him all to yourself when I leave."

While Sharon pats her grandson's back, she studies her daughter and son-in-law for the right moment to say what's been on her mind. When she finds it, she clears her throat softly and says, "I don't want to tell you two what to do, but Jack, you look like a fish out of water. Wouldn't you feel better if you were back at work? You're pacing around here like a caged animal."

Didi looks at Sharon, then at her husband. "You know, I think I agree," she says. "You should get your ass back to work, babe. I love ya, but you don't have to stay home with us; mom will be here for a while longer."

"But I want to be here," says Jack, "I—"

"Look," says Didi. "you're gonna be a great father, but you're also a great cop. And I know you're itching to get back out there."

"Well, I..." says Jack, looking at his wife in a certain way.

Didi smiles, "My eyes are up here, Jack."

"Yeah, but daaammn," Jack smirks. "Oops, sorry, mom."

Sharon waves her hand to dismiss Jack's remark, knowing that she's intruding on something.

"Well, if it's okay with you," Jack says to his wife, "I'll go back to work tomorrow. But if you need anything at all, Dee, you have to promise to call me immediately. No matter what's going on, I'll rush right back here."

At that moment, Mark wakes up and proceeds to let everyone know that he's hungry.

"Okay, here you go, mama," says Sharon, handing the baby over to Didi. "It's feeding time again."

Before Burley, Gomez, and Giancarlo enter the freight elevator up to Alan's apartment, John says, "Ally, this place is gonna blow your mind. It occupies the entire floor, and the view is fantastic. The décor is pretty opulent, too."

"Yeah, too opulent," agrees Hector. "The cost to live here must be outrageous. We need to find out how he was able to afford it. I'm willing to bet the Mets don't pay *that* well."

"Unless you're an athlete," interjects Allison. "Here," she says, passing out nitrile gloves and Tyvek shoe coverings. "Let's suit up for the crime scene."

When Burley pulls open the door at the fifth floor, Allison can't believe her eyes. "Wow, you weren't kidding!" she exclaims. "Did this guy win the lottery or something?"

As the trio makes their way through the apartment, the first things that catch their eyes are an overturned table in the living room and glass shards on the floor.

Allison walks over to the broken window. "You said the attorney was still here when you left?" she asks the sergeants. "Did you detect any issues between him and Alan?"

"They seemed to be in sync," responds John, looking around.

"Hi, guys," announces a crime scene investigator. "Glad you're here. We found blood on the frame of that broken table. Looks like there was a fight."

"Hey, I just thought of something," says Burley, looking at Hector. "Remember the delivery guy who entered the elevator when we got off? He was wearing one of those brown uniforms you see all over the place. But I don't think I saw a company truck parked anywhere downstairs. Did you see one?"

Gomez doesn't answer, so Allison jabs him in the arm. "What the hell are you lookin' at?" she asks.

Gomez bends down to brush shards of glass away from a broken frame lying on the floor. He shakes more glass off like newly fallen snow, then removes the picture from the frame. "Look at this," he says to Burley and Giancarlo. "It's a photo of Cummings in a military uniform with some other people. It was probably taken in Afghanistan."

Burley looks at the picture over Hector's shoulder. "Hey, that's Senator Callahan," he points. "But who's that guy dressed in black? He seems familiar, and he looks pretty chummy with Cummings."

Gomez looks at Allison. "When you interviewed Callahan, did he mention that he met Cummings while Cummings was deployed?"

"He said he met Alan at a cocktail party. I assume that was after Alan was discharged."

Hector studies the photo. "Oh, wait, I know this guy," he says about the man in black. "He was in Special Ops; his name is Serge Kaspin. Now he owns Black Horizon Incorporated."

Burley looks like he's seen a ghost. "Black Horizon? Those guys are mercenaries. They go wherever our government won't, and they do whatever can't be done 'officially.' What the hell is going on here?"

Allison looks around the apartment. "Okay, so now we may be getting close to knowing how Cummings afforded this place. Guess we need to speak to the senator again. Hector, tell the investigators that we're gonna take that photo with us. Let's do some digging on Black Horizon."

"Um, Kaspin left Black Horizon a while ago," says Hector. "They say he disappeared, but there are rumors that he's trading arms on the black market."

"Huh," says Allison, processing this new information. "This is starting to make sense. Cummings must have been working with Kaspin. That's how he could afford this apartment."

"Looks like Senator Callahan may be involved as well," adds Burley. "Let's get back to HQ."

While the threesome head down the freight elevator, Allison's phone jangles in her pocket. "It's Jack," she tells the others.

"Hi, Jack," she answers cheerfully. "Gomez and Burley are with me, so I'm putting you on speaker." Allison gestures at the men, then together, they ask, "How's it going, daddy?"

Jack laughs. "It's like being a eunuch at a porn convention. I can look, but I can't touch."

"What?" asks Allison, missing the reference to Didi's expanded bustline.

"Never mind," Jack replies, hearing the sergeants snickering in the background. "I got the 'all clear' from the missus to come back to work, so I'll see you guys in the morning. Any updates?"

"Yeah," says Allison. "The Stevens case has become a clusterfuck. The boyfriend we're investigating is now dead — thrown through the window of his million-dollar apartment. And adding to that drama is Callahan's ex-wife."

"Why is she involved?" asks Jack.

"She's also dead — dropped from a great height like Stevens, the senator's girlfriend."

"Geez!" comments Jack.

"That's not all," continues Allison. "You wanna know what's behind door number three?"

"I'm afraid to ask."

"You should be. Serge Kaspin, the owner of Black Horizon Inc., may be involved in this shit as well."

There's dead silence on the line. Then Jack responds while the muscles in his jaw tighten. "Ghosts making ghosts? Ain't that fucking great!"

CHAPTER TEN

Every morning, a familiar but jarring sound intrudes into the morning silence of Jack's bedroom, and he hates it. Although he knows it will happen, and in fact expects it, it sounds like a massive MOAB is exploding right beside his head.

"Fuckin' bastard!" Jack curses, preparing to hurl the offending object across the room like he's done so many times before. But when a loud, "Don't you dare!" comes from the baby's room, he places it back on the nightstand and shuts it off properly.

"I hate this thing!" he replies loudly. Then he sighs heavily and walks over to the nursery, still wearing his tighty-whities.

Jack smiles when he sees Didi feeding Mark in a rocking chair in the gaily decorated room. "Morning," he says. "That fuckin' clock's gonna be the death of me."

Didi heaves a heavy sigh; she's heard this a thousand times before. "I know you hate it," she says, "but you won't get up without it. And you promised not to break any more of them."

"I know," Jack replies, watching Mark fill up on his morning meal. Then he sighs again and walks to the bathroom, mumbling, "That kid is having a better morning than I've had in weeks. And shit, she still reminds me of the front bumper of a '58 caddy. I gotta get back to driving that again — soon."

Twenty minutes later, Jack sits at the breakfast bar dressed for work, but horny as a drunken sailor. While he sips his coffee, Didi sits down in the chair next to him and begins to rub his leg, checking periodically to make sure that Sharon isn't watching. Her mother is in the living room, walking Mark around while humming a nursery tune.

Didi looks stunning this morning, even without makeup. Her long, silk robe covers her swollen breasts, but Jack has no trouble imagining what's underneath. When he rises to the occasion, Didi whispers, "Wait a little longer, babe. We should be back to normal after my doctor appointment."

Jack squirms in his chair. "You know how to make it hard for a guy. I'm not gonna be able to stand up for a while now."

Didi kisses Jack's cheek and wickedly moves her hand higher, just as Sharon and the now sleeping Mark walk into the kitchen.

"Oops," says Sharon when she sees what's going on. Lowering her head to her grandson's ear, she grins and murmurs, "We gotta leave now, honey bun. Mommy and daddy are making nice-nice."

Later, Jack walks into the Homicide Department, his first day back after his son's birth. "They ain't Cuban, but they'll do!" he announces, proudly handing a cigar to everyone he passes.

Hearing Jack's voice, Lieutenant Conrad leaves his office to get one of Jack's fatherhood celebration gifts. "Did Didi kick you out?" he asks, grabbing a cigar from the open box.

"Yeah, I'm just a third wheel," Jack replies sullenly. "Didi and her mom are acting like little dictators..." he begins to say, until he sees his partner giving him a nasty look. "Whoops, I better rephrase that," he says cautiously. "There's a woman listening."

Jack keeps one eye on Allison while he puts his thoughts more diplomatically. "What I meant to say is that the women have everything under control."

Allison nods approvingly, but Jack leans toward the lieutenant, lowering his voice. "Actually," he confesses, "It's good to be back at work. This is the one place where I'm sure I know what I'm doin'."

The lieutenant chuckles, saying, "Welcome to fatherhood."

Jack smiles, then turns to look at the photographs now stuck to the whiteboard near his desk. He studies them for a minute, then blurts out, "Did you guys notice this?"

"What?" ask Conrad and Giancarlo.

"Look at these two pictures, the one of Catherine Stevens at the Statue of Liberty and the selfie Mrs. Callahan took at the museum. The same woman is in the background of each one. See here and here? We've seen this woman before, Ally. She's one of the volunteers at Callahan's office.

"Hey, you're right," says Allison, examining the photos again. "And... Oh, look at this other picture. It shows Cummings and Callahan on the battlefield, but she's there, too, standing next to Serge Kaspin. Could she be a chopper pilot?"

Jack cricks his neck — a move he makes when he's sure of himself. "I don't know about that, but I do know that we need to talk to the senator again. He's the only one in all of these photographs that's accessible to us."

"Well," says Conrad, turning toward his office, "it looks like you got three suspects now: Kaspin, the senator, and your mystery woman."

Before Conrad reaches his door, the elevator dings, and Sergeant Burley and Sergeant Gomez exit with two unfamiliar men.

"Oh, great. We must have hit a nerve," comments Jack. "The Feds are here."

The new father holds the cigar box open for his colleagues, who take one each. Then he closes it and looks at the FBI agents. "I'd offer one to you guys, too, but I know that most of you don't smoke. And if you're one of the few who do..."

Suddenly, Jack loses his train of thought. The younger of the two agents has captured his full attention.

Puzzled by the silence, Lieutenant Conrad looks at Jack to see why he stopped speaking. But he can't figure out what's going on, so he corrals the group for a meeting instead. "All right, everyone," he declares. "Let's go into my office."

The sergeants and agents follow Conrad; however Jack remains rooted in place.

"What's up?" asks Allison, picking up a notepad. "You look like you've seen a ghost."

"No, just the brother of one," responds Jack. "Let's go in."

Inside their boss' office, Jack makes a beeline for the younger agent. "You're Jacob, right?" he asks, greeting the man with a firm handshake. "When did you get discharged?"

"Good to see you, Jack," smiles Jacob. "I wasn't sure if you'd recognize me. I got out a few years ago, then decided to join the Bureau. What are the odds they'd assign me to New York?"

"Lucky for us," replies Jack warmly, still pumping Jacob's hand. "It's good to have you here. How are your parents?"

"They're fine. Thanks for asking."

Jack finally lets Jacob's hand go, then turns around to his office colleagues. "This is Jacob Assante," he explains with a wide grin. "He's Maria's brother!"

While Jack's coworkers react to the revelation with surprise and greetings, the other FBI agent stands on the sideline, watching everything.

Jack explains, "She worked with us undercover on a case involving a snake — a black mamba."

"Oh, yeah," says the agent. "I remember her going on and on about that case."

Allison looks more closely at Jacob. "Oh, I see the resemblance now," she says. "You have the same eyes! You have big shoes to fill, son."

"I know," replies Jacob. "The guys in the office are constantly reminding me of that."

Lieutenant Conrad knows how much his staff liked Maria Assante, so he allows the small talk to go on for a moment longer. Then he calls them back to work.

"Okay, everyone," Conrad announces from behind his desk, "let's get down to business. Which of you agents wants to tell us why the FBI is here?"

The senior of the two, a black man in his fifties, takes the lead. "Apparently, you already know Special Agent Assante, so that means I just have to introduce myself. My name is Senior Special Agent Bill Wilkens. We're here because we've been tasked with tracking down a guy named Serge Kaspin. He's number one on our most wanted fugitives list. He recently left his company rather abruptly, and we want to know where he is now. Anyone heard of Black Horizon?"

"Yeah," says Burley. "It's a mercenary group."

"That's right," says Special Agent Wilkens. "They're known for doing radical things around the world, and they've been on our radar for a while. We want to chop off the head of that snake, but Kaspin is slippery. He makes a lot of money off of other peoples' conflicts, but that isn't his only interest. He's also an international weapons smuggler, linked to several murders in New York, and he's connected to a para-military group headquartered in a small town in the Catskills."

"Sounds like a nice guy," snaps Hector. "We're also interested in him. He's in a photograph I took from the apartment of a guy who unexpectedly exited from a fifth-floor window."

"Oh, you mean Alan Cummings?" responds Wilkens.

"That's why we're here. We know that Kaspin had a relationship with him. Do you have that photo? We'll need to see it."

"Yeah, I'll get it; it's near my desk!"

Eager to display his prized find, Hector bolts from the office like a stallion from a paddock, while Wilkens continues his explanation.

"Jacob and I will be splitting duties on this investigation. He'll be working with you, and I'll be working with Detective Kurt Richter at the Thirty-fourth Precinct. They have a case that's overlapping yours, and we believe that Kaspin's involved in both."

"You know about Mrs. Callahan, too?" declares Allison. "Word gets around fast."

"Yes, that case is somewhat of a priority for us since it involves her ex-husband. We know there's a connection between Alan Cummings, Senator Callahan, Black Horizon, and a woman named Tonya Jefferson. We believe that some of them are still in contact with Kaspin, even though he hasn't been seen in public for a while."

Out on the floor, Gomez grabs the photo he found from the whiteboard, then starts to return to Conrad's office. But something makes him turn around. Looking over the other images on the board, he grabs one, and heads back.

"Here's the picture I was talking about," says Gomez as he hands the photo from the apartment to the senior agent.

Wilkens takes a long look at each person in the photo. Then he says, "Yes, that's Kaspin. And this is Tonya. She's standing next to Kaspin. She and Cummings were rumored to be close while they were in Afghanistan. Do you know they're both chopper pilots?"

Jack is puzzled. "So what if Tonya Jefferson's a chopper pilot who knew Cummings? Why are you interested in her?"

"We have reason to believe that she also works for Black Horizon."

"Oh, really? I think I saw her in Senator Callahan's New York office when we interviewed him there. Can you hand me that photo?" When he looks at the photo again, he says, "Yep, that's the woman I saw. I think she's one of his volunteers."

Hector is all ears. "Tonya gets around," he says. "She's also in the photo of Catherine Stevens at the Statue of Liberty. Here, take a look," he says, passing the other photograph from the whiteboard to Stenhouse.

Jack narrows his eyes while he studies the image, then passes it on to the FBI agents.

"Um, I don't mean to change the subject," interrupts Allison, "but you might like to know that I'm waiting for a call from Detective Richter. He's going to let me know what he's found out about Mrs. Callahan before Jack and I return to the senator's office to talk to him again. So if you don't mind, I'd like to go back to my desk."

"Wait," says Agent Assante. "You're going to have a long trip if you want to talk to Callahan. He went back to DC this morning."

Jack gasps loudly, then explodes with expletive after expletive. "FUCK! I hate that place!" he bellows. "I knew I'd have to go back there because of this case! Fuck, fuck, fuck! The bullshit in DC is so deep, the stink will never go away!" Then he points at the FBI agents. "Since we have to go there, I know you guys have access to private jets, so can you make one of them available for us? This case can't wait; dead bodies are cropping up left and right. It'll take hours to drive, and we need to talk to Callahan ASAP. If we don't get a line on these players soon, we may have even more dead people on our hands."

"Well..." says Wilkens hesitantly. "We do have aircraft at our disposal, but I'll need clearance if you're gonna use one of them."

"Okay, do whatever you have to," Stenhouse retorts. "Tell them that Jacob requested it. He's assigned to us, right? So there shouldn't be any problem."

Jacob smiles. "Then I guess I'm coming with you."

As Jack and his team file out of Conrad's office, the boss calls out, "What are you planning, Jack?"

"I got it," Jack replies over his shoulder. "I have a couple of theories, but I need more answers before I can share them."

At his desk, Jack delegates tasks. "While we're gone," he tells Hector and John, "Check Tonya Jefferson for helicopter rentals, and get her ass in here. Question her about Kaspin's whereabouts. She's ex-military, so she's gonna be tough. Don't take no for an answer."

In his Capitol Hill office, Senator Callahan looks through

a couple of folders before leaving for a meeting.

"So everything I need is here?" he asks his aide.

"Yes, be sure to bring all of it with you. I'll be at my desk if you need anything else."

While the senator gathers up the items he needs, a sudden vibration in his pocket startles him. Very few people have his personal number, so when his private phone rings, it's usually not good. He looks at the displayed number, then quickly closes his office door.

"Hello?" he asks cautiously. Then he listens while a computer-altered voice tells him something he doesn't want to hear.

The voice goes on and on, and he gets angrier and angrier. When he doesn't want to hear anymore, he barks, "Keep your damn mouth shut and take care of it, or I'll have to deal with it myself, and you won't like it when I do!"

CHAPTER ELEVEN

On the flight to DC, the clear air turbulence that the detectives and their FBI associate have been experiencing for the last fifteen minutes is making Allison keep a wary eye on her airsick bag. So when her ringtone suddenly jangles over Philadelphia, she's happy for the distraction, but she's also puzzled.

"Oops, I forgot to turn it off," she says, digging the noisy object out of her handbag. "You think they'll let me answer it?"

Jack shrugs. "No one's saying a word, so I guess it doesn't matter on a private jet. Who is it?"

"It's Richter. It's about time he got back to me. Hope he has something good."

Allison clicks on the call. "Kurt? What did you find out?"

"Looks like Tonya Jefferson is now our prime suspect. We found her name on a list of chopper rentals at a company in Jersey. She rented one the day before each body turned up."

Allison looks at Jack while she speaks to Kurt. "My guys are picking Jefferson up as we speak. You wanna get in on that interrogation?"

"Yeah, that'd be a good idea."

"Okay, call Lieutenant Conrad at the First. Stenhouse and I are on a plane headed to DC. We're gonna talk to Callahan again."

"All right. But if you're on a plane, how did you answer my call?"

"The plane belongs to the FBI, so I guess calls are allowed. Talk to you when we get back."

Jack looks intently at his partner while she slips the phone back into her handbag. "So, what did he say?"

Without warning, the plane suddenly lurches heavily in the turbulence, and Allison grips her armrests tightly. "Oooooh," she moans while the plane shakes and rocks side to side.

Jack knows Allison is nervous, so he tries to take her mind off the bumpy ride. "I'm gonna go out on a limb here," he says playfully. "I have a sneaking suspicion that you don't like roller coasters."

Allison responds to the jab through gritted teeth. "No, I do not like roller coasters," she mutters miserably. "I stay as far away from those damn things as I can."

When the ride stabilizes, Allison unwraps her fingers from the armrests. "To answer your question," she states, wiping sweat from her forehead, "Kurt says Jefferson rented choppers just before both victims died."

Jack is dazed by the new information. "Hoo-boy," he exhales. "We're working on the assumption that Cummings offed the women. But maybe it was Tonya. And there's still Kaspin."

A minute later, Jacob Assante returns from talking to the pilot. "We should be at Dulles in less than fifteen minutes," he tells them, taking the seat behind Stenhouse. "The Bureau contacted the senator, and he agreed to meet us in his office at one-thirty. So after we land, we'll have enough time to grab a quick lunch."

Stenhouse smiles happily. "Chicken and waffles on the Fed's dollar? Sounds good to me!"

Sergeant Burley looks up at the apartments above a sub shop on St. Nicholas Avenue. This neighborhood is old; empty storefronts dot the area, with occasional apartment units occupying the floors above. "She lives up there," he says while he parks the station's ancient Crown Vic across the street.

Sergeant Gomez knows the area is Hispanic, so he asks, "You think she speaks Spanish?" But Burley doesn't answer. He's already stepping out of the car.

At the corner, the men wait for a bus to pass, then cross the street. As they go, Hector notices a familiar woman on the opposite sidewalk. "That's her!" he says, pulling his partner the rest of the way.

The woman he spotted has just exited from an entrance to an apartment building. She's wearing boots, jeans, and a thick alpaca sweater against the crisp weather, and has a leather purse tucked under one arm.

Hector stops her by blocking her path. "Miss Jefferson?"

he asks. "I'd like to ask you a few ques..."

But Tonya doesn't want to hear what he has to say. Alarmed by the encounter, she pushes Hector aside, then bolts down the street.

"Crap!" the officers exclaim, breaking into runs to catch up.

The former servicewoman is fast. She dodges people in front of a store, then rounds the corner and turns her head to see if the cop is still following. But when she does, she runs straight into a man on a bicycle, and falls flat on her back.

"We're just here to talk," huffs Burley, winded and annoyed by having to chase their suspect. "Are you hurt? Here, let me help you up," he says, offering his hand.

But Tonya swats it away. "I have nothing to say," she states, rolling over to retrieve the purse she dropped.

"We'll see about that," says Gomez.

Hector and John help Tonya up from the sidewalk, then grab her elbows and escort her to the police sedan they left across the street.

Meanwhile, a couple of blocks north of the White House, Jack, Allison, and Jacob enjoy generous heaps of waffles with pieces of delightfully spicy chicken.

"This is great," comments Jack between mouthfuls. "But it goes best with beer, not the boring Arnold Palmers you two are drinking."

Jacob and Allison shrug as Jack, the irreverent SOB he is, toasts them with his beer mug.

"You know," says Jacob, "Maria talked about you so much that I feel like I know you. But I didn't believe all the stories she told; I thought she was exaggerating. However, even after the short time I've been here, I can see that she wasn't."

The mention of Jacob's sister wipes the smile from Jack's face. "Maria was a close friend," he says quietly, "and I think of her often. It's a fucking shame she's no longer with us." Jack sighs and takes a sip of beer. "Anyway, how's the Bureau treating you?"

"I'm doing well," Jacob responds lightly. "It's not as restrictive as the military, and that's a definite plus in my book. How are things with you?"

Allison shushes Jack with a finger on his lips. "I'll take this one," she says. "This guy just became a father! Can you see this idiot with a little one running around?"

"Wow, that's great!" declares Jacob. "Congratulations! I bet your wife makes a great mother. But from what I've seen so far, you as a father? Not so much."

Jack's smile returns as he recalls images of his new son. "Your sense of humor is just like your sister's," he laughs. Then he glances down at his Bulova. "You guys finished eating? We should head over to the Capitol. I don't want to keep the senator waiting."

At the First Precinct, John and Hector are sitting at a metal table in an interrogation room across from Tonya Jefferson. Detective Richter is also there, but he's watching from behind a two-way mirror.

Not surprisingly, Tonya isn't happy about being at the police station. She's shackled to the table, still refusing to cooperate. However, the sergeants are patient. They've been silent, watching Tonya while she ignores them and stares sullenly at the ceiling.

This continues to go on until Hector tires of the game. "We got nothin' to do for the rest of the day," he says, taking another gulp of a now warm bottle of water. "We can sit here as long as you like."

Tonya doesn't react, so John pushes the recorder closer. "This thing is on, you know, so you gotta say something. That's how it works. Or maybe we should just turn it off and leave you here alone until you decide to start talking. What do you think?" he asks Hector.

Hector shifts in his chair. "I think I'm gonna ask her one more time, and then I'm outta here. So let's try this again. Your name is Tonya Jefferson, is that right?"

Tonya frowns but nods affirmatively.

"Hey!" shouts Gomez. He's had just about enough, so he jumps into Tonya's shit. "This is a voice recorder, not a video camera! You gotta speak into it, right? Now, are you Tonya

Jefferson or not?"

Tonya leans back as far as she can in her chair without pulling on her shackles. "Yeah, that's me," she pouts.

"See?" smirks Gomez. "That wasn't so hard. Now let's get down to business. You served as a helicopter pilot in Afghanistan. That's pretty impressive."

Tonya looks surprised, so Gomez goes on. "Yeah, we know a couple of things about you, Warrant Officer Jefferson. We know that while you were overseas, you became pretty close to a fellow pilot named Alan Cummings. And when Senator Richard Callahan visited, you were pretty chummy with him, too. Oh, and Serge Kaspin of Black Horizons is also a friend of yours."

Tonya shrugs, unimpressed that the cops know these things. "So?" she says. "There's no law against talking to people, is there?"

"No," says Hector. "But the reason you're here is that you rented a helicopter the day Catherine Stevens was murdered."

"Who's that?" asks Tonya.

"C'mon, now," says Hector. "Your fingerprints were in the chopper you rented from Aerial Charters, and we're checking other evidence in the bird to see if it matches you or Miss Stevens. In addition to that, we know you rented another helicopter the night Mrs. Lena Callahan was murdered."

To prove what he's saying, Gomez pulls photographs from a folder and shows them to Tonya one by one.

When the pilot sees the bodies of Stevens and Callahan,

and the photo of her in uniform with Cummings, Kaspin, and the senator, her entire demeanor changes; her face goes pale, and her legs start bobbing up and down nervously.

"I didn't kill Mrs. Callahan," she declares firmly. "And that's all I'm gonna say without a lawyer. I got info you're gonna want, but you gotta give me a deal before I let you have any of it."

Tonya sets her feet flush to the floor, then leans back and smiles, confident that she now has the upper hand with the police.

Burley sighs and rises from his chair. "I'll take her to central booking," he says, disappointed that they got nowhere today.

Northeast of the Capitol, Stenhouse, Giancarlo, and Jacob Assante wait in the reception area of Senator Richard Callahan's office on the second floor of the Russell Senate Office Building.

"Who knows what stories are buried in these walls?" Allison wonders aloud as she taps her foot impatiently. "He does know we're here, right?"

Twenty minutes later, Senator Callahan pokes his head out of his office doorway. "Sorry about the delay," he says. "Come on in."

As the group files past, Callahan asks his assistant to

bring them some coffee.

Inside the office, the senator shakes hands all around, and when he reaches Jacob, Jack says, "You haven't met FBI Special Agent Jacob Assante. He recently joined our investigation into your wife's and girlfriend's deaths."

"I see," says Callahan, adjusting his voice to appear calm. "Please take a seat, everyone. My assistant found a few minutes for you today, but I'm going to have to leave soon; I'm needed back on the floor. There's a rather important bill that won't get passed without my vote."

Jacob seats himself in a plush chair around a highly polished coffee table, muttering, *Your vote may not be required much longer.* Then he opens a file folder and says aloud, "Let's get down to it, shall we? I don't want to waste any more of your time."

"Yes, let's get this over with," replies the senator condescendingly.

Jack clears his throat loudly to prevent himself from expressing his opinion about the senator's inflated sense of self-worth. "No problem," he replies instead. "New information has come to light since our last conversation, and we're here to ask you about it."

"All right," says Callahan evenly.

Jack crosses his legs, then casually folds his arms in his lap. "What is your relationship with Tonya Jefferson?"

Just as Jack suspected it would, the question makes a dent in the senator's façade — involuntary beads of sweat give away the man's true state of mind. "Um, I think I met her during one of my trips to visit the troops."

"How often did you make that trip, sir?"

"Just a few times," Callahan replies irritably. "And how is that relevant, Detective?"

"Well, there's been a development in the case. Tonya Jefferson was arrested today for the murder of Catherine Stevens, and possibly the murder of your ex-wife."

Now Callahan's face blanches, so Jack pushes on. "Sir, she's looking for a plea deal; she says she knows something that will interest us. Do you know what that might be?"

"I can't imagine," replies Callahan coldly. "I barely know the woman."

Jack clears his throat. "Senator, we know that Tonya had a close relationship with Alan Cummings, your girlfriend's boyfriend and a fellow chopper pilot, who is also a suspect in this case. But we can no longer question Alan since he's dead — also murdered. Isn't it funny how so many people around this woman you barely know are dying?"

"I, uh…"

Jack ignores the senator. "We have also found information that links Tonya to Serge Kaspin. Isn't it true that his company, Black Horizon, funded your trips to Afghanistan, and is a major contributor to your reelection campaign?"

"Now wait a minute!" Callahan declares hotly. "I don't know who set up those trips—"

Allison interrupts. "Is your career the only thing you're

concerned about? People are dying all around you, sir. We have a photograph of you with Serge, Alan, and Tonya, and you all look pretty friendly."

Jacob adds, "And in case you haven't heard, Serge Kaspin is wanted by the FBI for weapons trafficking, but he's disappeared; no one seems to know where he is. So we find it interesting that you've met him and two of the suspects in Catherine's and Lena's deaths."

"Look, I've talked to the police a couple of times already," declares Callahan, eyeing Jack and Allison. "You two were the first, then Detective Giancarlo came to my home with another detective — Richter, I think."

"This investigation is ongoing," states Jacob. "As we uncover more information, we'll be asking more questions. Sir, we came to your office today as a courtesy. If you weren't a senator, we would have taken you into the station for this interview, so we expect you to cooperate with us. If you refuse to answer more questions, or if you impede our investigation in any way, the photograph we mentioned earlier may find its way onto the evening news."

Senator Callahan narrows his eyes. "Is that a threat, Special Agent?"

"It's merely an observation, sir. Your constituents, never mind the general public, may not react favorably if they find out a United States Senator is hobnobbing with a weapons trafficker. Was I mistaken, or did I hear correctly that your ambitions extend to Pennsylvania Avenue?"

At that moment, Callahan's assistant interrupts them with a tray of coffee and cookies. "I baked these myself," she says cheerfully. "It's my mother's recipe. I hope you like granola chocolate chip."

Marjorie serves the group, then leaves and closes the door softly.

"I have no idea where Serge Kaspin is," says the senator. "I'm surprised to hear that he's disappeared."

While no one in the room believes that he's not in contact with the arms dealer, they move on to other things.

Jack asks, "How well do you know Tonya Jefferson?"

"I don't know her well at all. I know she and Alan were friends, but that's it."

Callahan's reply seemed overly smooth, so Jack continues to probe. "You don't know anything about Tonya Jefferson?"

"No. I already said that."

"Senator Callahan, your reputation with the ladies, including those on your staff, is no secret," says Allison. "It's well known that it was a major factor in your divorce. Now Miss Jefferson is an attractive woman, and for that matter, so is your assistant. So, was there anything going on between you and Tonya?"

Richard Callahan stands, balling his fists indignantly. "Look, I don't appreciate your inference, Detective!"

"No? What about the fact that you were having an affair with Catherine Stevens, Alan Cummings' girlfriend?"

Callahan frowns and straightens his tie. "I told you

everything I know," he declares curtly. "If you have any further questions, please direct them to my legal counsel. Now it's time for my committee meeting; I've given you more than enough time today."

Turning around, Callahan picks up his briefcase and walks to the door. "Marjorie will show you out."

When the senator is gone, Jack scoffs, "That went fucking well. Even hockey players don't sweat as much as he did."

Then Marjorie appears in the doorway, so before he leaves, Jack samples a cookie from the tray. "Mmm," he says, and takes another one.

On the ride downstairs, Jacob reveals his thoughts. "I'm gonna ask the DC office to put a tail on him," he tells the others, "and I'm gonna petition the FISA court to tap his phone and get his records. I think he may still be in contact with Serge, even though he said he isn't."

"He almost lost it when I brought up his sexual history," notes Allison. "But Jack, you acted as if you were sure that Black Horizon is funding his election campaign. And you also said Tonya Jefferson was arrested and wants a deal. What's all that about?"

Jack finishes the last of his cookie. "Fuck if I know," he smirks. "I made it up. I threw it out there to see if it would stick, and it did."

Jack's phone rings on their way out of the building. "It's Gomez," he says, raising the phone to his ear. "What's up, man?"

"We charged Tonya with the Stevens and Callahan murders. She says she has info and wants to know what it's worth to us."

Jack chuckles and winks at Allison. "I'm a fucking sooth-sayer!" he shouts at Gomez. "Thanks for making an honest man out of me!"

Hector is puzzled. "What the hell does that mean?"

"Nothing. See you guys in the morning."

Jack ends the call with a smile. "They actually arrested Jefferson, and she really does want a deal! Ain't that the shits?"

"That's good news!" says Jacob. "Look, guys, I'm staying in DC for a while, but the Bureau will fly you both back to La Guardia. And I'll get someone to drive you home from there."

"Huh. Guess it pays to be on the government's payroll," Jack remarks sardonically.

At the Capitol Building, Senator Callahan steps out of his meeting to make a call. "They were here," he says quietly. "They asked about all of it — you, Cummings, Jefferson, and my ex-wife. What the hell do I do now?"

Jack can't stop thinking the entire way home from DC, even though the FBI driver doesn't drop him off until after eight that evening. He's tired, but his thoughts keep bouncing around over the key issues of the case.

When he enters the elevator to the loft, he sighs and tries to quiet his mind. *That's enough!* he says to himself. *Time to start thinking about Mark and getting something to eat. Wonder if Didi's still awake.*

Instantly, Jack realizes what he's done. "Holy crap!" he mutters aloud. "I must really be a family man now! The wife used to be all I'd think of!"

When Jack exits the elevator's double door, he attempts to return to the old Jack. "Party's over!" he yells loudly, dropping his keys onto the hall table. "Time to get rid of the empty liquor bottles!"

But the only reaction he gets is from Sharon. "Shh!" she scowls. "The baby!"

Jack sheepishly lowers his voice to a whisper. "Oops!" he says. "I just thought…"

"Never mind," says Sharon, exasperated by her son-in-law and tired from a long day. "Are you hungry? I'll warm up the leftover meatloaf."

"Didi's meatloaf?" asks Jack, salivating like Pavlov's dog. "Shit, you don't have to warm that up!" he exclaims loudly. Then he lowers his voice again. "It's so good I'll eat it cold!"

Later, Didi walks into the kitchen, where Jack is digging into his dinner. "Hi, hon," she says wearily. "I just put Mark down for the night; he's been fussing all day."

Didi watches Jack wolf down his favorite meal for a moment, then she tilts her head and puts her hands on her hips. "No hello for me?"

Jack swallows a mouthful while he reaches for Didi's backside. "Come on, babe," he says impishly. "I'm starving, and it's your meatloaf!"

CHAPTER TWELVE

With a can of coke in one hand and a strong black coffee in the other, Jack walks into the First full of piss and vinegar. At his desk, he tries to use the extra boost he's getting from the beverages to connect the info on the whiteboard into something that makes sense, but a vision of his recently naked wife won't allow him to concentrate. So he gives up and rifles absentmindedly through a growing pile of papers.

"Rough night?" asks John when he notices the two beverages on Jack's desk.

Jack shrugs and sips the coke. "Didi missed me. What's the skinny on Jefferson?"

"Oh, bail will be set today. The DA will offer her a deal, but the terms depend on what she tells us."

Jack finishes the last of the soda, then tosses the can toward the recycling bin.

When the can hits its mark, John comments, "Your aim's getting better. I remember the days when you came in like this and you could hardly hold your head up."

"Yeah, I must be getting better at operating on only a few hours' sleep."

"How did your meeting with Callahan go?"

"Typical political bullshit. The FBI is getting a warrant for a wiretap and phone records. We have a good feeling that he's mixed up with Kaspin; we just need to find out how. Hey, I've been meaning to ask... How are you and Sylvia doing? Gonna marry that, or what?"

Burley laughs, "Slow down, will ya? Sylvia's great, and we've talked about it — hypothetically, you know? Maybe. I'm thinkin' about it."

"Don't think too long, Johnny boy," Hector interrupts when he joins them. "If you make her wait, she'll find someone else. She's not the type to sit around twiddling her thumbs."

"Maybe she's too hot for Johnny to handle," suggests Jack.

"I can handle her fine," John replies firmly. "We're just takin' it easy until..."

John lets his thought trail off when he sees Giancarlo entering the homicide area.

Noting the silence, Allison sets her purse down and looks suspiciously from one person to the other. "What?" she asks as the men scurry to their desks. "Did I interrupt something?"

"Nah," replies Jack, waving his hand while he gulps down his now cold coffee.

"Oh, I think I did. I know you guys. What's goin' on?"

"We were talking about you," fibs Hector. "We were saying what a good cop you are, even though you're a girl."

"Yeah, right," retorts Allison, not believing him for a moment. "Okay, you boys can keep your little secrets. Are you done now? Are you ready to get to work? I got interesting info from Richter."

John is eager to put the brofest behind him. "What is it?" he asks.

"Richter was busy while we were in DC." Looking at Jack, she asks, "You remember I told you that he said the chopper Jefferson rented the night Mrs. Callahan was killed was from a small regional airport in Jersey?"

"Yeah..."

"Well, witnesses confirmed that Senator Callahan was on the craft when they took off, and when they landed. Richter also found out that your hunch about Black Horizon is correct. The company is a major contributor to Callahan's campaign. Kaspin filtered his money through a special super PAC he set up just for that purpose."

"Ha! More truth from the mind of Jack Stenhouse!" Jack exclaims triumphantly. "I just *know* that Kaspin has a hand in all of this!"

"Yeah, I'm glad Kurt's on our team. He has a nose for digging up dirt. He also said the volunteers at Callahan's community office say our senator had affairs with many of his interns and volunteers."

"I'm not surprised," smirks Jack. "I bet Tonya was one of them."

Gomez breaks into the conversation to announce his own findings. "Kurt isn't the only one who's been busy," he tells them. "I did some digging of my own and weaseled info out of a Black Horizon employee. He said Cummings and Jefferson are on their payroll as helicopter pilots. And Forensics found some incriminating photos of Heatherton and Pino on Cummings' laptop. They were with Kaspin and Callahan at a party at a pretty fancy house."

"Huh, it's becoming clearer and clearer that they're all working together," says Allison.

"Yeah," agrees Jack. "Bet that party was at Callahan's place."

Jack looks thoughtful. "Hector, ask Forensics to send prints of those photos up here so we can take a look at them. And Allison, talk to Heatherton and Pino again, and take John with you. See if they'll tell you anything else about their relationships with the players. While you're all doing that, Hector and I will interrogate Jefferson. Depending on what she says, each of these women may need police protection. If any of them starts spilling the beans, I'm sure Kaspin will want to shut them up real quick."

At the apartment near NYU Law School, Jane Heatherton sighs when her phone rings, letting her hand hover over the doorknob. She was leaving for a job interview, so whoever's calling is interrupting her schedule.

"Hello?" she says, hoping whatever it is won't take long.

"Miss Heatherton, this is Detective Allison Giancarlo. I know you already spoke to two of my colleagues, but now I also need to speak with you and Miss Pino. It's urgent. I need to talk to both of you today."

Jane is surprised by the detective's serious tone of voice. "This sounds ominous. Is something wrong? I thought we answered all their questions."

"Yes, you did, but we have some new information that we need to confirm with the both of you."

"Oh. Well, Liz is at class right now, and I'm heading off to a job interview. I'll text Liz to let her know that you want to see us."

"All right. What time is good? The sooner, the better."

"Um, my interview is just a couple of blocks away, but I don't want to rush it. I should be free in, say, two hours, and I think Liz will also be available then." She checks her watch and says, "It's nine now, so that would be at eleven. Is that okay?"

"Yes, if that's best for both of you. Is there somewhere nearby where we can meet?"

Jane takes a moment to think. "There's a coffee shop on Sullivan and Third."

"All right, I'll be there with one of the detectives you talked to before. We'll get there early in case you can move up the time."

Allison ends the call and taps Burley on the shoulder. "John, we're going to meet Heatherton and Pino around eleven at a coffee shop near the NYU campus. Let's go."

"You want to leave now? It's only nine."

"Yeah. We can get breakfast before they arrive."

As John grabs his keys, Allison tells Jack that she's going to ask the desk sergeant to assign a mobile unit to keep tabs on Pino's and Heatherton's apartment in case they want to bolt.

Jack cocks his head. "That's a good idea, Ally. You're always thinking; that's one thing I like about you."

"Is that the only thing?"

Jack wags his finger playfully. "Don't push it, Giancarlo," he warns.

Jane is finally on her way to the Stern School of Business for her job interview. Regrettably, the call took longer than she liked, so as she hurries, she doesn't notice that a black SUV is following her from a distance.

While she walks, a man with mirrored sunglasses watches her from inside the car. "We have her, sir," he reports into his phone.

"Good. Keep her in your sights. She's meeting Pino later this morning, so we can take care of two birds with one stone. She'll be at a coffee shop on Sullivan and Third at eleven. I'm sending assets there now, so you'll be a backup."

When the call ends, the man turns to the SUV's driver.

"It's going down at a nearby coffee shop at eleven; it's at Sullivan and Third. Keep your eye on her in case things change."

CHAPTER THIRTEEN

On the way to the coffee shop where Allison and John arranged to meet the two law students, the day suddenly turns warmer, but this pleasant weather won't last. At this moment, a nor'easter is heading up the coast, and it's forecast to turn the Big Apple into a winter wonderland.

"Let's sit outside," says Allison.

Agreeing to the suggestion, John lowers himself onto a seat at a small table facing the intersection. The duo orders breakfast, and though they take their time eating it, they finish before the women arrive.

While they wait, they chat about various things, then fall silent. After a while, John taps Allison on the shoulder. "There's Pino," he says, pointing at someone crossing the street.

Allison rises and waves, beckoning Elizabeth to their table. "Good morning," she says. "You're Elizabeth Pino, right?"

"Yes, are you Detective Giancarlo?"

"Yes, I am, and this is Sergeant Burley, but I believe you've already met. Will Jane be here as well?"

"Yes, she should be here soon." Then Elizabeth directs

her gaze to Burley. "I remember you," she says. "What's this about? We already gave you our statements."

"Please sit down," says Allison. "We have additional information about Catherine Stevens' murder, including you and your friend's association with the case."

"What do you mean? There's nothing to add to what we already told you."

"We're hoping that we can jog your memories a bit. But let's wait for Jane to arrive before we go any further. Order anything you want, it's on us."

While the waitress takes Elizabeth's order, Jane turns the corner and heads for the café, dodging people as she goes. Behind her, a black Cadillac takes the same corner so fast that its tires squeal on the asphalt.

Alerted by the noise, John Burley looks for the source and is stunned to see a sunglass-wearing man pointing an Uzi out of the car's back window. "Get down!" he yells. "We got a shooter!"

To protect Elizabeth, John grabs her arm and pushes her behind him. Then he starts firing at the man with the Uzi.

As Allison spins around to see what's going on, she spots Jane coming toward them. But a second later, Jane lunges forward and falls to the ground from multiple bullets piercing her back.

As the speeding car passes the café, a continuous rain of 9mm rounds at 600 rounds per minute causes glass and bones to shatter, and forces everyone to scatter in all directions.

"Multiple shootings! Need assistance!" shouts Allison into her radio. "Officers down at Sullivan and Third!"

While the shooting is going on, Jack is at his desk at the First, staring at the wall clock that has just registered 10:48 a.m. "Hey, Hector," he asks, "when is Tonya due?"

Hector's response is interrupted by Lieutenant Conrad storming out of his office. Shouting at the top of his lungs, he waves a paper, saying, "There's been a shooting at Sullivan and Third! Multiple injuries and fatalities!"

"Hey! That's where Giancarlo and Burley went!" Hector informs him.

"Yeah, Giancarlo called it in! Get down to Presbyterian Hospital Downtown! They're in transit there now!"

"Are they okay? What the hell happened?"

"They took hits from a drive-by!"

Conrad refers to the paper in his hand for further details. "Pino, Heatherton, and four bystanders were also hit. Heatherton died at the scene with two others, and the rest are being transported as we speak."

Jack stares hard at the lieutenant. "If we find out that Kaspin ordered this hit, I'm gonna kill that bastard myself!"

"We don't know if he's involved," warns Conrad. Then he decides to leave that conversation for another time. "Look, I'll call Giancarlo's husband," he says. "Now get the hell out of here, you two!"

While the officers rush to their car, Senator Callahan moves away from the flow of traffic in the corridor outside the Capitol Building's Senate Chamber. His phone has just alerted him to a private text message. *Problem solved,* it reads.

Callahan stares at the phone for a minute, then breathes a sigh of relief. "Thank God," he mutters, as though a heavy weight were lifted from his shoulders.

At the same time, Doctor Stefan Goldson, chief ER physician at Presbyterian Hospital, gets an urgent message: *Multiple gunshot victims en route, including two police officers. ETA two minutes.*

Jack parks his Road Runner in an empty spot near the ER entrance. "This is the last place I want to be," he tells Hector. "Nothing good happens at hospitals."

"Oh, really? I seem to remember that you just had a baby."

"Oh, yeah, I guess that was good. But I was thinking about when I was shot."

"I remember that. You weren't a very good patient, were you?"

"No, I hate these places."

As they rush toward the automatic doors, ambulance techs are wheeling patients in, and nurses and doctors are barking orders.

Everyone ignores the two officers, so Jack stops a nurse. "My partners were brought in here," he says, flashing his badge. "Where are the two policemen?"

The young nurse stares at Jack, then spreads her arm wide at the controlled chaos. "I don't know, officer. We're a little busy here!"

An ER doctor passing by sees the frustration on the nurse's face. "Are you from the First Precinct?" he asks the men.

"Yeah. We need to see the officers who were brought here today."

"All right, but let's get out of the way for now," responds the doctor, leading the pair off to the side. As people rush around them, he explains, "We have a lot of trauma patients today. There are five gunshot victims — two officers and three civilians. One of the civilians was DOA, and the other two are heading to surgery now. One of the gunshot victims is a Sergeant Burley. Is he your partner?"

"Yeah, he's one of them."

"Well, he has multiple gunshot wounds, and he's already in surgery."

"What about Detective Giancarlo, a female officer?"

"She's being treated for a wound to her arm. I can take

you to see her."

The doctor leads them to one of the treatment rooms, where Allison is sitting on the edge of the bed with one arm wrapped from shoulder to elbow.

"What happened?" asks Jack, eyeing her bandages.

"It was a hit. A black Cadillac came blazing around the corner, then all hell broke loose. John got shot up pretty bad when he shielded Pino. But Heatherton didn't make it."

"We heard," says Jack.

"It was bad, but before John went down, he returned fire and hit the Caddy several times. I wrote down the plate number." Allison extends her palm to show her pals. "No paper."

Hector copies down the number. "I'll call it in, and I'll check on John and find out more on Pino. Conrad's gonna notify your husband, so he should be here soon."

When Hector leaves the room, Allison gingerly lowers herself off the bed. Jack notices that her sleeve was cut away and that there's blood on the side of her shirt. "They hit Heatherton as she was coming toward us," she says, "and then they concentrated their fire at John and Elizabeth. John's a hero, Jack. He sacrificed himself to protect Elizabeth."

Outside the room, a man cries out, "Ally? Ally? Where are you?"

"In here!" responds Allison, hearing her husband's voice.

"I'll leave you two alone," says Jack, heading for the door.

In the hallway, he turns around and pokes his head back in. "Don't be an ass like me," he warns Allison, wagging his finger at her. "Take some time off, and tell I.A. to fuck themselves if they want to bring you in too soon."

Jack searches for Gomez and finds him at the nurse's station. "Did you talk to the doctor?"

Gomez shakes his head. "Pino took a shot to the abdomen. She's critical, but they think she'll recover if there isn't any other damage. John wasn't as lucky, though. He has multiple gunshots to the chest, abdomen, and neck. All of them missed the carotid artery, but one bullet is near the spinal cord in his neck. He wasn't wearing a vest, but it wouldn't have mattered if he was."

"Is he out of surgery?"

"Not yet. I called Sylvia."

"Okay, stick around and keep her company," Jack tells him. "I'm sure Conrad contacted John's parents, so they'll probably be here as soon as they can book a flight."

"They're in Florida, right?"

"Yeah."

"What are *you* gonna do?"

"First, I'm gonna contact Assante to bring the senator in again. Then, I'm gonna talk to Jefferson. They're the only ones we can question about all this. After that, I'm going after Kaspin."

Hector frowns. "The FBI's been looking for him for a

while, so how the hell do you think you're gonna find him?"

"Well, I guess I'm gonna call the fucking ghost hunters. Call me when you get an update on John."

CHAPTER FOURTEEN

The ride back to the First is short and lonely. At a light, Jack drums his fingers impatiently on the steering wheel, hoping the light will change soon. When his ringtone trills, he looks over at the phone where he dropped it on the passenger seat. "Hi, Dee," he says. "What's up?"

"There was a news flash, and they said detectives from the First were involved in a shooting! Is everything okay?"

"Well..."

"Well, what?" asks Didi, her voice rising with concern. "Where are you?"

"I'm driving back to work. Allison and John were involved, not me."

"Oh, no! How are they?"

"Allison took some bullets to an arm, and John is in surgery. Ally's fine, nothing major, but we don't know about John. He got shot up pretty bad."

"Oh, Jack, I was so worried. What can I do?"

"Say a prayer for John; he's been in the OR for a while now. Hon, I'll be home late tonight. I'm gonna stop by the hospital again before I come home."

Within minutes, he parks outside the First, but decides to place a call before he leaves the car. "Hey, Jacob, it's Stenhouse," he says to the FBI special agent. "I got bad news. Two of my team were in a drive-by today. They were trying to interview Pino and Heatherton."

"Crap. Which ones were hurt?"

"Allison and John Burley. Allison was wounded in the arm. She's gonna be okay, but Burley's in surgery and it doesn't look good."

"That's tough. I hope they both recover soon. What about the interviewees?"

"Pino is also in surgery, and Heatherton didn't make it."

Jacob sighs into the phone.

"Pick up the senator," says Jack. "I'll be in DC tomorrow; I want to talk to him again. Then, I'm going for Kaspin."

Jacob says nothing for at least half a minute, and Jack wonders if he hung up. He was just about to ask if he's still there, when Jacob says, "Jack, you don't have to do anything about Kaspin. We're already working with the CIA and Interpol to find him."

"The CIA? Fuck the CIA!" shouts Jack. "So help me, Jacob, if Burley dies... That dickhead is mine, you hear? So back me up or get the hell out of my way! And Jacob?"

"Yeah?"

"Don't talk to that fucking Senator until I get there!"

Jack clicks End Call and flings the phone disgustedly back onto the passenger seat. "Fuck these cell phones, too!" he shouts into the quiet of his Road Runner. "There's nothing like slamming down a receiver!"

Jack storms into Conrad's office while the lieutenant is on the phone. "Geez, Jack!" the Homicide boss complains. "Don't you ever knock?" Then into the phone, he says, "Listen, I'll call you back."

When the receiver's in the cradle, Conrad looks over at his impulsive detective. "Before you say anything, Tonya's in Room Three with her lawyer."

Jack growls, "Burley's in surgery and it doesn't look good. I left Gomez at the hospital to give us updates. He's also going to speak with Pino when she gets out of surgery. They say she should be okay."

"What about Allison?"

"She'll be released today. Her arm will be out of commission for a while, though."

Lieutenant Conrad stands and looks at his department through the glass wall of his office. "If John doesn't make it," he says pensively, "he'll be the first detective to die in the line of duty in the history of the First Precinct."

Jack sucks in a breath. "That's not something I need to hear right now," he says angrily. "Did you reach John's parents?"

"Yeah, they're on their way; they should be here late tonight. Jack, that was Assante on the phone. Stay away from Kaspin, okay? The feds will handle that motherfucker."

"The feds can't handle an unplanned circle jerk, let alone Serge Kaspin! Did Assante tell you that they're gonna pick up Senator Callahan? I'm heading to DC in the morning to re-question that asshole."

Conrad shakes his head negatively. "Jack, just worry about Jefferson for now. Forensics says they found particles of Stevens' skin inside the chopper she rented the night Catherine died."

Jack cricks his neck and stands alongside his boss. "I guess I need to go have a chat."

At the interrogation room, Jack flings the door inward but doesn't enter. The noise jolts Tonya and her attorney, who look up to see Jack standing within the doorjamb with both palms on either side of it, like an actor in a movie poster.

Knowing that he's gained his suspect's attention, Jack slams the door shut and saunters over to the table, taking a seat opposite Tonya. Without saying a word, he stares into her eyes until she becomes uncomfortable.

When Jack finally breaks his stare, he looks over to the lawyer and realizes that the same attorney that represented Alan Cummings is working for Tonya.

"Well, look-a-here," Jack says with a smirk. "It's the man

in the skinny suit again. I wonder which one has you on re-tainer. Is it Senator Callahan, or Serge Kaspin? Oh, fuck, never mind. I don't give a damn."

Jack turns his sniper stare back to Tonya. "So, this infor-mation you say you have better be good, because things could get pretty dicey for you around here. We found samples from you and Stevens in the same chopper. You know — the one you rented the night she died?"

Jack expects Tonya to react in some way to the incrimin-ating evidence, but instead, she's as cool as a frozen margarita.

"Before I talk, I want involuntary manslaughter, and witness protection," she declares calmly.

Uncharacteristically, Jack takes a deep breath and tries to control himself. Normally, he'd hurl his customary insults at his suspect when she brought up witness protection, but for some reason, he doesn't.

"Alan Cummings and Jane Heatherton are dead," he de-clares evenly, "and Elizabeth Pino and two of my team mem-bers have bullet holes in them, along with several bystanders."

Jack worked hard to keep himself in check, but then he loses it, and his voice goes up several octaves. "And you say you want *protection*? Don't you know that it's just a matter of time before we confirm your connection to Kaspin? I know we're good, but do you really think you can outrun Kaspin and his goons forever? If we don't find him first, I'm not sure how long you'll stay alive!"

When Jack's outburst is over, the millennial lawyer clears his throat. "Detective, my client has information that will put both Senator Callahan and Serge Kaspin behind bars.

Therefore, what she said is correct. In exchange for her information, we will only accept Manslaughter II and protection. That's our final offer."

Exasperated, Jack runs his fingers through his hair. Then he looks at the surveillance camera above the two-way mirror, and talks to the mirror. "Lieutenant, can you contact the DA and find out if that's okay?"

Then Jack turns back to Tonya. "Look, I don't give a damn about Callahan, I only want Kaspin. So if the DA says it's okay, you have a deal. Now, give me something. What the hell do you know?"

Tonya leans over to hold a whispered conversation with her lawyer. Then she sits upright and looks at the mirror. "I can talk a little about Cummings and Stevens, but I won't say anything else until I hear back from the DA."

Jack nods in agreement, so she says, "Alan and I met in basic, then they sent us to Kandahar in the same unit. That's where we met the senator and Serge Kaspin. They visited the base often because Serge's company was supplying specialized weapons and other firearms to our unit, and the senator was a member of the committee that authorized the sale. Kaspin liked Alan from the start, and offered him a job after his tour was up. I got along with the senator because he likes pussy, so he offered me a position on his staff. No pun intended."

The joke falls flat because Jack is staring at Tonya, trying to get a read on whether she's lying or telling the truth. When he receives no clear sign of her intent, he asks, "Where does Catherine Stevens fit in?"

Once again, Tonya turns to her lawyer, who gives her the go ahead. "I love Richie," she says with a shrug. "Um, that's Senator Richard Callahan. He's a dog, but Stevens knew I wanted him, and she still fucked and sucked her way into his confidence. So, I killed her."

Jack is shocked by Tonya's indifference. "Just like that?" he asks.

Tonya shrugs again. "Richie likes to party, and so do I. When he met Pino and Heatherton, he persuaded them to have a group gang bang. But they were living in a shithole, so Richie started funding them. He doesn't like it when his women are struggling. Have you seen their apartment?" Jack nods, so she continues, "How the hell do you think those two bimbos could afford that crib without help? Anyway, Richie's ex found out about his women, and now she's dead. I don't know who killed her, but I know Richie wasn't happy that she knew, and I also know that Kaspin wanted her out of the picture."

"Senator Callahan had already divorced his wife by that time, so why did he care that she found out?"

"As a condition of the divorce, he made her sign a statement demanding that she wouldn't say anything about his sexual activities, but Lena was going to spill it all. She told him that she was going to write a book about his sexual escapades and his ties to Kaspin."

"What do you know about Kaspin?" asks Jack. He hopes to keep the momentum going, but Tonya has had enough.

"That's all I'm going to say," she declares, clamming up tighter than a witch's ass. "I'm not saying anything more unless the DA accepts my deal. If he does, I'll let you know about Kaspin, Cummings, and Callahan."

Confident that she has the upper hand, Tonya leans back

in her chair and tiredly cricks her neck.

Hector is pacing the hospital's surgical waiting area when Sylvia Stone rushes in, frantic and upset. "They won't tell me anything because I'm not family," John's girlfriend tells him. "How is he? What happened?"

"He's in surgery. He was shot, and we don't have any information on his condition yet. Allison was hit as well, but she's been released."

"Wasn't he wearing a vest?" Sylvia asks accusingly.

Hector sits Sylvia down on a small sofa. "They were conducting a routine interview with two college girls at a small coffee shop. It was a drive-by; no one could have predicted it."

"Detective Gomez?" interrupts a surgeon in hospital blues.

"Yes? How's Sergeant Burley?"

"Burley? I worked on Elizabeth Pino."

"Oh. How is she?"

"I'm sorry to say that she didn't make it. She had a stroke on the operating table. Sorry. Does she have family here?"

"No, we'll take care of notifying them."

"All right. Look, I'll check on Sergeant Burley for you."

Jack is in Lieutenant Conrad's office when his cell phone rings, and it's Hector.

"How's John?" he asks.

"We still don't know. Sylvia's here now, so I'll stay with her. But Jack, Elizabeth Pino died."

Jack sighs and mumbles something unintelligible. Then more coherently, he says, "Thanks, Hector," and ends the call.

"Pino died," he tells the lieutenant, "but nothing on John yet. What's taking that surgery so long?"

The rhetorical question hangs in the air while each man thinks the worst and neither of them wants to voice their fears.

When Inspector Rawlings enters the room, they seem relieved to discuss something else.

"Guys, I just got off the phone with the DA. He says he's hamstrung by the FBI on this case, so he can't decide about Jefferson until the feds give him the okay. They issued a warrant, and they're going to arrest the senator tonight on suspicion of crimes against the United States and murder. We put Tonya in a safe house until he can make a decision about whether he wants to agree to her terms or not."

Jack looks upset about the feds arresting Callahan so soon. "They're gonna pick him up tonight? I still have questions!"

The inspector takes a moment to consider his options. Then he looks at Jack. "You can talk to him tomorrow. Take the 6 a.m. train from Penn Station, and we'll get you a return flight home tomorrow night. I'll see if I can get Assante to pick you up in DC. You'll have the entire day to do your interview."

"Okay, I guess that'll work."

When the inspector's phone rings, he steps out of the office to answer it, and returns with a worried look on his face.

"What is it?" Stenhouse and Conrad ask with one voice.

"John's out of surgery, but he's in a coma. It doesn't look good, guys. I'll send our chaplain to the hospital to meet with his parents."

That night, Didi is waiting at the elevator when Jack pulls on the cord to open the doors.

"Hey, mama," he says tiredly, barely noticing that she's back in skinny jeans and is wearing her old maternity T-shirt with "Guess?" stretched across her chest.

Jack reaches for his wife, then Mark suddenly stops crying in the nursery.

"I guess he knows you're home," says Didi. "How's John?"

"Time will tell. He's in a coma, babe. No one knows how it's gonna play out. I gotta go back to DC tomorrow morning, but I'll be home at night."

"Okay," says Didi, rubbing her chest across Jack's. "What can I do to take your mind off things?"

Despite his weariness, Jack smiles. "Yesterday you said you wanted to wait until you saw the doctor."

"Well, surprise, I saw him today, and he gave me the go-ahead. Are you good to go? I know I am."

Jack grabs Didi's arm and leads her toward the bedroom. "Then let's get busy while Mark's behaving himself."

CHAPTER FIFTEEN

Early next morning, Jack buttons up his peacoat while he walks through Union Station. The weather in DC is colder than New York, so he wants to be prepared when he steps outside. As he goes, he recalls the last time he was here when his friend, FBI Special Agent Maria Assante, was the one picking him up.

When he opens a door facing Union Station Drive NE, Jacob sees him and waves from the driver's seat of a black Suburban parked at the curb.

"Hey, Jack!" calls Jacob, waving him over to the car.

For an instant, Jack pictures Jacob's sister rolling her eyes while shaking her head at him, then blinks away the image and climbs into the passenger seat.

"Did you get him?" he asks.

"Yeah. He wasn't too happy, especially since he's now the talk of the town, and not in a good way."

Jack unbuttons his coat because now he's hot. "You got the heat on in here?"

"Yeah, too much? I'll lower it." Jacob fiddles with the knobs while he keeps his eyes on the road. "I'm going to lead the interrogation, and you can observe. I'll bring you in later."

Jack nods, but what he's thinking is, *Shit, I can't get over how much he looks like his sister!*

At FBI headquarters, Jack is directed to a small room where a one-way mirror and a speaker allow him to follow along as Special Agent Assante questions Senator Callahan, with his attorney nearby.

To begin the interrogation, Jacob lays out photos of Catherine Stevens, Alan Cummings, and Mrs. Lena Callahan. "Take a good look," he says to the senator. "All of these people are connected to you, and they're all dead."

Callahan looks at everything but the photographs.

Undeterred, Jacob takes out two more photos and hands them directly to the senator. "Do you know these two young women?"

Playing it cool, Callahan glances briefly at the photos, then quickly hands them back. "They look familiar," he declares condescendingly. "They may be friends of Catherine Stevens."

Jacob frowns. "They say they know you quite well. In fact, they say you bedded both of them at the same time. Does that jog your memory at all?"

"I don't know—" begins the senator, until Maxwell Cauley pulls on his arm.

Callahan listens quietly while Maxwell whispers something in his ear, but it doesn't look like he wants to accept what he's saying. He shakes his head and tries to pull away, but Cauley insists.

Finally, after a few more whispered comments, Callahan replies grudgingly, "Yes, I know them."

At the senator's admission, Jacob narrows his eyes and sets his elbows on the table. Leaning forward, he declares, "Senator Callahan, both of those women were murdered yesterday in a shootout in Manhattan, and two cops and several innocent bystanders were also hit. Did you have anything to do with that, sir?"

"What?!" asks Callahan, appearing to be highly insulted by the question. "I'm a United States senator for crying out loud! How could you think I had anything to do with a *shootout*?"

Jacob isn't fazed by the outburst. "I find it disturbing, to say the least, that two more persons who knew you are now dead. And you should also know that Tonya Jefferson thinks you did have something to do with it."

Callahan takes a dim view of Tonya's accusation. "Really? Tonya Jefferson?" he declares, throwing up his hands in exasperation. "And you believe her? Special Agent, Tonya is an aide in my New York office. All the women in that office are jealous of each other. They all want my attention, and they do everything they can to get it. Sometimes I even have to lock my door; they'd do anything for some face time. I wouldn't be surprised if any of them lied just to get noticed."

Jacob doesn't believe Callahan for a minute. "So Tonya Jefferson would tell the cops that you kill people just for a chance to talk to you?"

"Well, umm, no… I mean, Tonya is—"

To shut Callahan up, Maxwell puts a restraining hand on his arm.

"Tonya is in protective custody," says Jacob. "She admitted that she killed Catherine Stevens, and now she's waiting for the DA to agree to certain terms before she reveals more."

"Whoa, wait a minute!" exclaims Maxwell Cauley. "Tonya confessed to killing Stevens? So what does Tonya have to do with my client? Why is he here, Special Agent? Nothing you've said so far links him to a crime."

Jacob snickers. "He's here because death is following him around like a shadow, and we believe that he and Serge Kaspin are behind this killing spree."

"You 'believe'?" scoffs Cauley. "Where's your proof? And when did Serge Kaspin become part of this?"

"I'll be honest, Kaspin is at the top of our most-wanted list, and we'd really like to put him behind bars. We know the senator is connected to him, so why don't you advise him to come clean?"

Looking back at the senator, he says, "The video of you being led away in handcuffs is all over the airwaves now, and it won't help you get reelected. Tell us what you know; help us get Kaspin. Then we can work something out for you."

In a prearranged signal, Jacob moves his case file from

one side of the table to the other, letting Jack know that he can now enter the interrogation room.

A minute later, Jack walks in and sits down next to Assante while Callahan confers with his lawyer.

When the senator looks up, he sees Jack, and reacts with indignation. "What's going on?" he shouts, pointing at Stenhouse. "Why is *he* here?"

Jack being Jack, he lets the senator know precisely why he's there, in no uncertain terms. "It's because of your association with Serge Kaspin, you mother f...!" he shouts, uncharacteristically biting his tongue. "I'm not gonna say what I really want to because of your position. But I'm here because I'm the gatekeeper of your own personal hell. Because of that shootout in New York, one of my sergeants is in a coma, my partner is shot up, and bystanders are either dead or injured."

"I told you! I didn't have anything to do with that—"

"Don't bother!" retorts Stenhouse, not letting the senator finish. "We know that Kaspin gave you a shitload of money for your campaign, so it's highly likely that he doesn't want anything to ruin your chances of getting reelected. He's just the kind of guy who would want to get rid of problematic people — people like Alan Cummings and those two women you don't seem to remember well. By the way, did you know that Cummings had a video of you with Jane Heatherton and Elizabeth Pino in some pretty compromising positions? Where's Kaspin?"

Callahan drops his head into his hands and seems to shrink before their eyes. "That bastard controls too much," he tells them. "I can't risk having him know that I talked."

Sensing a weakness, Jack presses on, hoping Callahan will crack. "We know you were in a helicopter with Tonya Jefferson the night your ex died," he says. "Did you two drop Lena in Fort Tryon Park?"

"Did I do *what*?" asks Callahan, chortling heartily. "Detective, Tonya flew us to a private party in Connecticut that night, and boy, did we make a grand entrance with that chopper!"

Jack looks dubious, so Callahan claims, "If you don't believe me, check our flight path with the FAA. Tonya and I spent the entire night at that party, and we had breakfast there, too."

Cauley stops his client from talking further. "That's enough," he says. "We have nothing more to say. Senator Callahan has a perfectly good alibi for every one of those deaths you mentioned, and you haven't presented any evidence of wrongdoing on his part. So I'm going to file for his release. Let's go, sir."

"Not so fast," warns Jacob Assante, rising from his chair. "We can hold him for another forty-eight hours, and you can bet that we're going to talk to him again."

Callahan raises his brows questioningly. "Can he do that?" he asks his lawyer.

Cauley shrugs in reply, so Jacob says, "Senator Callahan, I should remind you that you are being questioned under oath. Lying to the FBI is a felony."

Stenhouse and Agent Assante wait until the senator is escorted out of the interrogation room, then they look at each other like two cellmates with a tip for the warden.

"Callahan didn't kill anyone," declares Jack.

"No, but he knows who did," states Jacob.

The men chuckle softly, knowing they've come to the same conclusion.

"Well, I'm glad we got that cleared up," says Jack. "But how are we gonna tie him to Kaspin?"

"We have that money trail linking them together."

"Yeah, but that's not gonna be enough."

"There's also an international warrant out on Kaspin for illegal weapons trafficking, and when the press gets wind of Callahan's involvement with him, it's gonna ruin the senator's political career."

"Well, I'm not so sure about that," contends Jack. "There's not much that seems to derail corrupt politicians nowadays."

Jacob concurs. "You're right about that," he says. "But there's one more thing. Your forensic guys found a safe deposit key in Cummings' apartment. When we find out which bank it belongs to, maybe there'll be something in it we can use."

"Let's hope. We don't have much else."

Jacob rises from his chair. "I'll drive you back to the airport now. When you get back to New York, get a statement from Tonya. I'll work on Callahan for as long as we have him here."

On the way to the airport, a cell phone comes alive at an old warehouse in Nyack, New York.

"Go ahead," says a voice.

"Jefferson is in police custody at a safe house on Staten Island."

"Handle it," the voice orders.

Back in Manhattan, Sylvia Stone hasn't moved from John Burley's bedside. As soon as she saw him, she pulled a chair up close, and she's been talking to him and holding his hand ever since, even though he's still in a coma.

For as long as she's been there, no one else has been in the room except doctors and nurses, so when a uniformed police officer enters with an older couple, Sylvia knows something's up.

"Oh, my god!" cries the woman, her hand flying to her mouth in shock. "My poor baby!"

While the man comforts her, he asks, "Are you Sylvia?"

"Yes."

"We're John's parents."

"Oh! I'm happy to meet you," responds Sylvia, standing to greet them.

"We're glad you're here," says the man. "I'm Frank, and this is my wife, Connie. The last time we talked to John, he said he wanted us to meet you, but this isn't the way we imagined it would be."

Suddenly, a thud, barely audible over the beeping monitors, catches their attention. Turning to the bed, they're shocked to see John looking at them with one eye.

As Sylvia runs to the bed, John lifts one hand, then drops it to let them know that he's aware of them. He's on a ventilator, so he can't talk.

"Nurse, nurse!" shouts Frank joyfully.

In front of a vacant cape cod on New York's Staten Island, a truck from All Things Air Conditioning and Plumbing parks in a short driveway. The cape cod is across the street from the unassuming dwelling where police are guarding Tonya Jefferson.

When the truck's engine shuts off, two men in repairman uniforms climb out of the truck — one heading for the house and the other making a beeline for the for-sale sign on the lawn.

The man on the lawn replaces the "For Sale" wording with a large "Sold" banner. "This place will do nicely," he mutters.

A few minutes later, one of the officers guarding Tonya peeks out of the living room window during one of his periodic checks of the surrounding area. "Hey, Jimmy," he calls out. "I guess we're gonna have new neighbors. The sign across the street says 'Sold,' and there's a repair truck in the driveway."

The two "repairmen" inside the empty house waste no time getting ready for their current job. They set up a tripod in the living room and tighten a suppressed Remington 700 SPS rifle and a Leupold Mark IV scope onto it. Then they chamber a .308 Winchester round and point the weapon at the house across the street through the closed blinds.

"Detective Giancarlo? What are you doing here?" asks Inspector Rawlings when Allison walks off the elevator.

"I'm going stir crazy at home, sir. I'm better off if I work. Besides, with Burley down—"

"Detective," interrupts Rawlings, "you were just involved in a shooting, and your arm is still injured. If something happens to you while you're here, we'll have two officers out of commission. Go home."

Passing by them, Lieutenant Conrad is also surprised to see Allison. "How's your arm? You feel well enough to work?"

"Yeah, I'm okay. It's too boring at home."

Allison's boss looks at her skeptically. "Did your doctor say it was all right?"

"Well…"

"Look, I know it's tough to feel that you're out of the mix, so I'm gonna trust you to pace yourself. Take it easy, you hear?"

"I will," Allison replies. "I can't wait to get these bandages off."

"Actually, I'm glad you're here," confesses Conrad. "I need someone to go to Presbyterian Hospital. Burley regained consciousness."

"Wow, that's great!" Allison exclaims happily. "Hey, Hector!" she calls out to the sergeant at his desk. "Burley's conscious!"

While Hector runs over to get more details, Conrad adds, "It's fantastic news! Check it out and report back to me. And while you're there, have them look at your arm again."

"What's his condition?" asks Hector.

Conrad replies, "Don't know yet. Allison's going over there to find out."

Hector nods. "As long as you're all here, the FBI says Alan Cummings had his safe deposit box at the Chase branch on Delancey Street. They're in the process of getting a warrant, so I'm gonna head down there." Turning to Allison, he tells her that he'll accompany her down to the street.

When the officers are in the elevator, Rawlings pulls Conrad aside. In a low voice, he says, "I was on my way to see you. I've decided to promote Giancarlo to our terrorism unit when this case is wrapped up. She's good; she needs her own team."

Conrad agrees. "Yeah, I guess it's time. I agree that she's good; we've depended on her a lot. The entire Homicide Department is gonna miss her, especially Jack."

"Jack will be okay," states Rawlings. "I'm moving others around as well, so we can get him another partner. Let's go to my office. There's more to discuss."

CHAPTER SIXTEEN

As Allison approaches John Burley's hospital room, Sylvia Stone steps into the hallway with John's parents. "Allison!" she says, concerned by the officer's tightly bandaged arm. "How do you feel?"

"Oh, I'm pretty sore, but I'll be okay."

"Glad to hear that. Allison, these are John's parents, Frank and Connie Burley. They arrived today from Florida."

"Hello," Allison smiles. "I work with John. I'm Detective Giancarlo."

Connie smiles back at her. "John talks about you and the others he works with a lot. We heard about what happened; I'm so glad you're okay."

The mention of the shooting suddenly fills Allison's mind with images she'd rather forget, so she expresses her thanks with a forced smile. "You should be very proud of your son," she says. "He did all he could to protect others. How is he doing?"

Frank is still riding a high after seeing his son regain consciousness. "This morning, he raised a hand and opened one eye," he says happily. "The doctor is in there now, checking him out."

While the group waits for the physician to finish his assessment, they make awkward chitchat.

After a while, a dark-skinned Sikh emerges from the room.

"How's our son?" asks Connie eagerly.

The doctor takes Connie's hand. "Mrs. Burley, John is awake. His blood pressure is good, his breathing is clear, and there is no sign of infection. So we will take him off the ventilator. These are all good signs. However, he has restricted movement on his right side, and we do not know why yet."

Crowded around the doctor, John's parents gasp, and Sylvia asks in a shaky voice, "Is it permanent?"

The doctor looks at the group solemnly. "John lost a lot of blood before we could get him into surgery. He also has internal injuries from the bullet's fragments. We got most of them out, but not all. It is possible that he could have had a stroke; we just do not know at this time. We will be conducting tests in the coming days."

Amid whimpers and moans from John's family and friends, the doctor adds, "I am cautiously optimistic, as long as there are no complications." Then he stops and looks intently at Allison and her bandaged arm. "You were here yesterday, weren't you? Why are you up and around today? Come with me; I am going to have one of our residents examine that arm."

While Jack flies home from DC, no one on his plane is happy when the pilot announces that heavy air traffic at La Guardia will keep them circling the airport for a while.

When they go around for the third time, the pilot activates the passenger address system again. "We're coming upon an area of weather, so there may be some turbulence while we wait for clearance to land. Flight attendants, please remain seated."

Jack checks the time and notes that since it's already afternoon, it wouldn't be worth it to go to the First when they finally land. So he settles back in his seat and looks out the window.

The sea of grey clouds surrounding the plane offers nothing to catch his eye, so his mind takes over with a wide range of thoughts. While they bounce around his head like a Mexican jumping bean, he thinks variously of John Burley, Didi, Mark, Serge Kaspin, Catherine Stevens, and Maria Assante.

Suddenly, turbulence jolts the plane, so he closes his eyes tightly. Around him, others gasp and grab their armrests, then the pilot clicks on the PA system again. "We're going through a snow squall, folks, but we're on final approach, so it won't be long before we land. Thanks for your patience."

When the metal bird touches down, it's not as gentle as usual. However, the relieved passengers erupt in a round of applause anyway, grateful to be safe and on the ground.

Jack stays seated while the mix of people grabbing overhead carry-ons causes the usual confusion. He has no luggage, so there's no need for him to hurry.

Everyone wants to get off the plane quickly, however, when two overserved men up front disagree about something, they delay the process.

When shouts erupt and their flailing arms take up the narrow aisle, Jack sighs and tries to make himself invisible. Behind them, the rest of the passengers react with varying degrees of disgust and frustration. "Get off the plane!" some shout, while others yell, Stop it, you idiots!" But the men aren't willing to give up; nothing ends their fury, even when the flight crew struggles to separate them.

Frustrated, the stewards look around for help and spot Jack, who's still trying to stay under the radar.

"Aren't you a police officer?" asks one of them. "We need another body over here!"

Reluctantly, Jack makes his way into the crowded aisle. "NYPD, let me through!" he shouts as he plows through annoyed passengers.

When Jack reaches the brawlers, he puts the nearest one into a chokehold, and pulls him from the one he's pummeling. "Get the other guy!" he orders the pilot and copilot when they arrive to help. Soon, Homeland Security officers grab both assailants and push them off the plane.

When peace is restored, the passengers applaud Jack's help, and pass his pea coat forward so he can get off the plane.

To Jack, it's "just another day at the office." Nevertheless, he waves to acknowledge the appreciation and heads for the exit. When he passes a flight attendant, she mouths, "Call me," and hands him a note.

Inside the busy terminal, Jack dodges man, woman, and beast as he speedwalks to the taxi stand. On the way, he stifles a yawn and realizes that he's tired. *Man, it's been a long day*, he reflects. *I'll be glad when it's over.*

Unfortunately, the line at the taxi stand is long, and he fumes inwardly. *Guess I'm gonna have to pull rank if I wanna get home at a decent time*, he decides.

When the next cab pulls up, Jack flashes his badge at the people waiting and steps to the front of the line. "Hey!" they grumble at him, flashing half peace signs in disapproval. "We've been waiting an hour!" But Jack is too tired to care.

While the cab snakes through cars and busses trying to leave airport property, he clicks on Didi's number, but she doesn't pick up. "Hey babe," he tells her voicemail. "I'm back, but I'm gonna stop by the hospital to check on John. I'll pick up some Chinese on the way home."

Jack sits back in his seat, then remembers his overflowing pocket. Fishing into it, he takes out bits of paper and cards that women have handed him recently. As he looks at the various names and phone numbers, he smiles, then crumples them all up and stuffs them back into his pocket. *I'm gonna get rid of these soon,* he promises himself.

Jack, Allison, and Sylvia converge in the waiting room while Frank and Connie Burley confer with the attending physician. The mood among the group is tense, so Jack tries to lighten it. Out of the blue, he asks Sylvia, "So, when are you two getting married?"

The women among them are shocked by Jack's insensitivity. While Allison stares daggers at him, Sylvia widens her eyes in surprise and disbelief.

"Let's just get him healed first, all right?" she retorts angrily. "And anyway, he hasn't asked me, you moron."

Jack shakes his head, unaware of the distress his question caused. "I know he wants to, but… Look, if I were you, I'd ask *him* as soon as you can. I know John, and if you wait for him to find the right words, you could be waiting a very long time."

Sylvia looks away, lost in thought, so Jack turns to Allison for conversation. "I see you're as stubborn as I am," he says, ignoring her continued frown. "Glad to see you up and around so quickly. How's the arm?"

Allison sighs, then winces while she tries to get comfortable in an uncomfortable chair. "It hurts like hell, Jack. How did you cope when you got shot?"

Jack shrugs. "It wasn't easy, but I had a good nurse, remember?"

"Yeah, yeah, I remember we all had to leave your room

when Didi popped in. I assume that's the 'nurse' you're talking about."

"That's the one," Jack replies with a dreamy grin. "She was such a great 'nurse'!"

Allison rolls her eyes at Jack's familiar subtext, then changes the subject. "Oh, I forgot to tell you. Our guys found a key to a safe deposit box in Cummings' apartment, and the FBI tracked it to Chase. They're getting a warrant; Gomez will be with them when they peek inside."

"Okay," says Jack, reluctantly tearing himself away from a pleasant memory.

"What's new with you?" presses Allison. "Did you talk to Callahan?"

Jack rubs the back of his neck wearily. "That phony bureaucrat has a serious fear of Kaspin. He can incriminate the bastard, but he won't. Not now, anyway. The FBI still has him, but they can't keep him for long. He'll probably get a deal, but who knows what'll happen to him? Callahan's life probably isn't worth a damn to Kaspin."

"You have any leads on that snake yet?"

"No, but there's an angle I want to try."

Sylvia stands and paces the waiting room; concern for her boyfriend won't let her keep still for long. "John's semi-paralyzed on one side," she states pensively, "and the doctors don't know what's going on."

Then Sylvia begins to cry, and Allison rises to comfort her, moving her to another side of the room for privacy.

As the women talk together, Frank Burley walks up to Stenhouse with a halfhearted smile. "You must be Jack. I'm John's father, Frank."

"Pleased to meet you," Jack replies, as Allison and Sylvia join them, hoping he has more news.

Frank looks at his son's worried friends. "I'm happy to know that you all care about my son, so I want you to know what the doctor said. John didn't have a stroke, but one of the bullet fragments is next to his spinal cord, and it's causing partial paralysis on his right side, and numbness in his fingers. They want to go in and remove it, but it's in a tricky area."

"Oh, my God," gasps Sylvia. "When are they going to operate?"

"I don't know. John is talking, but one side of his face is weak. He wants to see you all, but you'll have to make it short. He gets tired pretty easily, and my wife is with him now."

Sylvia hastily wipes her eyes. "I'm gonna stop in the restroom before I see him. I want to freshen up, so John won't know that I've been crying."

A few minutes later, John sees his colleagues entering his room behind Frank, and he perks up immediately. "Hi, boss! Hi, Ally!" he mumbles through a crooked mouth. "That's the guy I told you about," he says to his mother and father. "He gives me nothing but grief!"

Jack is happy to see that John's in a good mood, so he tries to keep the joke going. "Damnit, Burley," he says, "you'll do anything to get attention, won't you? Get the fuck out of that bed and get back to work, you lazy bum!"

John begins to laugh, but a burst of pain stops him short. "Damnit," he mumbles, moaning slightly. "They want to cut me open again, just when I'm starting to feel better. Look, I can move my toes."

"Honey, you heard the doctor," says John's mother. "He said you could be paralyzed for good if they don't take that fragment out."

John stiffens from another jolt of pain. "Yeah, but they're not sure. They don't know what would happen if they just left it in there. I'm not sure I want the operation, mom. Not right now, anyway."

When Sylvia enters, she hears John saying that he doesn't want an operation, and she gets upset.

"Why is everyone from the First Precinct so stubborn?" she asks with worried frustration. "John, I want you around for a long time. Don't you think you should let the surgeon go in there and get that thing out?"

While Sylvia moves to John's bedside, his father says, "We have to be cautious. The surgeon told us there's a chance the operation itself could leave John paralyzed. But he also said there's a chance the fragment could move on its own to a better place; a safer place."

"Or, it could move somewhere else, and he could be paralyzed permanently," his mother warns.

Listening from his bed, John mumbles, "That's why I want to wait. If I decide to let them take it out, I want to be stronger when they do the operation."

While everyone chimes in with an opinion, John cuts

through the noise with a quiet, "Can you take it outside? I'm getting sleepy again." Then he crooks his finger at Jack. "Where's my burger and beer?" he asks with a lopsided grin.

Jack, Allison, and Sylvia laugh at the inside joke, but John's parents look perplexed. To continue the gag, Sylvia adopts a look of mock solemnity. "I'm going to leave now," she declares, "but I want you to know that I'll be here early tomorrow for your sponge bath." Then she remembers John's parents, and leans down to whisper in John's ear. "And your mom and dad shouldn't be here for that."

Knowing what Sylvia means, John's pulse and blood pressure suddenly spike, and the attached monitors wail in confirmation, provoking even more laughter among the friends, and more confused looks between the parents.

It's nearly seven p.m. when the weary detective enters his apartment with a bag from Sum Luc's. "Hope you like sweet and sour pork," he says to his mother-in-law as he places the large bag on the table. "Where's Dee?"

"She'll be out in a minute. Mark is finally sleeping, and she wanted to make herself a little more presentable."

When Didi walks in, she walks up to Jack and hugs him tightly.

"What's that for?" he asks. "Should I bring Chinese home more often?"

Didi only pulls him closer. "I was thinking about John, then all the memories from when you were shot last year came flooding back. How is he?"

"There's some paralysis on one side. A couple of bullet fragments are pressing against his spinal cord."

Didi exclaims, "Oh no! Isn't there something they can do?"

"They want to take them out, but the operation is delicate and there's no telling what could happen when they go in there. John doesn't want the surgery, and I don't blame him. But if they leave the fragments in, they could move around and cause permanent paralysis later."

"Wow, that's tough. Is John sure about no surgery?"

"Well, he said he doesn't want it right now — he doesn't feel that he's strong enough for another operation. He's leaving the door open for later, though. I think he just wants to get out of the hospital."

Jack heads to the kitchen for a cold Guinness, and as he takes a long gulp of its dark goodness, Didi shakes her head. "Do you remember how you rushed back to work way too soon after you were shot? How'd that go?" she scolds. "And I heard that Allison is already back at work. Wasn't she shot when John was? What the heck is it with the cops at the First and their macho shit? All of you are crazy! Are you channeling John Wayne? You know, if John is going to risk his health, he should ask Sylvia to marry him first!"

Jack nearly chokes on his beer. "Shit, I told Sylvia that she should ask *him*!"

"Ha," laughs Didi's mom. "That's what I did! I got tired of waiting for my Mark to ask me, so I just went for it!"

CHAPTER SEVENTEEN

Like most mornings, residents across the five boroughs stir when millions of bedside alarms ring. But today, it's different in the Stenhouse residence. A much noisier sound awakens them, and this is one that Jack can't ignore or throw against the wall like he usually does when he doesn't want to get up. The Stenhouse's best wake-up call is now little Mark, the newest member of the household.

When Mark begins to cry, Didi's eyes pop open and she jumps out of bed, leaving Jack to stretch tight muscles under the covers. "When did the doc say we can move him to his own room?" he asks lazily.

"Maybe after another month or so," Didi replies, undressing Mark at the changing table. "What's your schedule today? You have time for breakfast?"

"No," says Jack, on his way to the bathroom. "I'm going to the safe house this morning to help escort our witness back to the First. Gotta leave early; it's in Staten Island."

By seven, a bright late winter morning brings Big Apple temperatures into the forties, and the city's day gets started in earnest. Roads, trains, busses, and taxis are filling up, and people are moving around, everyone in a hurry to get where they're going.

On a quiet street in Staten Island, Jack parks his Road Runner's wheels on the sidewalk, unaware of two sets of eyes watching him. Across the way, a Leupold scope casts an unwavering stare in his direction, while a nearby suppressor peeks through faded blinds.

Jack cuts the engine, then calls the guards posted inside the safe house. When he gets the okay, he heads up the short walkway.

While he waits for the door to open, the hairs on the back of his neck stand up, so he turns around and searches up and down the street for something unusual.

"What're you lookin' at?" asks the undercover officer who lets him in.

"Nothin', I guess," replies Jack while the man closes the door. "Just got a weird feeling for a minute."

When Jack is out of view, the hired gun pulls his head away from the scope. "Damnit," he snarls at his partner. "We have another cop to deal with."

Inside the safe house, Jack greets Tonya, then waits while his fellow officers slip her into a Kevlar vest.

When she's ready, Jack's hand hovers over the doorknob. "I'll go out first," he says. "Make sure Tonya stays between you." Then he slowly opens the door to check the street. It's still quiet, but the work van in the driveway across the way bothers him. "I saw that van when I pulled up. Isn't it a little early for union guys to be on the job?"

"It was there yesterday, too," responds one of the officers. "They just sold the house, so maybe they're doing repairs."

"Maybe," says Jack. "I don't see anyone around, so let's go."

Jack is the first out, followed by an officer who makes sure to keep Tonya close behind him. Then the second officer leaves the house.

When everyone is clear of the door, a thwack suddenly rings out, and Tonya drops like a stone.

"Fuckin' shit!" shout the men, racing to hunker down behind their SUV in the driveway. "Where'd that come from?!"

Behind them, Tonya lies in a pool of blood with parts of her head splattered over the front of the house.

Jack barks, "Call for backup! The shooter's probably in that house with the van!"

Assessing the situation, Jack quickly orders the closest officer to provide cover. Then he motions to the one coated with Tonya's blood. "Follow me! We need to get close!"

Ducking down, the two men creep to Jack's Road Runner, then dart across the street. On the other side, they keep close to bushes and shrubs while they make their way to the "sold" house.

Suddenly, a man opens his front door to leave for work. "Get back inside!" they shout at him.

For an instant, the homeowner stares open-mouthed at the two men in Kevlar vests crouched in front of his low privacy wall. Then he retreats inside and slams the door.

"Bet they're long gone," grumbles Jack as they approach the work van. "Go around back. I'll give you a ten-count, then I'll go in."

Jack waits for his colleague to get into position while working to shake off thoughts of the shotgun blast that sent him to the hospital not too long ago. "That's not gonna happen today," he vows. Then he starts his countdown.

When he reaches ten, he jumps up and runs to the front of the house. With his back to the wall, he inches his way to the door and tries the knob. As expected, it's locked, so he kicks the door in, knowing the other officer will do the same at the back of the house.

The men have their guns ready, but there's no need to use them. The house is empty. A sweep of the interior reveals nothing but a sniper rifle mounted to a tripod in the living room.

When backup police vehicles roar into the neighborhood, the two assassins are slipping into a waiting Cadillac three blocks away.

"It's handled," they announce to the stone-faced driver.

"Are you absolutely sure?" he demands.

"Yes, tell Mr. Kaspin he has nothing to worry about. It's done."

Later that morning, Lieutenant Conrad is waiting when Jack enters the Homicide Department. "In here!" he calls from his doorway.

After what just happened, Jack isn't in the mood for bureaucratic bullshit. "Yeah, yeah, I'm coming," he growls. He knows Conrad wants him to recap his morning, but he's angry, and he doesn't want to explain it to his boss.

Conrad stands in front of his door while Jack storms past. "I know you're pissed," he says, "that's why I'm standing here. The last time you were in this mood, you broke the glass of the door."

Conrad shuts the door, then asks, "What the hell happened, Stenhouse? It was supposed to be an easy transfer."

Jack frowns and stares into space. "Can't say for sure, but I'm willing to bet it was Kaspin's goons. We found a suppressed Remington in the house across the street. It was one shot and done. I'm gonna find that fuck, and I hope he resists."

Conrad sits down heavily at his desk. "I'll tell Rawlings," he says gloomily. "Dead bodies just keep piling up on us. Wait till the mayor finds out."

Jack retorts, "Fuck the damn mayor. We have to assume that Kaspin has ears inside the department, so we have to be careful about everything we do from now on. When I find that fucker, I'm gonna cut his balls off, just for fun."

Conrad has heard Jack talk this way many times before, so he sighs again and dismisses his detective. But before Stenhouse clears the doorway, he thinks of one more thing to say. "Jack!" he calls out, and Stenhouse turns around. "Keep it clean! Don't do anything illegal!"

Jack gives his boss an innocent smile, then heads for the whiteboard near his desk.

When Hector and Allison enter the department, they find him adding Tonya's name to a growing list of victims in their case.

"Jefferson, too?" they ask in shocked surprise.

"Yeah," Jack responds with his back to his friends. "Someone snitched about the transfer this morning, so Kaspin sent a sniper."

"Holy crap!" responds Hector. "Now we have a snitch to worry about along with everything else?"

"Are you surprised? Nothing is going right about this case," Jack grumbles. "Meanwhile, what was in the safe deposit box?"

Hector holds up a flash drive in an evidence bag. Then he digs it out and inserts it into the USB port of his laptop. "It's a journal. There are dates and dollar amounts, some with notes saying 'Delivered.' It may be records of Kaspin's arms sales, but there's no indication of who they went to."

Allison flexes her wounded shoulder. "Run it by Interpol," she says, trying not to move her arm too much.

"The FBI has the original; they burned me this copy. They're already coordinating with Interpol, so if we can't get anything more out of Callahan, we'll be getting nowhere fast."

Jack seats himself at Hector's desk and starts to scroll through the file. Suddenly, he stops and gasps. "Ha! Got ya!" he shouts, pointing to the screen. "Lookie here, folks, I just found Callahan's name in the file!"

"Whoa, what does that mean?" asks Hector.

"Well, it's not good. Ally, contact Assante in Washington and let him know that Callahan's name is in here. They may already know, but it won't hurt to double-check, in case they haven't gone through the file yet."

"Wait, before you do that," says Gomez, "how's John? Conrad told me that he's conscious now."

Allison sadly shakes her head. "He *is* conscious, but bullet fragments are lodged near his spinal cord. They want to go back in and remove them, but the surgery is risky. He's not sure if he wants to go under the knife again so soon, but if they leave them in, they can float around and cause paralysis."

Hector is shaken by the news. "How's he doing right now?"

"He's weak on the right side, and his fingers are numb. But he may be regaining some movement."

Then Giancarlo reaches for her desk phone, but Stenhouse stops her. "Can you look through that file some more?" he asks. "And make another copy of it. There must be more info in there. Meanwhile, Hector and I are going to Tonya's apartment."

"We are?"

"Yeah. I want to snoop around."

Tonya Jefferson's studio apartment is on West 109th Street, near Riverside Drive. When Jack and Hector get there, the first thing they do is check in with the building superintendent. They tell him why they're there, then they follow him up the stairs. It's one of the city's older buildings, so there's no elevator.

At the third-floor landing, the building manager suddenly stops.

"What's going on?" asks Jack, after almost bumping into him.

"That's her apartment, but I don't know who that guy is," says the manager, pointing at a man exiting a unit down the hall.

Immediately, the cops draw their weapons, shouting, "NYPD! Freeze!"

Hearing the order, the startled stranger drops to his knees and places his hands behind his head. "Whoa!" he calls out. "What's wrong? Don't shoot!"

Jack approaches the kneeling man with a pair of hand-cuffs at the ready. He clicks them on, then pulls the man to his feet. "Why were you in that apartment?" he asks.

"I've been trying to reach my sister, but she's not an-swering her phone. I have a key to her place, so I came over to see if she's okay. You can check my name, my ID's in my back pocket. I'm Jerome Jefferson. The apartment belongs to Tonya, my sister."

Jack hesitates. "Are there any sharp objects in your pockets that I need to be aware of?"

Jerome shakes his head, so he reaches in and removes a wallet. Then he does a thorough pat-down.

Jack squints at the guy's driver's license in the dark hall-way. "Well, the ID matches," he tells Hector. "Mr. Jefferson, I'm going to remove the cuffs now. Don't make any sudden moves. I don't want Sergeant Gomez to have to shoot your ass."

When the cuffs are off, Jerome rubs his wrists and leans against the wall, shaken by the confrontation. "What's my sis-ter gotten into?" he asks, looking from one officer to the other. "Do you know where she is?"

Jack glances at Hector, then turns to Jerome. "I guess you don't know," he says. "But before I say anything, I gotta check. You say your sister is Tonya Jefferson?"

"Yeah. What's going on?"

"Tonya was charged with murder a couple of days ago, and she's been in police custody since then. Didn't she call you?"

"No! She was charged with *murder*?"

"Yes, but I'm sorry to tell you that she was killed this morning."

"What?! Now she's *dead*? How the hell did that happen if she was in police custody?"

"It happened while she was being moved to First Precinct Headquarters."

Jerome crumbles to the floor. "I told her they were no good!" he sobs, holding his head in his hands. "I told her to leave that group! Oh, god! Tonya!"

Jack, Hector, and the manager wait quietly while Jerome cries for his sister. Then he calms down and rises to his feet.

"Let's go inside the apartment to talk," says Jack, laying a comforting hand on Jerome's shoulder.

Tonya's unit is small. It only has a kitchen and a living area with a closet, a bed, and a tiny bathroom.

Jack unbuttons his pea coat. "Before we talk, we're going to look around, if it's all right with you."

"Yeah, go ahead," sniffles Jerome, dropping tearfully onto a small sofa.

While Hector checks the closet, Jack flips open a laptop and hits the power button.

"Hey, Jack," calls Hector from the closet. "Look what I found!"

Jack looks up to see Hector holding an automatic P90 assault rifle. "There are hundreds of rounds in here, including extra clips. I don't know what she was preparing for, but there are also tactical vests, some armor, and... Damn! Jack, you gotta come over here!"

At the closet, Jack stares agape at packages of Semtex, C-4, and boxes of electronic detonators in a footlocker on the floor. "Holy shit on a shingle!" he exclaims. "What the hell kinda war was she plotting?"

Hector points to a closed aluminum case. "Wonder what's in that?"

"Take a look, then call the bomb guys to take care of this shit," orders Jack. "I'm gonna check the laptop."

Kneeling down, Hector uses one hand to pull a hand-held radio from his belt while he opens the aluminum case with the other.

"Crap!" he shouts, jumping to his feet and backing away. "We need to evacuate the building! There are IEDs in there! Holy shit! It's a good thing I looked before I used the handheld!" Turning to Jack, he says, "I'm gonna hafta call this in on a landline! If I use the radio, this place could blow up!"

"Are you kidding?" exclaims Jerome, rising from his seat to take a look in the closet.

But Hector bars his way with an outstretched arm. "Stay back!" he shouts. "That stuff is dangerous!"

Jerome grabs both sides of his head. "Hell," he moans. "It must be that fucking paramilitary group she got involved with! They're always spouting all kinds of patriot defense crap!"

Jack and Hector stare wide-eyed at Jerome, then Hector tears himself away and rushes into the hallway. "I hope the super has a landline!" he calls back over his shoulder.

As Hector disappears, Jack pokes his head into the hall. "After you call it in, tell the super to help you knock on doors!" he shouts out to the sergeant. "We gotta get people out of here!" Then he grabs Jerome's elbow. "Come with me," he orders. "We're going to the precinct to talk about that militia group!"

Down at street level, sirens announce the arrival of the bomb squad and other law enforcement personnel.

"That was quick!" notes Jerome as they watch police vehicles screeching to the curb. "I've never seen the cops respond so fast!"

"Well, explosives do tend to get people moving," comments Jack, a little too cynically for Jerome.

With a wary glance at the detective, Tonya's brother says earnestly, "I hope they get it all out."

The pair stays long enough to watch SWAT officers bringing cases of IEDs, plastic explosives, detonators, P90s, and hundreds of 5.7 x 28 mm rounds out of the building.

Then, lazy snowflakes begin to fall on evacuated residents and curious bystanders, and Captain Johansson, SWAT unit leader and a mountain of a man, approaches Stenhouse with a grim look on his face. "This is a strange one," he says, nodding toward the pile of weaponry in police vehicles. "Looks like she was prepping for battle."

"That's what I think," responds Jack, craning his neck to look up into the hulking man's face. "Some of those rounds are military-issue; armor-piercing."

Captain Johansson sighs. "Guess you can buy anything if you have enough money. ATF and the feds will be scouring that apartment for days." Then the captain looks around and leans close to Jack. Lowering his voice, he says, "I noticed a laptop up there, and it was on. Here." Pulling the device from under his tactical vest, he passes it to Jack. "If the feds get their hands on it, you'll never see it again."

"Thanks," says Jack, tucking the computer under his jacket.

"You got it," Johansson replies. "The building's clear now, so people can go back in." The captain starts to lumber off, but suddenly stops and turns around. "Hey, tell Didi I said hello," he waves.

Jack is puzzled, but cordial. "Will do," he replies, waving back at the tough sasquatch. *How the hell does he know my wife?*

Jack brings Jerome to the First and leaves him with Allison Giancarlo. Then he drops Tonya's laptop off at Forensics.

While he's doing that, the weather outside gets worse, but none of them know it. The flurries that he and Jerome encountered at Tonya's building are now morphing into a full-blown snowstorm, and people are getting ready to leave work early.

Back upstairs, Jack asks Allison to jot down pertinent information while he questions Jerome.

"Are you okay to start?" he asks him. "You need anything? Water, soda? We have coffee, but I wouldn't recommend it. It's probably been sitting in the pot all day."

"I guess I'm ready," Jerome replies quietly. "What do you want to know?"

To begin, Jack asks him to tell them about the militia group his sister was involved with.

"They call themselves the New Patriot Guard. I think they meet upstate, in a small town called Durham. She didn't really want to talk about it, and I didn't press her. There's a lot she kept close to the vest after leaving the military. But a guy named Serge something is the leader, and that fucking Senator Callahan is involved as well."

"Did you know that Tonya had a relationship with Serge and the senator?"

"Well... I know she had an affair with the senator. She met them both in Kandahar.

"Hmm. Tell me more about the militia group."

"Like I said, Tonya didn't talk about it too much."

Jack rubs his chin in thought. "That's interesting," he says. "Back at the apartment, it seemed like you knew a little more about them."

"Well, I don't. I just didn't like the sound of it. Look, I'd like to go now. I have to call my parents. I don't know how I'm gonna tell them Tonya's dead."

Jack isn't ready to let him go just yet. "I know you want to leave, but is there any other information you can give us? Anything at all?"

"I don't think so."

Jack sighs. "All right. Here's my card. We'll be in touch, but please call me if you think of anything."

Jerome takes the business card with a trembling hand. "What about...?" he asks hesitantly. "What about her...body? What happens now?"

"Someone will call you when they're ready to release it. Then you can make funeral arrangements."

"Our condolences to you and your family," says Allison kindly.

Jerome starts to leave, then turns around. "Wait," he says. "Didn't you say that Tonya was killed while you guys were bringing her here?"

"Yes," Jack replies.

"So what happened? You guys fucked up! Who's in charge here?"

Allison and Jack glance at each other. "That would be Lieutenant Conrad," offers Allison.

"I need to talk to him!" Jerome declares, his voice growing hard. Then he shoves Jack's business card at Allison. "Write down his number!"

While Allison complies, Jack glances out of a far window. "Wow, look at that snow!" he exclaims. "The weather turned bad real fast!"

Jerome follows Jack's gaze, then moans. "Oh, crap! I gotta get to work; I drive a snowplow for the city! But I also have to call my parents! Shit! This is really a helluva day!"

Jerome leaves the department in a hurry. Then Jack turns to Allison. "How's the arm? I notice you're holding it a little stiffly."

"It throbs, it hurts, and it itches, all at the same time. You remember what that's like, right?"

"Yeah, the itching was the worst. I remember it fondly," Jack smirks.

Allison reaches into her sling. "I bet," she says. "But let's change the subject before I go crazy. How's Didi? Is she okay being at home with Mark all day long? Being a new mommy can be stressful."

At the mention of Didi, the hulking SWAT captain pops into Jack's mind. "Oh, ah, she's fine," he says. "Thank God for her mother. I hope she can stay with us for a while."

"Doesn't your mother-in-law have anyone to go home to?"

"No, she's a widow. She got a boatload of life insurance money when her husband passed, and she's enjoying herself with it."

"Nice," says Allison wistfully. "Wish I could enjoy myself."

"Me, too. If I had half her money, I'd burn mine. But listen, you better get outta here. The ride up north's gonna be nasty."

Allison rolls her eyes. "Come on, Jack," she says with a shake of her head. "I know you're a good 'ole Florida boy, but you've been here long enough to know that it's uptown. I have a long drive...uptown."

Jack rolls his eyes as well. "You live north of here, right? So I can say north, uptown, or up yours. Take your pick."

To prevent Allison from replying, Jack quickly adds, "Before you go, did Interpol have anything to say about those dates we found in the flash drive from Alan Cumming's safe deposit box?"

Allison narrows her eyes and punches Jack's arm. "It's uptown, you ass." Then she reaches for her notepad and turns the pages. While Jack rubs his arm, she says, "Ah, here it is. When Lieutenant Conrad told me about the arsenal you found at Tonya's place, I called Interpol and spoke to an inspector named Jean Claude Brisbois. He said an arms shipment that contained similar weapons was stolen in Sweden, so I gave that info to the 24th Precinct. We'll have to work with them, since her apartment is in their district. Now, I'm waiting for the P90 serial numbers from Forensics. When I get them, I'll call Monsieur Jean Claude back to see if they're from the Swedish heist. Oh, and I'll also tell Assante about Tonya's connection to the militia."

Jack stands up from his desk, still rubbing his arm. "Damn, you punch hard," he says. "See ya tomorrow...maybe. I hope the streets are plowed by then."

Jacob is meeting with Richard Callahan again. "Special agents found a key to a safe deposit box in Alan Cummings' apartment, and when they opened it, they found several interesting items, one of which was a flash drive."

"So?"

"It contains a file that Cummings used to record some pretty detailed information. Do you know anything about that file, sir?"

At the mention of the file, all the blood seems to drain from Callahan's face, and he doesn't respond. Instead, he turns to his lawyer and holds a whispered conversation with him for several minutes.

When the discussion ends, Attorney Maxwell Cauley asks, "Where are you going with this line of questioning, Jacob?"

FBI Special Agent Jacob Assante stifles a smile, knowing that he must be getting somewhere. "Where am I going, you ask? Hell, I'll be going home, Counselor. Your client, though? He'll be going to Petersburg."

Maxwell Cauley knows that the senator probably doesn't understand Jacob's comment, so he clarifies it for him. "Petersburg is a federal correctional facility for low- and medium-security inmates."

Jacob looks hard at the senator, who is now white as a

ghost, and pulls out a typed document from a folder. Reading the form, he says, "Senator Callahan, your name is scattered throughout the journal on that flash drive, along with the names of Serge Kaspin, Elizabeth Pino, Jane Heatherton, and Tonya Jefferson. Also in that journal are lists of dates, with notations beside each one indicating deliveries made and monies received."

Jacob looks up when he hears a sharp intake of breath. But Callahan's face is a total blank, so he continues. "We know that you, Kaspin, and Tonya belong to a paramilitary group called the New Patriot Guard. We're in the process of investigating them now, and we'd appreciate any information about them that you could provide to us." Jacob pauses, then says, "But before we go any further, I have some distressing news for you."

"Ha," says Callahan. "You have distressing news? What else are you going to tell me, Special Agent?"

Jacob pauses again. "I know that you were close to Tonya Jefferson, so I'm sorry to say that while Ms. Jefferson was being moved between police facilities, she was shot, and she died from her injuries."

Callahan gasps and hangs his head down to his chest as sweat beads up on his forehead like a pig in heat. "Look," he says, "no one is safe with that bastard! If I decide to talk to you, I'll need protection — armed guards and a new identity. I'm sure Kaspin knows that you're questioning me, so he'll have no trouble ordering another hit if he feels threatened. All of them will kill me, and they could do it right in this building!"

Jacob smiles. "So you're saying that Serge Kaspin ordered the murder of Tonya Jefferson?"

"Um, I, uh—"

"Don't answer that," Cauley cautions.

Sensing vulnerability, Jacob cuts to the chase. "Tell me what you know about Kaspin and the New Patriot Guard and be ready to testify to everything you say. The FBI can make you disappear. You'll be safe."

"Not if they get to me first," Callahan states with a sad shake of his head.

That evening, Jack cradles his sleeping son on his chest. It's one of the few times he gets to hold the boy so close, and it makes him happy, like a protective papa.

The household is unusually quiet. As soon as the dishes were done, Didi's mom retreated to her room, so the little family is alone for a while.

"Can you make me a Daniels and coke?" Jack asks Didi, careful not to make any sudden movements that would wake the baby.

"Sure," says Didi, and when she reappears, she brings Jack's drink and a hot chai tea for herself.

Jack sips his favorite beverage, trying to enjoy the break in activity. But his mind is going a mile a minute. He's still bothered by his encounter with the SWAT captain that morning.

Looking over the rim of his glass, Jack studies his wife and considers how to approach the subject. The idea that Didi knows the big guy is galling, and he's itching to know how. He ponders several opening lines, then decides to just come out with it.

"Captain Johansson says hello," he announces into the silence.

"Oh?" replies Didi, widening her eyes while she casually lifts her cup to her mouth.

Didi's reaction seems a little forced, so Jack gives his wife his sniper stare. "He was at a crime scene with Hector and me this morning. The guy's as big as a building, Dee. How do you know him?"

Didi smiles at Jack's critical look, knowing her husband's moods. "Aw, you're jealous!" she says. "How cute. Yeah, the man is quite a mountain, isn't he? His wife is only five feet tall, and she must weigh all of 100 pounds, soaking wet."

"Okaayy..." says Jack. "But how do you know *him*?"

"Hon, he came into the shop one day to buy lingerie for his wife, and we got to talking. He showed me a photo, so I'd get an idea of her size. His wife is so petite that I was actually a little worried for her! I couldn't help hoping that she's always on top, 'cause he'd surely crush her!"

Jack imagines the scene, then blurts out a relieved laugh, startling Mark. And just like that, the interlude of calm in the Stenhouse family is over.

"I'll take him," says Didi, to Jack's relief. Jack loves holding his son, but he's unsure about what to do when he cries.

Didi brings Mark over to the sofa, where she sits down with a couple of pillows to nurse him back to sleep, hopefully for the rest of the night.

While Mark enjoys himself, Didi looks out of the window at the snow that's blowing in all directions. "Damn, Jack, how are you going to get to work tomorrow? This storm looks awful."

"Yeah, it's really coming down," agrees Jack, looking out of another window at the city blanketed in white. "I'll see how bad it is in the morning. What are you going to do about work?"

"I already called Sonia and told her that I'm going to close the shop for the day. Maybe we can both sleep in tomorrow," she adds hopefully.

"From your lips to God's ears," says Jack wistfully. "We have a hungry boy who doesn't know what a clock is, and I have a case that won't wait. But anyway, every time we're in the same bed, you make it hard to sleep."

CHAPTER EIGHTEEN

At 6 a.m. the following day, Jack rolls off his wife for the second time, then stares at the ceiling. It's cold, and he doesn't want to leave the warmth of the bed or the touch of his wife, who's snuggling on his chest.

The two lovebirds try to keep reality away by cowering under the covers, but Mark's cooing soon draws his mother's attention.

"Aw, look at him," she says to Jack lovingly. "He found his feet!"

The infant is babbling contentedly while he tries to put his feet into his mouth. "Good thing I put him in that warm sleeper. He pushed the blanket clear off him!"

Didi pushes the covers away and snags her robe off the floor. "You're not gonna drive this morning, are you?" she asks Jack as she lifts Mark out of his bed.

"I don't know. Did they plow our street yet?"

The question goes unanswered as Jack tosses back the covers and pulls on a pair of pants. Then he heads to the living room after first stopping at the thermostat to crank up the heat.

"Morning, Mom," he says to Sharon while she spoons grounds into the coffee maker. "Make it strong, so I can wake up."

"Why? You've been awake for a while," she replies with a knowing glance. "Did you guys have fun?"

Jack gives two thumbs up, then looks out the window at his street. "Fuck! It's not plowed yet! There must be a foot of snow out there. I'm gonna have to hoof it down to Houston Street."

Disappointed, Jack returns to the bedroom to call Lieutenant Conrad, and while the phone dials his boss' home number, he heads back to the kitchen to see if the coffee is ready.

"Morning, Lieutenant," he says when Conrad answers. "My street is snowed in, so I'm gonna need a pickup at Houston and Suffolk if I'm gonna get to work today. Unless I can get the day off, that is."

Conrad isn't impressed by his detective's problem — he received the same amount of snow at his house. "Dream on, Stenhouse!" he grumbles. "I'm stuck, too. It takes longer for the county to get off their duffs out here on the island, so I'll be in late. But I *will* be there. Have a nice walk. I'll have a uniformed unit pick you up at 7:30."

When the call ends, Jack flashes his finger at the screen.

Along with the rest of the city, the other members of Jack's team are dealing with the snow this morning. Across town, Hector is plowing through snowdrifts on his way to the subway, while Uptown, Allison drinks a second cup of coffee as her husband shovels her car out of the snow piled outside their building.

At seven a.m., Jack fills up a reusable travel mug with coffee, then buttons up his pea coat over his Tony Lamas and chinos. He kisses each member of his "fan club," then heads down the elevator to Suffolk Street. It's a bright, sunny morning, so he dons his mirrored sunglasses before opening the lobby door.

"Daaamm," he gasps as a burst of frigid air hits his face. "It's times like these that make me miss the palm trees lining A1A at Fort Lauderdale Beach!"

Though Jack's building manager cleared the sidewalk in front of his building, the snow beyond it is deep. "Crap," he says, knowing that he's going to have to do something he hoped he'd never do. With a curse against the weather, he leans down, balances his coffee mug in one hand, and tucks first one, then the other leg of his pants into his boots to block snow from slipping in. When he's done, he pulls back his sleeve to check the time: 7:15 a.m. "I better hurry," he mumbles.

Looking ahead, Jack notes that some of the sidewalks on the way to Houston Street are clear, while others are piled high with snowdrifts. Cinching his collar closed, he shivers and trudges onward, all the while mumbling, "The Florida heat is bad, but *this* is FUBAR!"

As Jack steps in and out of large snow drifts, the only sound he hears in this ordinarily bustling town is the crackling swoosh of compacting powder under his feet. No one else is outside yet, except for a maintenance man shoveling the sidewalk in front of an art gallery.

As he passes, Jack raises a gloved hand in a warmer-than-he-feels good morning, and continues on, not stopping until he reaches Houston Street.

The road there is plowed, but there is no movement as far as he can see; the city is eerily quiet. To keep himself warm while he waits for his ride, he sips his coffee and stomps his feet.

Several minutes later, Jack hears a low roar drifting over the snowy landscape. Turning toward the sound, he's surprised to see a black, six-wheeled MRAP with large blue FBI emblems lumbering up Houston Street. When it stops in front of him, he hauls himself aboard, grateful for the vehicle's strong heater.

"Looks like you guys are prepared for World War III; so glad you're on my side!" he jokes. "Ahh, this heater is great!" he adds, pulling his pants out of his boots. "What are we, five feet off the ground?"

The driver smiles while he turns the beast around. "Agent Assante sent us. We'll be at the First in fifteen minutes."

The deep Manhattan snowfall has affected most businesses, and even the First Precinct is almost deserted. Scattered around the building are a few of the hardier cops, but at the moment, Jack is the only one in Homicide.

The first thing he does is make a fresh pot of coffee. Then he sits down at his desk and dials Agent Assante.

"Thanks for the ride," he says when the agent picks up. "That's some beast, and it really came in handy this morning! The city got a ton of snow last night. Did you get any of it in DC?"

Jacob walks out of Conrad's empty office with his phone up to his ear. "Not much," he responds, laughing when he sees Jack's expression.

"What the hell? How did you get here from DC?"

"I took a company jet to La Guardia, then an MRAP to get here. It's the same one I sent for you. Look, Jack, we have a busy day ahead of us. I want to pay a surprise visit to the New Patriot Guard compound in Durham. ATF and Homeland Security have been monitoring that group for weeks, and agents from ATF will join us there. Is your crew coming in? I want them there as well."

Jack raises a skeptical brow. "You want to go to upstate New York today, in this weather?"

"Yeah. We can go wherever we want in an MRAP."

"Well, I guess you're right. And they probably won't expect a visit from anyone under these conditions. But are you sure any of them will be there? The storm was supposed to cover the entire state."

"They have enough barracks for one hundred people, and they keep militiamen there 24/7. We know this because ATF has men inside, and Callahan spilled his guts."

"He did? What did he say?"

"He said Kaspin runs the group, but he's never been there. None of the members have ever seen him in person; he only communicates with them via Skype or some other digital link."

"Hmm, that's going to make it harder to nab him."

"I know, but we're gathering more information as we speak. Callahan verified that Kaspin was going to bankroll his campaign, however, there was one stipulation: Callahan had to join the Patriot Guard."

"Yeah? Wonder what that's about."

"I don't know. But about six months ago, Kaspin became more militant than he already was, and said he wanted to organize a coup to take over Washington. That worried Callahan, so he told Kaspin that he wanted out of the Guard."

"Oops."

"Exactly. Needless to say, Kaspin didn't take that news too well. He was angry, and he told Callahan that he had several people killed already: Callahan's wife, Lena; Alan Cummings; Jane Heatherton; and Elizabeth Pino, so he'd have no problem killing a 'pussified' United States Senator, either."

Jack turns to stare at the whiteboard behind his desk. "Does Callahan know where Kaspin is or where he hangs out?"

The FBI special agent studies the whiteboard. "That looks good. Seems like you've captured everything we know so far. But to answer your question, Kaspin's no dummy; Callahan said the man is untraceable. Whenever Kaspin calls the Patriot Guard, his signal is routed through servers all over the planet."

"Can you guys figure that out?"

"Yeah. It'll be a bear to work on, but we've done it before. We know he's been spotted in Nyack, New York; Washington, DC; and Brussels, Belgium. We sent Cummings' journal to Interpol, so maybe they can get something out of it."

Jack frowns at the mention of Interpol. "That organization leaves a bad taste in my mouth; they fuck up way too often. All of them think—"

"I know," says Jacob, cutting Jack off. "They think their shit don't stink."

"They don't think we know what we're doing, and it gets to me, ya know?"

"I know, but so far, we're doing pretty well for ourselves. We confiscated one of Kaspin's helicopters from that small air-park in northern Jersey, and the ground crew said two men who fit descriptions of militia members took Mrs. Callahan out to a bar the night she was found dead."

"Really? That's news to me."

"Well, I'm sharing it now. We have to be careful about the info we have. Hey, what's the latest on Sergeant Burley's condition?"

Jack finishes his coffee and tosses the cup toward the garbage can, but misses. "There are bullet fragments near his spine, and if they move to a bad place, he'll be paralyzed to some degree. But if they go in to remove them, there's a chance that something may go wrong, and he'll be paralyzed permanently."

"Wow, tough break."

"I know. He's a good friend and a great cop. The shooting was bad and he's recovering, but he'll be out of commission for a while. Meanwhile, Allison Giancarlo is okay. She's up and around — a little stiff and sore, but she'll heal."

Jacob picks Jack's cup up and throws it into the garbage can. "Today's raid will go down as soon as we get enough personnel to report in. Conditions out there suck."

"So why do we have to go today? Can't we wait?"

At that moment, Hector arrives and slips past them, asking, "Where are we going?"

Jacob turns to greet Hector, then continues talking with Jack. "That group has been getting ready for action for a while, and we're not sure what they're up to. So we have to go in today; it's all arranged. We hope to round up at least some of them and disrupt whatever their planning."

"What the hell's going on?" asks Hector while he takes off his coat.

"We're joining the feds to raid a militia compound that Kaspin runs," replies Jack.

"Under these conditions? It'll be a fucking Chinese fire drill, and we'll get nothing!"

Jacob purses his lips at the lack of confidence, but says nothing.

Behind them, the elevator dings, and Inspector Rawlings steps out. "My office!" he calls to Jack and Jacob. "Conrad is stuck on the Island, so you'll have to deal with me today. Sergeant Gomez, bring Giancarlo in with you when she gets here."

Though the sky is now bright and clear, the temperature has only risen into the thirties in the small town of Durham, where twenty-five men and women of the New Patriot Guard are waiting to hear from their leader. The group's members, all of them dressed in black, are sitting at attention in neat rows in a large, heated auditorium. The room is quiet, but there's a substantial amount of tension in the air.

Before the meeting begins, a senior officer strides to the front of the room, where a large screen is flanked by an American flag and a picture of Nathan Hale.

"Patriots!" he shouts in a voice brimming with passion. "Our training will soon be put to the ready! We *must* take this country back from the anarchists and socialists before it's too late!"

At answering shouts of agreement, the officer pumps his fist in the air until quiet resumes. When the group is ready to hear him again, he says, "When we launch our offensive, we'll be uniting with other patriots nationwide. However, before we can do that, we need to weaponize. This morning, our founder will inform you of your mission...*our* mission. So now, before he speaks to us, you have one last chance to make a decision: Are you committed to our cause, or not? If you can't be behind us one hundred percent, you need to leave this compound now. There can't be anyone in our organization who isn't ready and willing to give up their life for this country!"

The officer waits while the seconds tick by. Then slowly, one man, and another, stands. Each of them looks around hesitantly, then turns to the door.

While the others watch in silence, armed men escort them out, and the door closes behind them.

The officer waits until the two are gone, then he shouts, "Good riddance to those cowards! Now, the rest of us will carry on, and together, we will stand strong in defense of our freedoms! Semper Fi!"

Once more, the room erupts in passionate shouts, and the officer tells them to get ready to hear their leader. Then, amid excited murmurs, the screen flickers to life while two muffled gunshots go off in the distance.

Inspector Rawlings would have preferred to have Hector and Allison in this meeting, but he doesn't want to wait any longer. So he tells Jack to update them later. "I want to make sure everyone is aware that Interpol expects a ship loaded with the latest Russian and Chinese military weapons to arrive here from Eastern Europe in the next ten days."

"Oh, great," remarks Jack, not happy at all that his job is getting harder by the minute. "Where will it dock?"

"They're pretty sure it's headed for the New York/New Jersey area because Kaspin has ties here."

Jacob concurs. "Our intel says he's well-connected to this area."

"And they also think there's at least one case of EMP devices on the ship."

Jack looks shocked. "EMPs? That'll cause entire areas to shut down!"

"That's for sure," agrees Jacob. "EMPs are powerful pulses of electromagnetic energy. If any of those weapons go off, nothing that runs on computers will work: no cars, cell phones, water or power utilities, and who knows what else. That's the main reason the raid's going down today. That shipment may be intended for the New Patriot Guard, so we're gonna head them off at the pass."

CHAPTER NINETEEN

Mercenary Serge Kaspin holds onto the sides of an oak podium in the media room of a mansion on Rhode Island's coastline, while a young intern finishes her morning task. While she rises from her knees, Serge packs his manhood back into his boxers and adjusts his jeans. When he's presentable, a media guru at a nearby computer terminal gives him a signal, and he begins to speak to his men.

"Fellow patriots, it's my pleasure to address you today. The mission that you have been training for is about to start! In exactly twenty days, you will be tasked with unloading a cache of weapons that we will use to bolster our cause. With that cache, we will launch our assault on Washington, DC to shut down that city of evil!

"Now I'm sure you know that our task will not be easy, and that many of you will pay the ultimate price. But this is something that we *must* do! With your help, our constitutional republic will rise like a phoenix, and once again be the shining city on the hill! Many small-minded persons have tried to shut us down, but I know you're committed, and you won't let them stop us!"

Those remarks get an enthusiastic response, so Serge pauses to allow his audience to express themselves.

After an acceptable time, he motions for silence and

says, "Unfortunately, as we get closer to our target date, the efforts of those people will increase. My sources inside ATF have already warned me that there will soon be a raid on our compound, so I need to ask for a small group of volunteers to stay behind to defend the camp while the rest of you go to a location that I will reveal later. I know you understand that this may be a suicide mission, but it's necessary; we need to keep our cause on track. Many outside our group don't understand what we're trying to do here. I promise that those of you who stay at the camp to defend what we've built will not regret it. If you pay the ultimate sacrifice, your families will be well taken care of, and your names will go down in the history books!"

Serge waits again, then says, "Colonel Anderson will inform you about your tasks for the next week, and two days before the mission, he'll fill you in on the final plans. God bless you all, and may God bless our magnificent constitutional republic!"

Serge gives a rousing patriotic cheer, then motions to his media man to end the transmission.

"Don't ya love it when a plan comes together?" he tells the computer geek with a smile. "Now, tell Rebecca to come back in here for round two. I'm pumped! I need to let off steam!"

Hector ushers Detective Giancarlo directly into Inspector Rawlings' office as soon as she arrives at the station.

"Good, you're both here," says Rawlings. "Let me recap

what we already discussed."

While the inspector goes over the latest information, Agent Assante receives a phone call, so he moves to one side of the room. As he listens, his face contorts and he yells out a loud, "FUCK!" then ends the call.

Surprised, the others stop talking, and Jacob looks over to see everyone staring at him. "They know we're coming!" he explains with disgust. "We have a mole, damnit! Someone leaked our plans, and the ATF agent on site says the majority of the members are moving to an underground facility. They also asked a small contingent of men to stay behind to put up a fight."

"We already suspected a mole when Tonya was killed," says Jack. "Maybe it's the same guy."

Rawlings asks, "What's the agent gonna do?"

"I dunno. I hope he's safe. Damn that fucking Kaspin!"

Jack probes for more. "Who else knows about this operation?"

"My boss, the assault crew, Homeland Security, ATF... Too many to track down at this point."

Jack is worried. "Are we still gonna go through with it?"

Despite everything, Jacob remains resolute. "Yeah, we have to," he replies, his mouth set in a thin line. "Let's hope we can capture some of the militiamen. Maybe they'll lead us to the snitch."

The meeting is over, so everyone begins to file out. But

the inspector isn't finished yet.

"Hold on a minute," he says to Jack, calling him back inside. "What's going on with the rest of the case?"

"Well, this Kaspin thing has sort of taken over. But we're still working on the other parts of it."

"You mean the other murders? How many are there now?"

"Um, there's Catherine Stevens, Lena Callahan, Alan Cummings, uh…Jane Heatherton, Elizabeth Pino…and Tonya Jefferson."

"Is that all?" asks the inspector, his voice going hard.

Jack knows things aren't going well. "Sir, we're working every angle we can, and so far, it all points to Kaspin."

"Well, you know what to do. Find the bastard, will ya?"

"Right."

When Kaspin's face fades from the screen at the Durham compound, Colonel Sam Anderson takes over the meeting. "All right, you heard Kaspin!" he says, his voice booming over excited murmurs. "I need ten volunteers to stay behind!"

When twenty of twenty-five hands rise in the air, the colonel thrusts out his chest with pride. "I expected nothing less from all of you!" he bellows, beaming proudly. "But I only need ten, and I want people with no family obligations. So raise your hand only if you fit that bill."

At that, twelve hands drop, leaving eight in the air, including the mole, the man who's been leaking law enforcement plans to the group.

When no other hands go up, the colonel looks disappointed. "Thank you," he says to the ones who volunteered, "but I still need two more. If no one else comes forward, I'll have to choose myself. I know there are single people here."

Regrettably, no one raises a hand, so the colonel randomly selects two others, one of whom is undercover ATF law enforcement officer Leo DeSantis.

When the colonel points at the officer, he tenses. *"Oh, shit,"* he frets, nervous as hell. *Maybe he knows who I am! If he wants me out of here, I won't be able to report on the main contingent's activities.*

Thinking quickly, the ATF operative tries to fix the problem by concocting a reason to go with the others, while warding off any doubts about him at the same time. "Colonel Anderson, permission to speak, sir."

"Go ahead, soldier."

"Sir, I'm highly decorated ex-military, familiar with all types of weapons. I feel I'll be more useful if I go with the others to DC. Sir!"

Anderson frowns and narrows his eyes. "I hope you're not questioning my decision, soldier. My choice is final. You're single. Are you committed to our cause or not?"

DeSantis sees Anderson glancing at the men standing near the door, so he realizes his answer is critical to his well-being. "Yes, sir!" he responds enthusiastically. "I will defend our base, sir! Semper Fi!"

"Good," smiles the colonel, "then we're set. Before the rest of you leave, you'll receive written instructions about the location of our underground facility. Now, pack up your gear. We need to depart this location ASAP. You're dismissed!"

Jack, Hector, and several members of Jacob's team stop at a remote location in Cairo, New York after a two-hour ride in the MRAP. The assault team chose this area as a staging location because it's secluded and only fifteen minutes from the New Patriot militia encampment. They're scheduled to meet with ATF and Homeland Security here.

As soon as the others arrive, leaders from each department gather in a tight group to discuss final plans.

While they're doing that, their teams are happy to wait in the warmth of their MRAPs. "Good thing the storm passed by this area," says Hector. "Did you notice how the snowpack dwindled the farther north we traveled?"

"Yeah," says Jack, looking out the window at a light dusting of snow on the trees. "I heard that Manhattan, Boston, and the eastern coastline got the brunt of it."

Moments later, Jacob climbs back into the MRAP. "Time to go," he says. "Everything's set."

As the assault team travels north on Route 145, their presence is noticed by everyone on the road, including the main contingent from the New Patriot Guard campground. "Look at that!" the militia members laugh, pointing at the caravan of large MRAPs lumbering in the opposite direction. "They're not even bothering to disguise themselves! They must be pretty confident that they're gonna catch us off-guard! What a joke!"

Miles more go by with nothing to look at, so Jack ponders the mission ahead and asks himself, not for the first time, *Why do I keep getting pulled into government bullshit? I'm a cop in the Big Apple, for cryin' out loud! I don't need the extra pressure.* Jack sighs, then remembers his family. *Besides, I have a young son now, so I shouldn't be taking extra risks.* And with that last thought, he comes to a startling revelation: *Maybe it's time I got out of this business.*

Jack sighs again, then looks at his somber colleagues and gets an idea. "Hey, why so glum?" he shouts at their grim expressions. "Are we there yet? I'm bored and I'm hungry, and I have to go potty!"

Just as he intended, Jack's outburst breaks the tension, causing everyone in the vehicle to burst out laughing.

But the minute light chatter resumes, Jacob calls for attention. "Okay, everyone! We're just outside the compound now, so heads up, and let's keep it safe out there!"

A quarter of a mile later, the MRAP caravan pulls off Route 145 onto a winding road. Up ahead, a farmhouse with several adjoining buildings soon comes into view, and the team notices a trail of tire tracks in the light snow leading to Route 145.

When the caravan passes a line of vehicles parked along the road with multiple empty spots devoid of snow, Jacob observes, "There must have been more cars here overnight. This is probably where those tire tracks came from."

Further on, a Ford F250 with a snowplow blade attachment sits motionless in the road.

Jacob takes in the undisturbed snow cover and a lack of footprints or any other signs of inhabitants. "It doesn't look like anyone tried to plow this area," he reflects. "I wonder if anyone's still here."

"It does look deserted," mutters Hector. "But it's so pretty. With the light snow everywhere, it could almost be a Currier and Ives print."

When the armored vehicles reach the farmhouse, no one gets out. Everyone stays put while the team leaders confer with each other on their radios about what to do next.

While they continue to talk, a man exits the farmhouse with a white towel in one hand and an ATF badge in the other. "DON'T SHOOT!" he shouts. "I'M ATF AGENT DESANTIS!"

When the man gets closer, the ATF leader recognizes him and orders, "Stand down, he's one of us!" Then he exits his MRAP and motions for Jacob to follow him.

"Glad to see you're okay," he says to his field operative. "Where's Ricks?"

"He's keeping an eye on the militia members who remained behind to defend the place. The majority already left. Besides us two, there are only eight here now."

Jacob looks upset. "How many left before we got here?"

"I guess about fifty. They're going to regroup somewhere else. Their leader gave them written instructions about where to go."

"Do you know where that is?" asks the ATF leader.

"No, they didn't tell us. I know the militia has an underground encampment somewhere, so I guess they're moving there."

Jacob looks crestfallen. "So we just missed them, and they're still out there somewhere."

"Yeah, but I did overhear them mention Schenectady," says the field operative.

Jacob brightens and pats the ATF guy on the back. "All right, that's something we can use. Now let's work with what we have. Can you help SWAT round up the ones who are here? Maybe we can get something useful out of them."

The ATF guys nod and move off, so Jacob walks toward Jack and Hector, who've been some distance away during the conversation.

"Most of them bugged out, except for a handful," he tells them. "It seems the Guard is moving underground. We're not sure where they'll pop up next."

Jack frowns and spits in the snow. "I bet Callahan and the fucking mole know where they'll be."

Just then, Jack's stomach growls loudly. "Ooh," he says, rubbing his abdomen. "Did any of you have breakfast before we left? I know I didn't."

That afternoon, Gomez and Stenhouse saunter back into the First without their usual banter. Seeing their bleak expressions, Giancarlo knows things didn't go well. "What happened?" she asks.

Jack throws his pea coat over the back of his chair. "They knew we were coming, and the militia is going underground. Literally."

"What do you mean?"

While Jack sits down, Gomez explains. "They have an underground facility somewhere upstate. The Feds had two undercover agents inside the militia, but they were left behind with a small squad to slow us up, so neither of them knows where the group went. One of them mentioned Schenectady, but that's the only clue we have."

"Jeez," whines Allison. "Why can't anything ever go smoothly with this job?"

"Oh, why don't you just admit that you love our daily mysteries," chuckles Gomez. "It's what keeps you coming back every day, am I right?"

"Shut up, Hector" replies Allison gruffly.

Jack watches the two from his desk and laughs, knowing they're only teasing.

"There is one good thing," continues Hector. "ATF has eight of the Guard's members in custody."

"Yeah, well, let's hope they talk a blue streak," says Giancarlo. "But I wouldn't bet on it. Anyway," she continues, "I don't have good news, either. Interpol says they lost track of the missing weapons shipment, and they have no idea where it is now. They don't know what ship it's on or where it's going. So now we're dead in the water."

"We still have the arrested militia members," offers Hector hopefully. "Maybe they know something."

Until this point, Jack had just been listening to the conversation, but now he taps his fingers on his desk and smiles like the cat who ate the canary.

"What?" asks Allison, noticing Jack's odd expression.

"I know who can help us, and so do you," he says with a mischievous grin.

Giancarlo rumples her brow and looks at Jack questioningly, until a light goes off in her head. Then her eyes go wide, and she asks, "Oh, no... You don't mean Vito Lucchese, do you?"

Jack smirks, "Yeah, your uncle Vito. The mob controls all the ports in the tri-state area; nothing goes down without them knowing about it. So... Looks like we need to pay your old uncle a visit."

"Vito's in Sing Sing, you ass, and you know very well that we helped put him there. So why on earth do you think he'd talk to us?"

"I have a pretty good feeling that he wants to get out, don't you?"

"Yeah, but—"

"Now, now," says Jack, patting Allison's shoulder playfully. "Don't go worrying your pretty little head about old Uncle Vito. You won't have to do a thing. I'll contact Jacob; he'll get the ball rolling."

Allison brushes Jack's hand off her shoulder. Retorting irritably, she reminds him, "If we're not careful, that 'ball' could easily be our heads!"

CHAPTER TWENTY

Friday can't come soon enough for Stenhouse. This morning, he wakes well before dawn, too excited about his upcoming meeting with Allison's mobster uncle to stay asleep any longer. He's eager to get to work, but he's also not looking forward to another walk in the cold. Suffolk Street was still covered in a white, gloppy mess when he got home yesterday, and he wasn't happy about it.

Jack slides out of bed as quietly as he can. It's earlier than usual, so he doesn't want to wake Didi or his son. The boy is fast asleep in his bassinette, and he wants him to stay that way.

Fumbling in the dark, he finds his pants and slips them on. Then he feels along the walls, making his way slowly through the dark apartment to the living room window where he can check on the condition of the street below. He knows that if he has to walk to the corner again, he'll have to start out early to allow extra time for another pickup.

Though Jack is being especially quiet, the best-laid plans of mice and men oft go astray. So, as he blindly makes his way through the darkness, his toe somehow finds a leg of the coffee table, and the encounter doesn't go well.

"FUCK IT ALL!" he suddenly screams, crumpling to one knee in excruciating pain.

The first indication that Jack had about something being wrong was a loud thud of impact. Then immediately after that, he felt a searing spasm that radiated from his foot to the center of his brain. "Owwwww, oooooh," he moans, grabbing his foot to make sure it's still there.

The tough detective is in too much pain to do anything else, so he stays on his knee. Moaning softly, he rocks back and forth as lights come on in the guest room and the bedroom. Then all too soon, his moans are overpowered by loud, startled cries coming from the bassinette. "Shit," he says through gritted teeth. "He's awake."

When the pain subsides enough for Jack to get up, he hobbles to the window, his original destination this morning. "Fuck!" he yells again, not caring this time if he wakes anyone or not. "That's just fucking dandy!" he shouts, bending over from renewed pain in his foot.

Without warning, the room light comes on, momentarily blinding him.

"What the hell's going on?" asks Sharon, yawning as she shrugs into a robe.

"Damn, fuckin' shit," replies Jack, a bit more sharply than he intended. "Sorry, mom," he apologizes. Then he begins to limp around to walk off the pain. "I got up early. I was trying to be quiet so I wouldn't wake anyone."

"Well, so much for that," retorts Sharon, tying the sash of her robe. "What happened?"

"I stubbed my toe on the coffee table! It was so dark in here that I couldn't see where I was going!"

"Ouch. Are you okay?"

"Yeah, I'll live. But it hurts like a sonofabitch! I wanted to see if they plowed the street, because if they didn't, I'd have to get out early for another ride in. And wouldn't you know it, the fuckin' street's clear, so this was a total waste of time!"

Sharon laughs. "You're just like my late husband, cursing like a drunken sailor."

Jack rolls his eyes at his mother-in-law. "Is that a good thing or a bad thing?" he asks, then says, "Wait, I don't want to know. But listen, now that I'm up and I have all this extra time, I'll make breakfast today... After I apologize to my wife and son, that is."

"Sounds good to me," declares Sharon. "I'll put on the coffee."

Jack is still limping, so as he hobbles over to the bedroom, he stops short at the door, unsure of what he'll find inside. With Mark still screaming, he imagines that Didi isn't in a particularly good mood, so he wants to be careful.

Peeking his head around the open door, he sees Didi pacing back and forth with Mark on her shoulder, trying hard to calm the boy down with pats, rubs on his back, and gentle rocking back and forth.

Jack waits until Mark settles down. Then he takes a deep breath and enters the room. "Sorry, babe," he says woefully. "I stubbed my toe, and it really hurt. Are you hungry? I'm making breakfast today."

Jack waits for the verbal onslaught that he expects, but instead of being angry, Didi only smiles. "I heard you out there.

You're just like my dad," she says, giving Jack a strange look. "Are you alright?"

"Yeah, it still hurts, but I don't think it's broken."

"That's good. There's an ace bandage in the hall closet and an icepack in the fridge if you need them."

"Right."

"Hey," says Didi, still rubbing Mark's back, "if you're going to cook, can you make eggs in a blanket? When dad made breakfast, that was mom's favorite. It'd be nice."

"Yeah, okay. I can do that."

Didi smacks her lips. "Yum! Now I'm hungry! So let me feed Mark while you cook. He should be done by the time the eggs are ready."

Didi expects Jack to head to the kitchen, but he remains standing in the doorway. "What?" she asks, wondering why he's still there.

"I can't cook yet," says Jack with a wicked grin. "I want to stay and watch!"

The instant those words leave Jack's mouth, he has second thoughts, but Didi is amused. Stifling a laugh, she shouts, "You're hopeless!" while her husband grins foolishly and ducks to avoid being hit by her fuzzy pink slipper.

Jack's early start at home means that he's the first one at the precinct again. So while he waits for the others to arrive, he drinks cup after cup of coffee and hobbles around his desk, thinking about the case. He still feels the effects of his unfortunate collision with the coffee table, but it doesn't bother him enough to take his mind off his meeting with Lucchese.

Finally, the elevator dings, meaning someone else has arrived, but Jack doesn't notice.

"Good morning!" yells Lieutenant Conrad when he steps onto the floor. But Jack is concentrating, so he just waves and continues pacing. However, the next time the elevator chimes, the person who exits succeeds in capturing Jack's attention.

"Morning, Detective," says Senior FBI Special Agent Bill Wilkens while he swings a white bag in one hand.

Jack looks up, surprised to see the senior agent. "Where's Jacob? I expected him here this morning."

"Assante is in DC, so I'll be working with you today."

"Why is he there?"

"The assistant DA assigned to Detective Richter's case at the Thirty-fourth Precinct filed murder charges against Kaspin, so I told Assante to interrogate Callahan again."

"Why? You think Callahan's gonna talk now? I doubt he'll say anything. He's too afraid of Kaspin."

"Well, we have to try, don't we?" Wilkens replies gruffly. "Anyway, we still have Lucchese. I heard that you're going up to Sing Sing, so I'm going with you. If he helps us with Kaspin, the DA says he'll look into getting him released early."

"Oh, great," replies Jack sarcastically. "I miss Assante already."

"Grow up, Stenhouse," responds Wilkens. "I set up our meeting with Lucchese in the warden's office. He plays chess with the chief once a week, so it won't draw attention if he's out of his cell. We have to be there by ten, though, so we'll need to leave in about an hour. By the way, why did you want to meet with Lucchese? What makes you think he'll help us?"

Jack smiles. "He wants out, right? Also, I'm sure that once we, or actually Detective Giancarlo, tells her uncle that Kaspin's men shot her up, well, we know how loyal Lucchese is to his family."

Wilkens is shocked. "Holy shit!" he exclaims. "Giancarlo is Lucchese's niece? I'm gonna have to take a minute to digest that." Then he remembers the bag in his hand. "Here," he says, presenting it to Jack. "I thought you'd like some muffins this morning."

Jack lifts one brow, but takes the bag and looks inside. "Ooh, they're double chocolate chip! How did you know?" Reaching in, he takes one that looks especially tasty.

While Jack enjoys his treat, Gomez and Giancarlo walk into the department, one behind the other. When Jack sees them, he cocks his head in their direction. "You know, it's really interesting," he says, chewing his muffin. "You two always seem to walk in together. What's up with that?"

Gomez has heard this remark many times before. He knows that Jack's fishing for a reaction, so he purposefully ignores him. Instead of responding, he points at the bag on Jack's desk and asks, "What's that?"

Unwisely, Giancarlo takes the bait. She gives Jack the side-eye while rubbing the middle finger of her good arm against the side of her nose, provoking hearty laughter from her partner.

"Fuck you, Stenhouse," says Allison, while Jack continues to laugh. Then after flipping him another bird, she motions to Hector. "Pass that bag over here, will ya?" she asks.

Jack slaps a hand against his knee with unrestrained glee. "You just can't let it go, can you?" he asks, chortling triumphantly. "That's why I love you!"

It takes a moment longer for Jack to calm down. When he can speak again, he says, "Ally, we're heading over to Sing Sing at 8:30. Agent Wilkens is coming with us because Jacob is in DC."

"Okay," says Allison, still upset with Jack, but happy with her muffin. "Where did these come from?"

"Wilkens brought them in."

Allison turns around to look for the special agent, and when she spots him at the vending machine, she calls out, "Hey, Wilkens! Thanks for the muffins! Where is ATF questioning the militiamen?"

"They're at their Brooklyn office!" he replies, punching the button for hot chocolate.

When his drink is ready, Wilkens takes a sip and walks back to Jack's desk. "Holy crap!" he hollers, spitting the chocolate into his cup. "This is too freakin' hot! What do you have that machine set at, scalding?"

None of the officers pays much attention to Wilkens when he rejoins them, still blowing on his cup. They all know that they have to wait before they can drink anything from that vending machine.

Looking at his notes, Jack says, "Gomez, while Ally and I are going up north, go over to Brooklyn to check on those eight guests ATF is holding."

When Jack stops speaking, he hears a faint cough from Allison. "Oops," he says, glancing at his friend. "I meant to say, we're going upstate, right? Sheesh. That don't roll off the tongue of this southern boy. You Yanks have a funny way of talking."

Sing Sing Correctional Facility is a maximum-security prison located in the small village of Ossining, about thirty miles north of New York City. Situated on the east bank of the Hudson River, the prison is known for the phrase "sent up the river," because in its early days, many criminals arrived there by boat.

Jack, Allison, and Senior Special Agent Wilkens are pleased when the drive to the prison doesn't take as long as they thought. Even though the storm passed this way, the highways have been plowed, and traffic is moving smoothly.

It's a different story when they arrive in Ossining, however. Some of the town's streets are clear, but many are not. So the going is slow.

Eventually, Jack turns onto Correctional Facilities Road, where the massive concrete walls and guard towers of the prison jut out imposingly from the landscape.

"Isn't it weird to see a prison in such a pretty location?" asks Allison. "You'd think it would be more inland, not on prime land near the water."

"Maybe the builders wanted to let the inmates know what they're missing," suggests Jack.

Jack wonders about the prison's occupants, noting the high walls topped by barbed wire and protected by guard towers. *Bet there are a lot of scumbags in there. Glad I'm only visiting!*

Jack parks the car, then the trio walks to the entrance to state their reason for being there.

"The warden is expecting you," declares the first corrections officer they meet. "Go over to the visitor window."

At the window, each member of the group goes through the typical screening procedures. When they're finished, a short, balding man emerges from behind a locked gate.

"Welcome to my prison," the undersized man says, looking over each of them with a critical eye. "I'm Warden Seymore Quigley. Leave your weapons here. Mr. Lucchese is in my office."

While Jack waits to turn in his firearm, he takes note of

the warden's rather old-fashioned outfit. The man looks out of place in wingtip shoes, pinstripe pants, matching vest, and stiff white shirt. The outfit seems like something straight out of the thirties, which makes Jack wonder about the guy's approach to running the prison. *If he has a photo of a chain gang in his office, I'll shit a brick,* he reflects.

When the group is cleared for entry, the warden walks them through several gates and down various hallways, where inmates on work programs stare at them all — especially Giancarlo.

"Good grief," mumbles Jack at the catcalls and whistles that trail behind them. Most of the taunts are directed at Allison, but plenty of them are for the two men.

At long last, the warden opens a door to a separate building where another concrete hallway leads to a door marked "private."

"Here we are," announces Quigley, opening the door and bidding the others to enter. "This is my reception area."

In front of them, an older woman seated at a large desk greets Warden Quigley. "Mr. Lucchese is waiting for you inside," she says. "And you have a couple of messages."

Quigley accepts several sheets torn from a phone message pad from his secretary's outstretched hand. "Thank you, Dorothy," he replies.

While the warden talks with his secretary, Jack and the others take in their surroundings with raised brows, shocked by the stark difference between this area and the rest of the prison. There's no concrete in this room, only plush carpeting, paneled walls, and upscale furniture.

"Holy crap; seems like another universe," mutters Jack, to nods from Allison and Agent Wilkens.

When Quigley finishes his conversation, he turns back to the group. "Ready?" he asks.

"Yeah," replies Jack, eyeing the two guards stationed outside the door to Quigley's inner sanctum. Jack surmises that the warden must have handpicked these men; they're huge and well-muscled. If he didn't know any better, he'd swear they were uniformed Bigfoots.

The warden opens this last door and stands beside it to let the visitors pass him by. When they're all inside, he says, "I'll leave you to it. Knock when you're finished."

"Thank you," Agent Wilkens responds, closing the door as the warden leaves.

When Wilkens turns around, he sees Allison and Jack staring at Vito Lucchese, who's sitting at a small table with his back to them. The mobster looks different, even from this angle. Instead of sporting his usual custom-tailored suits, he's dressed in baggy prison greens, and his hair looks like it needs to be cut. He also appears to be absorbed in a chessboard, which seems out-of-character for this modern, sophisticated criminal.

However, things change when the door closes. Knowing they're alone, Vito rises from his chair and turns around to face his inquisitors.

When he sees Giancarlo, he smiles and opens his arms wide. "Allison!" he says happily. "I knew you would come! Kiss your old uncle hello!"

Though Allison complies, it's with great reluctance. She inches over to Vito like a child who doesn't want to do her parents' bidding. But Vito pretends not to notice. When she draws near, he puts his arms around her and squeezes tightly. However, Allison is stiff as a statue, and the encounter is awkward.

A moment later, Vito backs away from his niece. "What is this?" he asks, noticing that Allison is favoring one arm. "What has happened to you?"

When Allison doesn't respond, Vito looks at Stenhouse and Wilkens for answers. But they remain silent, so he drops his arms to his side. "Very well," he says. "Please, everyone sit down."

"I am pleased to see you," says Vito to Allison charmingly. "What can an old man do for you?"

Jack clears his throat to answer the question. But Vito stops him with a raised hand. "No!" he bellows. "I will only respond to my niece!"

Stunned, Jack backs down, glancing quickly at his partner. *This is going to be interesting,* he thinks.

Sitting beside him, Allison sighs, knowing that her uncle won't change his mind. "Vito, we..." she begins. She doesn't get any farther because Vito suddenly rises from his chair and stands over her with his arms folded tightly across his chest.

Allison knows her uncle is annoyed. Inhaling deeply, she begins again. "Uncle Vito, my arm is sore because I was shot by men working for Serge Kaspin, a wealthy mercenary and weapons trader. They also shot civilians and a fellow officer, who's still in the hospital. He's still alive, thank God, but he's badly injured, and some of the civilians are dead. That's one of the reasons we're here. We've come to ask for your help in appre-hending Kaspin."

Vito smiles like the Cheshire cat. "Ah, you need my help?" he asks in a tone as smooth as butter. "*Mia cara*, you give me way too much credit. What can I do? I am a legitimate businessman."

Allison has dealt with her cagey uncle before, so she disregards his protest and presses on. "*Zio*, Kaspin is bringing a large shipment of illegal weapons into the tri-state area. We know they're arriving by ship, but we don't know which port they're heading for. With your control of the docks and your influence over the longshoremen, we hope you can help us find them."

Vito laughs and unfolds his arms. "I know nothing about illegal weapons shipments," he says. "However, it upsets me that this Kaspin has hurt you."

Vito pats Allison's head affectionately, but she dismisses his attempt to win her over. Instead, she looks at her uncle with a wry grin. "Zio, we're here to make you an offer you can't refuse."

At the iconic line, Vito bursts into wild and unrestrained laughter, which ends in a coughing fit.

Concerned, Allison asks, "Do you need water?"

"No," coughs Vito, composing himself with a handker-chief. He wipes his eyes, then looks at Allison warmly. "Ah, it feels good to laugh again. Everyone is so serious in here. Now, my dear, tell me what I can do for you."

Allison senses that she's back on Vito's good side, so

she says, "We believe Kaspin is planning an attack against the United States. He controls an armed militia, and we think he needs this shipment of weapons to carry out his plans. We'd like you to tell us where this shipment is headed and when it's scheduled to arrive."

"Hmm," replies Vito. "If I do this for you, what will you do for me?"

"We'll tell the union to make sure their members aren't present when the weapons are transferred to Kaspin's men. That way, no longshoremen will be implicated. And if the information you supply is correct, you'll be released from prison."

"Hmm," repeats Vito, gently patting Allison's head while he continues to stand over her. "You never come to see your uncle, and you never eat at my restaurant. You are family, but you have abandoned your cousin and me, and you sent me to this prison on trumped-up charges. Now you want something?"

Vito looks at Jack and Agent Wilkens. "My dear, you have not introduced me to your associates, but I believe I know one of them. Detective Stenhouse, how is your arm? You were also involved in a shootout not too long ago. I seem to remember something about an armored truck. Oh, and I must congratulate you and Diedre on the birth of your son. You named him Mark, a strong name. Detective, you must bring your family to my restaurant for a free dinner, and Allison, you and Vincent should join them. I have not seen your husband in a long time."

Jack is pissed that Vito knows so much about him and Dee, but he holds his tongue because the mob chieftain is now staring hard at Agent Wilkens.

"Uncle," says Allison, following Vito's gaze. "That is FBI Agent Bill Wilkens. He's here to observe this interview."

Vito nods and gives Wilkens a Mona Lisa smile, revealing nothing of what he's thinking. Then he sits down and directs his attention back to Jack. With a gallant flick of his wrist, he says, "Detective Stenhouse, I admire your patience and restraint. If I were you, I would have beat the shit out of me as soon as I walked into this room."

Once again, Jack is angry, but he refrains from commenting. So Vito turns back to Allison. "Mia cara, I will help you, but you must promise to come to my restaurant. And when you do, you must be a Lucchese, not a detective. Detective Stenhouse, you will enjoy the food there. It is exceptionally good, and I know how much you like to eat well."

Despite himself, Jack smiles slightly, which pleases Vito.

"Now, back to business," says Vito, turning to Allison. "I will tell your cousin Michael to call you when he has the information you need. But understand this: he will only give it to you after he confirms that I am on my way home, a free man. Capeesh, mia cara?"

Vito leans over and pinches Allison's cheek with a wide grin. Then he says, "I am done now. Send Seymore in so we can have a last chess match before I leave this place."

Rising from his chair, Vito walks over to the table where the chessboard is waiting to be played. Then he sits down with his back to the law enforcement trio.

"Guess that's it," mouths Jack.

Realizing they'll get nothing else out of the mafia chief,

Wilkens knocks on the door to signal the end of their session.

However, Allison isn't ready to leave. She's grateful for Vito's cooperation, so she kneels next to his chair and puts her hand on his arm. "Thank you, Zio," she whispers.

In response, Vito pats Allison's head again. *"Ciao, bella,"* he whispers back.

When the group returns to the reception area, Warden Quigley asks, "Did you get what you want?"

"We're hopeful," responds Agent Wilkens, looking at Allison.

"All right," nods Quigley. "I'm sure you'd like to get out of here now, so I'll lead you back to the entrance. It wouldn't be a good idea if you got lost."

The walk back through the facility is long and loud. Once again, catcalls, insults, and threats ring out from the inmates they pass on their way.

When they finally exit the prison, all of them breathe huge sighs of relief. Jack says, "I've never been so happy to be outside in my life!"

"Me, too," responds Allison, turning her face to the sun. "But Jack, before I burst, you hafta tell me how the hell you kept silent in there. You must have wanted to kill him when he mentioned Mark and Dee!"

Jack eyes Allison thoughtfully, but doesn't say anything. Instead, he climbs into the Road Runner, puts his key into the ignition, and starts up the beast. Then he hits the horn twice — his signature move — and only then, replies angrily, "If we didn't need that bastard's help, I would have choked the living shit out of him, and he knows it. So let's get out of here now, before I do something stupid."

Draping one arm over the passenger seat, Jack steps on the gas and backs out of the parking spot like a man in a hurry. When he's clear of other cars, he flips the Road Runner around like a NASCAR race winner, causing blue-grey tire smoke to fill the lot.

"Whoo-hoo!" he shouts, pealing out of the parking lot to approvals and cheers from the corrections officers in the tower above.

CHAPTER TWENTY-ONE

The *Koto*, a Panamax container ship registered in the Netherlands, is on its way to Red Hook Container Terminal in Brooklyn. The ship is carrying three thousand containers of cargo registered as women's and men's apparel, electric bicycles, televisions, household goods, and exercise equipment. However, also included in the freight, but not showing up on any official manifests, are two containers for Serge Kaspin.

Not far from the terminal, Colonel Sam Anderson of the New Patriot Guard glares at his Rolex, upset and uncomfortable. He's been waiting for over an hour for Anthony DeMaria, the local union representative of ILA, the International Longshoremen's Association.

Anderson isn't pleased by the wait, especially since he's dressed in a black business suit and tie. He's more used to fatigues, so he keeps tugging at his shirt collar, trying to relieve the pressure on his neck.

"It's now four o'clock on a Friday," he fumes. "I've been waiting over two hours, dammit! It's so late now, that even if he walks in the door this minute, my drive back upstate's gonna be awful!"

Anderson glowers at the closed door, willing it to open. But it takes fifteen more minutes before DeMaria finally arrives and waves him into his office.

While Sam is relieved that his meeting is finally going to begin, he's also pissed at the amount of time he's wasted. However, he knows better than to voice his feelings. He needs this guy, so he has to keep his thoughts to himself. Accordingly, in as pleasant a tone as he can muster, he says, "Mr. DeMaria, thank you for seeing me today," and offers his hand in greeting.

Anthony shakes Sam's hand and sits down at his desk. "My secretary tells me that you insisted that she fit you into my schedule today. So let's get down to business, Mr. Anderson. What can I do for you?"

Sam Anderson places his aluminum attaché case on the floor at his feet, then reaches into his suit jacket. "I'm with the NSA," he says, producing a phony ID card. "We have a special shipment coming into Red Hook on the *Koto*, which is scheduled to dock here in thirty hours. The ship is carrying two containers of highly classified cargo, so due to national security issues, those containers must be offloaded by my men only. The ones I'm interested in are marked in yellow, so they can't be missed."

Once again, Sam pulls bogus documents from his suit jacket and hands them to DeMaria. "Our men will observe while your workers go about their usual duties when the ship arrives. However, as soon as those containers are visible, my men will take over, and all union personnel must exit the pier — Red Hook Terminal must be completely evacuated. To make sure that's done, we'll set up a fake medical emergency; our men will pose as medical and Homeland Security personnel. We expect this to begin around ten p.m. on Monday evening, and we expect to be finished about four hours later. At that point, we'll turn control of the terminal back to you."

The entire time Anderson was speaking, Anthony DeMaria was sitting back in his chair listening, not making a sound. However, as soon as Anderson stops, DeMaria bellows, "Are you out of your fucking mind? There's no way I'm gonna let you people into my port to do my stevedores' work! And I'm sure as hell not gonna give you control of my terminal! I don't give a rat's ass who you are or what's in those containers!"

Sam isn't surprised by the longshoreman's reaction. He knew the union rep wouldn't be pleased, so he continues with his well-rehearsed plan. "I understand your reluctance, Mr. De-Maria. But we need to shut down the area from all outside influence during the time we're working. Our operation will take place at night, after normal hours, and we expect it to conclude by approximately two a.m. on Tuesday. We know this will disrupt the usual business at your terminal, so the government is prepared to compensate you financially for the disturbance." Reaching down, Sam picks up his aluminum case and places it on Anthony's desk.

Tony looks at the locked case, knowing what's happening. "What's the combination?" he asks.

"53712."

Anthony spins the tumblers, then flips the top open, and with his face hidden from view, stares wide-eyed at stacks and stacks of Euros. "How much is in here?"

"One million."

"Are you fucking kidding me? The United States government wants to pay me off in Euros?"

Colonel Anderson smiles. "This is a covert government operation, hence the Euros. I'm sure you won't have any trouble converting them, and you can distribute them wherever you see fit. So, can we count on your cooperation, Mr. De-

Maria, or will we have to do this another way, which I can tell you won't be as pleasant?"

Anthony DeMaria grins, then places the case on the floor next to his chair. "I'm always happy to do business with the government," he replies, delighted by his sudden good fortune. "Give me a number to call when the *Koto* arrives in port."

Sam writes a phone number on a slip of paper that DeMaria slides across his desk. Then he rises and shakes Anthony's hand. "Don't fuck this up," he warns, keeping tight hold of Anthony. "Uncle Sam won't like it."

Anthony watches the colonel leave, then he closes his office door and phones Ferro di Cosenza Ristorante, an Italian restaurant in Little Italy.

"This is Tony DeMaria," he says. "I need to speak to Michael Lucchese."

Anthony waits briefly, then speaks again. "Mr. Lucchese, it's Tony at the port. I think I just got the information you asked for. Container ship *Koto* will dock in thirty hours, and that special cargo you asked about will be offloaded between ten p.m. Monday and two a.m. Tuesday. A guy came in posing as a fucking NSA agent, but it wasn't hard to figure out what's going on. He's Serge Kaspin's man. Oh, and he left me a little 'gift' that I'll share with you." Anthony listens, then says, "Glad to help, Mr. Lucchese."

The wall clock says it's 4:40 p.m., but Agent Wilkens and

Lieutenant Conrad still haven't ended their meeting. They've been upstairs with ATF and the DA for the last three hours.

"How much longer they gonna be in there?" Hector asks while finishing up some paperwork. Jack only shrugs in reply, so while he shoves the last of the papers in a folder, he says, "Look, I'm tired. I'm gonna head home."

"All right," responds Jack while he watches Allison packing up her things at her desk.

Hector follows Jack's gaze. "You leaving, too?" he asks Allison. "I hear the traffic's crazy out there. "It's gonna take you forever to get home tonight."

"Well, I'm not going home right now," she replies. "I'm going to the hospital to visit John, then Sylvia and I are going out to dinner."

Jack grins at Allison impishly. "You going to the Ferro di Cosenza restaurant? I hear you're sure to get a great discount there."

Allison purses her lips and flashes Jack half a peace sign, something she does a lot. "You should go, too, you know," she reminds him while she grabs her coat from the coat rack.

Just then, the elevator door opens, and Lieutenant Conrad steps out onto the floor. "Gomez, Stenhouse, and Giancarlo, in my office," he commands.

With a sigh, Allison re-hangs her coat and follows Hector and Jack into their boss' office. Trailing behind them are Agent Wilkens and Inspector Rawlings.

When everyone's inside, Wilkens says, "Let's get down

to it. We have a Go for Kaspin. Michael Lucchese gave the information we asked for to the District Attorney's office, so his father's being released."

"What did he tell them?" asks Jack.

"He said the container ship *Koto* is scheduled to arrive at the Brooklyn Red Hook Terminal sometime this weekend, probably by midday on Sunday. Its manifest shows three thousand containers, two of which are marked in yellow for Serge Kaspin."

Allison is skeptical. "Are we sure the info's legit?"

"Yeah. Mikey got it from Anthony DeMaria, a union rep, and a soldier in the Lucchese crime family. DeMaria said a guy posing as an NSA agent visited him at his ILA office in Brooklyn. He knew the guy wasn't who he said he was because of the photos we gave to Vito."

"Who was he?" asks Jack.

"It was a someone named Sam Anderson, from the New Patriot Guard. DeMaria said Anderson paid him a 'fee' to have his longshoremen stop unloading the *Koto* as soon as they get to the yellow containers. When those containers are accessible, he wants the terminal evacuated so his team can offload them themselves."

Hector asks, "What happens when they get their stuff?"

"We're not sure yet. But the militiamen the ATF arrested at the upstate compound said the Guard's plan is intended to go into effect around ten Monday night. So we set up a team comprised of ATF, FBI, and Homeland Security, and we'll also use intel and guidance from Interpol. SWAT teams from the

First and the 76th Precincts will assist, as well as units from local precincts and Port Authority police. The militiamen told us to expect at least fifty New Patriot Guard members armed with automatic and semi-automatic assault weapons."

Lieutenant Conrad interrupts, "This sounds like it could develop into a helluva war. Stenhouse, I'm gonna assign you and Gomez to the FBI unit. Allison, I want you to monitor the mission from the mobile command center with your French friend."

The look on Giancarlo's face makes it clear that she's highly disappointed by this arrangement. However, before she can verbalize her objection, Inspector Rawlings jumps in to prevent a shouting match.

"Allison," he says, trying to sound reasonable, "you're still recuperating from your gunshot wound. You're not at one hundred percent yet, and we need assets on the ground who can give us one hundred and ten percent and more. That's why we want you to stay in the command center. Honestly, if it were up to me, you wouldn't be there at all, but Lieutenant Conrad insists that you be a part of the team."

Giancarlo seems somewhat pacified, so Wilkens continues with the rest of the briefing. "By the way," he says, "Agent Assante will be joining the assault team as well, and I have one more thing to tell you. Michael added a prerequisite before he'd give us the information, and we accepted it, provided they'll stay out of this."

"Great," moans Jack. "What did he ask for?"

"He demanded that we assure him that we won't confiscate or investigate the 'fee' that Kaspin paid through Anderson to gain access to the Port. Any other questions, Detective?"

"Yeah. Red Hook Terminal is huge. How can we cover that entire area? I bet it spans more than eighty acres, and containers will be stacked all over the place like cordwood. So it's gonna be near impossible to find the ones we want."

"I know it won't be easy," agrees Wilkens. "But we're gonna deploy more than two hundred men, with most of them posing as dock workers. We're gonna stage in an abandoned building near the port, and we'll enter it slowly during the day and early evening, so we won't draw attention from Kaspin's spies. ATF will pose as terminal security so they can interact with Kaspin's men."

Jack has another question. "What's the timing on all of this?"

"Anderson wants the terminal evacuated by about ten o'clock Monday night so his men can take over. We'll put undercover officers around the port — on Hamilton Avenue and along Van Brunt and Imlay Streets. Harbor units will also patrol the waterway, and there'll be airborne assets as well. This won't be easy; we expect casualties. We know Kaspin's men will put up a fight."

Allison looks at Jack, then turns to the others. "You know Lucchese will have men there as well, right? If Kaspin turns up himself, I know for a fact that Vito's men will go after him. So this could turn into one giant foul-up, with bullets crossing every which way."

Wilkens takes a deep breath. "Have you heard the saying, 'Keep your friends close and your enemies closer'? Lucchese said they won't interfere, so I guess we'll just have to wait and see."

Allison smirks. "Right... You hold onto that thought."

Jack looks hard at Agent Wilkens. "What's the size and tactical range of those EMP weapons Kaspin wants to get his hands on?"

Wilkens furrows his brow while he thinks. "The Israelis designed two types. One has an effective range of half a mile and fits into an attaché case. The other is effective at five miles and has to be carried by two men. Why?"

Jack cricks his neck. "If Kaspin sets one of those things off, especially the larger one, we and the rest of New York and New Jersey will be in deep shit. It won't matter how many assets you've deployed. And even if he only uses the smaller one, all of Brooklyn will be fucked up. This operation can go wrong in so many, many ways!"

Wilkens nods in agreement, which causes everyone to look at each other in silent desperation.

Into the tension, Jack says, "Lieutenant, I assume that we'll be reporting here around seven p.m. on Monday?"

"Yeah, that sounds good."

"Well, I said I 'assume,' but you know what they say about that, right? It's just like this raid we're organizing. We may think we're covering everything, but with all our planning, unexpected things always find a way to make an ass out of you and me. This could all be FUBAR... And if it goes wrong, a lot of people will be affected, not just us. Just sayin'."

Everyone knows the detective is right, so no one says anything when Jack and his team start to walk out of the office.

However, when they're out of earshot, Inspector Rawlings points at Jack. "Agent Wilkens, that man said what I've been feeling all along. This can go oh so wrong, and if it does, the end result may cripple this entire city!"

While March blossoms, the snow melts fast. But it's still cold outside, so Didi bundles Mark up before they leave the house.

"Jack!" she calls out, "Mom and I are taking Mark to the playground! Want to come along?" Didi is tired of staying inside, and she's been dying to take her young son to a small playground at Suffolk and Houston.

Jack has just stepped out of the shower, so while toweling off, he answers, "I have to go to the store! I'll meet you there in half an hour!"

Didi wonders what her husband needs to shop for, but when Mark clamors for a toy, she shrugs off the thought. "All right, all right," she says to her son. "Here it is, you little rascal."

While Jack dresses, all he can think about are EMP devices. Like a former Floridian prepping for a hurricane, he knows that his family should be prepared if they lose power, so he begins to make a mental list of everything he wants to buy.

Outside, Sharon says, "It's such a beautiful day. The air is crisp and the sky is clear. There's not a cloud around."

"Yeah," agrees Didi, soaking up the sunshine. "The weather report says it's in the high forties now, and should reach about sixty today."

Soon, they hear the sound of children playing. "Ah, here it is," says Didi, stopping to fix Mark's hat.

Sitting in his stroller, little Mark doesn't know where to look first. The neighborhood sights, smells, and sounds are all new to him, and every bit of it is exciting.

"Oh, look," says a passerby, nudging her friend when they see the baby. "Such a handsome boy! What's his name?"

"His name is Mark, after my late father," replies Didi proudly.

The women chat amiably for a while, inevitably giving the young mother some unsolicited advice. Then, before they continue on their way, one of them says, "Enjoy him while he's still small! They grow up way too fast!"

Didi waves goodbye, then pushes the stroller into the park. "Mom," she says, "it feels great to get out of the apartment. Thanks for staying with us so long."

"No problem, honey," Sharon responds, looking at her grandson. "I'm happy to be here."

"Welll...I'm glad you said that because I'm thinking about going back to work soon. Can you stay a while longer?"

Sharon smiles. "Sweetie, I'll stay as long as you like. And to tell you the truth, I've been thinking about what you said about selling the house and moving closer to you. I don't need that big place any longer, and I do want to be near you and Mark."

While Didi gives her mom a warm hug, Mark stops chewing on his teething toy. With wide eyes, he watches in fascination as a colorful ball rolls his way, and a young boy squeals delightfully after it.

That evening, Jack turns over to snuggle when Didi joins him in bed after finally getting Mark to sleep. While he breathes in the scent of her hair, he says, "On Monday, I won't be going into work until early evening."

"Oh? That's odd," replies Didi softly, hoping not to wake Mark. "Why? What's up?"

"We have something going down late that night. That's why I went shopping today. Babe, I bought some emergency items."

"Emergency? What emergency?" asks Didi, still speaking softly but now sitting up on one elbow.

"Calm down," replies Jack, reaching for Didi's hand while lowering his voice to match hers. "There's an outside chance that there will be a power outage, so like a good Florida boy, I got prepared."

Didi pulls her hand away. "I know you," she says. "If you're getting prepared, there's something I should be worried about. But what could cause a power outage in New York?"

Jack wants to tell his wife, but he thinks better of it. All he says is, "Gomez, Giancarlo, and I will be joining some federal agencies in a raid against some of the people involved with my case. They've been tracking criminals who've been trying to get access to some powerful weapons. It's the same bastards responsible for shooting Burley, Giancarlo, and the two women at the coffee shop, among others. They're trying to get a device that can shut down the power grid."

Didi's eyes go wide. "You mean an EMP device? That's some serious shit, Jack! Everything will shut down — power grids, banks, computers, cars, planes; anything controlled by computer chips!"

Didi stops and looks Jack in the eye. Holding his gaze, she pleads, "Promise me you'll take the Road Runner, no rides in that day. Your beast won't be affected by an EMP blast."

Jack pulls his wife close. "That's why I love you," he murmurs, slipping his hand under the covers.

CHAPTER TWENTY-TWO

When Monday rolls around, Jack tries to get a little extra sleep, but Mark has other plans. Waking up to loud babbling noises from the next room, Jack rubs his eyes, and is surprised to see Didi already dressed and putting finishing touches on a business outfit.

"Where are you going?" asks Jack, puzzled by not seeing her in the bathrobe he's gotten used to these past few months.

Didi gives her husband a withering stare. "Weren't you listening? I told you I'm going to work today. I need to get out of the house for a while. Being stuck inside is driving me crazy."

"What about Mark?"

"Mom has everything covered. She's feeding him breakfast now. Listen, Sonia is here. She's gonna drive me in, so can you pick me up? I'm not gonna stay until closing, and you're not going in until late."

"Yeah," says Jack, stretching his arms over his head.

"Thanks, babe."

Didi leans over to give Jack a quick kiss, but he tries to grab her backside. "Hey!" she says, slapping his hand away. "I gotta go!"

"Okay," sighs Jack. "Close the door, will ya?"

Disappointed, Jack rolls over and tries to go back to sleep.

Near the small hamlet of Central Bridge, about twenty-four miles west of Schenectady, seventy-five militiamen are trying to keep warm in a nameless cave system off a private dirt road. Deep in the cave, they're waiting for final orders from Serge Kaspin and Colonel Anderson.

Kaspin found the cavern several years ago, purely by chance. While staying in the area to hide out for a time, he took a hike to cure his boredom, and stumbled upon a large hole partially covered by brush. The opening sparked his curiosity, so he switched on the flashlight he kept with him, and went inside.

When he entered the gap in the rocks, he was happy for the warm hooded jacket he was wearing that day — the farther he walked into the darkness, the lower the temperature became. Sometime later, he measured it, and found that it registered fifty-two degrees Fahrenheit, no matter what time of year it was.

While Kaspin explored the hidden chambers, he came upon hundreds of orange and golden yellow stalagmites and stalactites, which he found pretty to look at. But what ultimately fascinated him about the cave was a vast open area. It appeared to be a natural arena, and that gave him an idea.

As he explored it by flashlight, he knew the size and natural acoustics were perfect for his needs. He believed he could conceal all his followers there, and in the large space, he'd be able to talk to them without using an electrical sound system. The only thing he'd have to provide was illumination, and for that, he could use battery-powered lights and oil lamps. Moreover, he later realized that the cavern was unknown to the locals, which was even better.

Serge has been planning to use this underground space for a long time, so it's a sweet moment when he finally addresses the followers who've gathered there at his command.

"Fellow patriots," he roars, "tonight, our hard work will finally begin to pay off! I know it wasn't easy for you to get here, but this cave system will provide the stealth we need to put the finishing touches on our mission plan!

"Until now, I've kept the final details from you. I've been cautious, only sharing my thoughts with a few people. But tonight, I'm ready to share them with all of you! Because you're here, you've proven your willingness to defend our Constitution against all odds, so I trust that you will carry out our plan!

"Patriots, our nation is in trouble! Our beloved Constitution has been maligned so much over the years that it's become almost unrecognizable! That's why we must act, and we must act now! These are drastic times; no one is listening to the pleas of reasonable people! So it's time for extreme measures!"

When the wild applause dies down, Serge continues. "Our mission will begin tonight at Red Hook Container Terminal in Brooklyn. We're confident that no one will hinder us, because thanks to Colonel Anderson, we've obtained assurance from the longshoremen's union boss that all workers and port security personnel will look the other way while we're there.

"Our plan will go into action at ten p.m. At that time, we will issue a false report about a medical emergency that will force the terminal to be shut down, and all personnel on duty will have to leave. As you are aware, some of our people have been training as emergency Medivac crisis workers. When that emergency is declared, they will take control of the port from the union bosses, and Colonel Anderson and I will drive military cargo trucks to a ship that is holding containers marked specifically for me. We will begin to offload the cargo at midnight, and if our operation runs smoothly, we should be on our way in two hours. When that phase of my plan is completed, we will regroup here before our assault on DC.

"Warriors, I have complete faith in your abilities and in your dedication to our cause. At this crucial hour, I leave you with these words from General George Patton:

"Battle is the most significant competition in which a man can indulge. It brings out all that is best and it removes all that is base. You are not all going to die. Only two percent of you right here today would be killed in a major battle. Every man is scared in his first action. If he says he's not, he's a goddamn liar. But the real hero is the man who fights even though he's scared. Some men will get over their fright in a minute under fire, some take an hour, and for some it takes days. But the real man never lets his fear of death overpower his honor, his sense of duty to his country, and his innate manhood.

"Semper Fi, soldiers!"

At three o'clock, Jack gets ready to pick Didi up at her

boutique before he has to go to work.

He dons jeans and an NYPD sweatshirt, then fastens his badge and Glock at his hip and combs his hair. When he's done, he walks quietly past Mark and Sharon, who are asleep on the couch.

Must be nice, he muses, pausing to pat his son's back. Then he wonders about the baby's future. *I sure hope he doesn't want to be a cop*, he thinks, knowing how risky his job is.

When Jack reaches the boutique, he parks his car and steps carefully through piles of speckled snow left at the street corner by the city's snowplows.

Didi is behind the counter when her husband opens the door. "You're right on time," she says. "We had a quiet day today. Sonia's gonna stay late; she's gonna teach her first pole dancing class tonight. And her sister will be here, too."

"Damn!" frowns Jack. "Wish I could stay to watch!"

Sonia laughs while she sorts through nearby clothing racks. "You're welcome to come in any time!" she says.

Jack's face lights up a little too much at the invitation, which spurs Didi into action. Striding over to Sonia, she hugs her tightly. Then she grabs her husband's arm and pulls. "Let's go, stud," she commands. "We hafta get home!"

After dinner, Jack looks longingly at Didi and Mark,

who's cooing loudly while studying his mother's face. "I don't want to leave you guys, but I feel better knowing that I bought supplies in case you need them. They're on the kitchen counter. It's going down around midnight, so keep the flashlights and oil lamps handy. If I can, I'll call you when it's over."

At the elevator door, Sharon waits to call the car up to their floor. "Don't do anything stupid," she warns her son-in-law in a stern, motherly tone.

"Okay, mom. I'll try to be a good boy," he winks.

When Jack gets on the road, he's happy that the evening rush hour is almost over. However, traffic in the Big Apple never really goes away, so it's around seven when he gets to the Homicide Department.

"Glad you could make it!" tease Giancarlo and Gomez from their desks.

"Hey, I'm right on time!" he replies, draping his coat over his chair.

"Hey, guys, c'mon in so we can get started," waves Jacob Assante from the lieutenant's office.

"Okay, here we go," Assante says after they file in. Raising a laser pointer, he shines it at one section of a large map. "Our team, along with ATF and Homeland Security, are already in place here, at the old Kramer warehouse at the intersection of Van Brunt and Carroll Streets." Moving the light, he highlights several other areas. "We'll also have assets at the main entrance at Bowne and Imlay Streets, and at Wolcott Street, Clinton Wharf, Union Street, and Atlantic Avenue."

"You think that'll be enough?" asks Jack skeptically.

"Yeah, it should be. Now, to make sure the port is clear before their guys come in, our men inside their organization told us they're going to declare a "medical emergency," which will force the port to be shut down and quarantined. We think this is when Kaspin and his men will go in, so we're watching the Brooklyn Bridge and the Brooklyn-Battery Tunnel to see if we can spot them before they get there."

"Sounds good so far," says Lieutenant Conrad. "Do we have any leads on the underground facility?"

"As a matter of fact, we do," replies Jacob, pleased to impart something positive. "The militia members from the camp told the ATF that it's in a cavern, of all places, somewhere west of Schenectady. Unfortunately, those militiamen weren't given the exact location, so our men are searching for it with help from local authorities. The area they're looking through is large and mostly undeveloped, so we don't think we'll get anything that could help us tonight."

"All right, guess we should head out," states Conrad. "I'm sure some of Kaspin's men are already at the port."

"Yeah, and don't forget about Lucchese," Allison reminds them. "He probably has men there as well, and remember, they'll be looking for Kaspin, too. No matter what Michael said."

"Ha," declares Jack. "If they get a bead on that bastard before we do, I, for one, won't stop them."

"Stenhouse…" Conrad warns with a stern look.

"I know, I know," Jack replies. "Standard procedure and all that. It's just wishful thinking, boss."

CHAPTER TWENTY-THREE

Just after six that night, trucks painted with EMT and Hazmat logos head south on Taconic State Parkway from the wooded area around the cavern. They want to reach Brooklyn's Red Hook terminal by ten, so they're hoping for light traffic.

At the same time, Serge Kaspin and Colonel Anderson set off in a caravan of four military 6x6 trucks filled with armed men. Serge doesn't expect to reach Brooklyn until midnight because he's taking a more circuitous route than his other followers. His group's vehicles are easily recognizable, so he wants them to stay off as many major highways as they can.

At the Brooklyn staging area, Stenhouse, Gomez, and Assante sit at a square folding table in SWAT armor and helmets while one hundred others from ATF, Homeland Security, FBI, and NYPD mill around, waiting for the action to start.

The three of them are playing crazy eights with a deck of cards someone handed them.

After a few hands, Hector lays his cards down on the table.

"What's goin' on?" asks Jack. "You tired of playing already?"

"Nah, I'm just havin' a hard time concentrating. And it's not because of the mission."

For a moment, Jack looks confused. Then he says, "Oh, I get it," and holds up one of the cards from the draw pile. Looking at its back, he says, "I've seen naked women in my time, but whooee, these ladies are hot!"

"I know, right?" agrees Hector.

"Makes me wanna call Didi in the worst way."

The men chuckle sympathetically, then play several other hands before calls finally start coming in from agents in the field.

Special Agent Bill Wilkens takes each call, then makes an announcement.

"Okay, people!" he shouts loud enough to grab the team's attention. "It's now 23:30, and we just got two reports! They issued the 'medical emergency,' and it's supposed to be smallpox! They say it infected the crew of the *Koto,* so the terminal's being evacuated now by Kaspin's port security impostors. In addition, a convoy of military vehicles is approaching the Brooklyn Bridge, and if it's who we think it is, they should be here soon. Be alert, folks, and remember, you are *not* to engage them until *after* they've offloaded their cargo! And our top priority is to take Serge Kaspin alive!"

"What?!" bellows Jack, scraping his chair away from the table and jumping to his feet. "Hold on a minute!" he shouts. "Our priority is *not* Kaspin's life, it's to prevent him or anyone else from setting off one of those damn EMP devices!"

Wilkens nods, and then, not at all bothered by being corrected, shouts, "Yes, Stenhouse is absolutely right! Everyone, keep a close watch on the containers and the rest of the cargo! We must stop Kaspin or anyone else from deploying those weapons! Stay safe out there!"

Jack is satisfied by Wilken's clarification, so he grabs his duffel bag and motions to Hector and Jacob. When they gather round, Jack reaches into his bag and hands each of them a small, steel and copper-lined pouch. "Put your cell phones into these," he tells them. "They'll protect your phones if one of those EMPs goes off."

When the first of the New Patriot Guard caravans enters the main entrance to Red Hook, a phony security guard waves them through, and thirty minutes after that, the entire terminal is deserted — except for Patriot members, ATF undercover agents, and soldiers from the Lucchese crime family.

Without delay, the first wave sets about the duties they trained for these past few months. First, they swarm the *Koto*. Then, they start the sophisticated process of offloading the two yellow containers. The Guard members work together so well that it seems like they've operated container cranes before.

Though law enforcement knows what's going on at the dock, they can't move on them yet, and they're getting anxious. Serge Kaspin still hasn't arrived, so they need to tamp down their enthusiasm until he gets there.

But Jack and his gang are getting tired of playing cards.

"I'm done," says Jack, throwing down his hand. "I can't sit here anymore." While the others stretch their arms and legs, Jack paces around the table checking his watch every few minutes.

"That's not gonna make the time go any faster," chides Hector.

"I know, but it makes me feel better."

Finally, Serge leads the last column of patriots into the terminal's entrance gate, past a lone man lurking in the shadows.

When the watcher is certain it's the mercenary, he activates his phone. "Mr. Lucchese, Kaspin just entered the gate. Our men are ready."

Just past the entrance, one of Kaspin's trucks stops, and several men jump out. Moving fast, they take over the main gate while the rest of the vehicles spread out around the terminal.

But Serge drives directly to the *Koto.* He's determined to

watch his precious containers being moved to the dock.

As the ship looms into view, Kaspin and the colonel get their first glimpse of their followers in action, and Kaspin can't contain his excitement. "I've been planning this for years," he shouts with satisfaction, "and it looks like it's going perfectly!" Then he slaps the colonel on the shoulder and laughs.

Meanwhile, it's go-time at the law enforcement staging area. "We're on!" shouts Agent Wilkens. "Our target is inside the terminal!"

As soon as the two marked containers are off the ship, Anderson and Kaspin unlock each one. Then, they start carrying EMPs and other weapons to their truck.

After a while, each of them receives warning texts on their phones, and Kaspin reads his out loud. "Cops are here!" he shouts angrily. Then both of them hear gunshots ringing out from every corner.

"Shit! Sounds like they're all over the place!" growls Anderson. "Let's keep loading as many weapons as we can!"

Wilkens' assault team is amazed at how fast they were spotted. "Seems like they knew exactly when we got here!"

many of them say, as the situation quickly escalates into a full-blown melee.

While bullets whiz by from all directions, Jack shouts to get Hector's attention. "This is crazy! But we gotta find Kaspin!"

Hector nods and follows Jack as he sprints forward into a haze of cordite and burnt gunpowder. Running in zigzag patterns, they do their best to dodge the bullets flying around like a swarm of locusts.

While the assault team is occupied with the firefight, the mercenary and his righthand man keep busy. They've already loaded the EMP weapons and multiple boxes of guns into the back of their 6x6, and now, they're preparing to leave with their haul.

As the sound of gunfire grows closer, the rebels strap down the larger EMP.

"Doesn't sound good," says Kaspin, knowing the tide may be turning against them. "If we get separated, take this truck to my Rhode Island estate. Don't go to the underground facility; it may be compromised."

With a nod, the colonel continues to fasten the last strap of the destructive EMP weapon. He works quickly, hoping they can get out of there as soon as possible.

When the gunfire comes even closer, Kaspin jumps off the back of the truck to check on the situation. However, before he can figure out what's going on, two men approach him from behind and taser him into unconsciousness. Then they carry him off into the darkness.

Colonel Anderson didn't see what happened, so when he's ready to leave, he looks for his boss. "Serge! Where are you?" he yells, ducking as dozens of bullets fly past his head.

When Kaspin doesn't answer, the colonel assumes the worst. "Hellfire! This doesn't end here!" he screams, then makes a snap decision.

Anderson knows the Patriot Guard is putting up a valiant effort, but he's also realistic about how much they can take. So he grabs one of the smaller aluminum attaché cases and climbs out of the truck.

With the truck as a shield, he places the case on the ground and opens it. Then, with no hesitation at all, he activates the countdown clock with a special key he and Kaspin carry around their necks.

While an "EMT" vehicle with Kaspin in the back streaks out of the terminal's main entrance, Anderson sets the timer for one minute and leaves the device on the ground. Then he steps up to the door of the truck and climbs in.

At that same moment, Jack and Hector round the corner of a forest of shipping containers stacked nine feet high.

"That must be Kaspin!" whispers Hector, pointing at a dark figure climbing into the 6x6.

"Must be!" agrees Jack.

While Jack and Hector look on, the vehicle makes a slow U-turn and drives toward their position. So the men raise their guns, and when it's within range, they fire.

But what comes next has nothing to do with their actions.

Suddenly, a whoosh of blue ionized air spreads across the port and expands widely, charging headlong into the borough of Brooklyn. The unusual phenomenon affects everything in its path: static electricity fills the air, streetlights go dark, police and Coast Guard helicopters fall out of the sky, patrol boats go silent, radios stop working, and all communication halts abruptly.

Gomez can't believe his eyes. "They did it!" he exclaims. "We're fucked, man!" Then he points at the still moving 6x6 cargo truck. "That rig must be old surplus; the burst didn't affect it at all! Kaspin's getting away!"

When there's no comment from Jack, Hector turns around to find him, but he's nowhere to be seen. Jack bolted away at the first sign of the blast, and he's now running toward the Kramer warehouse where he parked his Road Runner.

Meanwhile, Anderson is now outside the terminal. He's driving the 6x6 as fast as he dares around multiple vehicles stranded on roadways along the Brooklyn Queens Expressway and the Brooklyn Bridge.

Though stalled cars are everywhere, they don't deter him. At a particularly tight spot, he merely jams his foot down on the accelerator and rams his way through them all, causing one of the vehicles to catch fire near a tanker truck.

Fortunately, Jack's car is also functioning. He's glad he took Didi's advice and drove his Road Runner to work that evening, but he's also angry. "Fuckin' shit," he mutters as he sets off after the unknown driver of the 6x6. "I gotta catch up to that bastard!"

Faced with the same stalled vehicles, Stenhouse weaves in and out of them looking for a moving truck. Eventually, he spots it up ahead. "Got ya!" he shouts happily. "I'm right behind ya, bastard!"

But Jack's excitement is short-lived. The very next moment, a fireball erupts from the tanker in front of him. "Shit!" he yells, and slams on his brakes so hard that the beast goes into a stunt-worthy U-turn.

"Damnit!" Jack bellows, pounding his fists on the steering wheel in frustrating anger. "The fucker's getting away!"

Beyond the fire, Anderson continues his escape past the limits of the EMP pulse.

But Stenhouse is still within the blast zone. Reaching into his pocket, he tries his hand-held radio but gets nothing, so he removes his cell phone from the metal-lined pouch. When the phone turns on, his hopes rise, but there's no signal. "Fuck!" he shouts into the darkness. "I forgot about the cell towers!"

Outwitted by the limits of technology, Stenhouse steps out of his vehicle to survey his surroundings. In the distance, he sees a distinct line marking where city lights have stayed on and where they've gone off. "What a perfectly fucking shit storm!" he shouts into the silence. "When I find Kaspin, I'm gonna blast his ass! Twice!"

Jack climbs back into the Road Runner, then points the vehicle back to Red Hook. He goes the wrong way on I-278 but it doesn't matter, as his vehicle is the only one moving on the roads. For all intents and purposes, southeast Brooklyn is dead in the water.

The raid at Red Hook is winding down when Jack pulls up to the pier near the *Koto.* In the distance, the lights of Manhattan are still shining brightly. "At least he didn't set off the big one," he mutters.

While Jack continues to look at the only lights still glowing, Jacob Assante approaches him from the rear. "Hey, Stenhouse," he calls out, breaking Jack's meditation.

"Hey. How'd we do?" responds Jack, turning around to face the special agent.

"Well, it could have been better. We arrested numerous militiamen and confiscated the two containers, but a lot of the weapons are missing. And they set off an EMP in the United States, so that's on us."

"I know. This is bad, but it could have been a lot worse. Who knows what else they would have done if we weren't here? What about casualties?"

"We lost a few of our men, and a bunch of militiamen are dead. There are also some injuries, but none too bad. Ambulances are in bound from Manhattan and Queens, and city busses are on the way. We're gonna use them as prisoner transport vehicles."

"Okay," replies Jack while staring mindlessly at the *Koto.* "But Kaspin got away, Jacob. He's probably heading up to his underground cave right now."

"No, buddy," Jacob retorts, placing a hand on Jack's shoulder. "Kaspin didn't get away. Lucchese's men said he was in that EMT vehicle that left during the melee. So it's not likely that we'll ever see him again."

"Well, fuck!" yells Jack, looking at Jacob. "Then who the hell was in that damn truck?"

Assante shakes his head. "We don't know yet, but we'll find out. We have eyes in the sky, and sooner or later, someone will talk."

Assante joins Jack in staring at the darkness of Brooklyn. "It's gonna take a while for the power to come back," he states pensively.

Jack lowers his head to rub the back of his neck. "Yeah. I just thank God they didn't deploy the larger weapon, or all of Manhattan would have been fucked as well. You think we'll get sued? A lot of people are gonna be pissed; their cars and other electronics are ruined. It'll cost a fortune to replace all that stuff."

While Jacob murmurs his agreement, Jack pats the fender of his Road Runner. "So there's nothing like going old school, baby," he adds. "It's times like this when I can confidently say, take your fancy Beemer and shove it."

At Little Italy's Ferro di Cosenza Ristorante, Michael and Vito Lucchese stand in front of Serge Kaspin with their arms folded across their chests. The powerful arms dealer doesn't look happy; he's in an unusual situation – instead of being the one in charge, he's gagged and tied to a chair, unable to move.

Vito smiles at their captive and drops his arms to his sides. "Mr. Kaspin," he says pleasantly, "I understand that you have a problem with the government. That is interesting, because I do as well. Now normally, I would not like to interrupt someone from teaching those bastards a lesson. However, I cannot ignore something that you have done. Do you know why you are my special guest today?"

Kaspin is unable to say what he wants, so he simply looks up at Vito with hatred in his eyes.

"Hmm, you are angry, and I understand that," remarks Vito affably. "You are a powerful man, but here you are, tied to a chair. It is frustrating, no?"

Kaspin is incensed by his current circumstances, so he lets out a litany of curses. However, none of them are recognizable through the duct tape holding an old sock in his mouth.

While Vito patiently indulges his prisoner's invectives, he reaches into his pocket for a cigar and pops it into his mouth. Then he continues as if nothing is wrong. "You need to know that you are here for a very good reason," he says. "You tried to kill my niece, a beloved member of *mia famiglia*. That is my concern today."

Kaspin is confused.

"Oh? You do not know? It was at the coffee shop at Sullivan Street and West Third Avenue. She is an NYPD detective, and she is one of many innocent persons your men shot that day. Do you remember now?"

Whether Kaspin remembers or not, he knows he's in trouble, so he squirms and tries to break free of his bonds. But one of the burly men standing behind him won't have it. To stop him, he smacks the side of Kaspin's head, causing the arms dealer to emit a muffled shout.

Looking on, Michael Lucchese approves of his soldier's reaction, but he's also eager to get in on it. Moving closer, he punches Kaspin in the stomach with a balled fist, then watches with satisfaction as he doubles over and gasps for air.

"You remember now, you freakin' asshole?" Michael bellows. "We don't take kindly to people messin' with our family!"

Behind him, Vito sighs in exasperation at his son's hot temper.

But Michael's on a high. "You done with him, pop?" he asks impatiently.

"Yeah," responds Vito with a dismissive wave. "Get him outta my sight."

Happy to get things going, Michael orders the men to take Kaspin to a hotel construction site at the Meadowlands. "He'll make a nice addition to the foundation," he tells them.

Kaspin knows what's in store for him, so his eyes go wild. He screams and jerks his chair around, looking desperately from Michael to Vito, but the two men are already on their way out of the room. Panicked, he wets his pants and screams again, with nothing but muffled noises for all his efforts.

Hearing the commotion, Michael turns for one last look and sees the growing wet stain on Kaspin's pants. "Shut that guy up," he orders the men. "I don't want anyone hearing him."

Instantly, one of the soldiers smashes a forty-five into the side of Kaspin's head. Then two of them pick him up, chair and all, and carry him out of a side door.

When the door closes on the crime family's latest problem, Vito notices the reminders their victim left behind. "Ah, shit. Get someone in here to clean up this rug," he commands Michael. Then he thinks better of it. "Never mind. Just replace the rug."

While Michael pops out to give the order, Vito rubs his belly. "I am hungry enough to eat a horse," he mutters, waiting for Michael to return. When he comes back in, he says, "When you are done here, bring a bottle of Lambrusco to my table. I am in the mood for a good meal with my son tonight."

As soon as the raid is over and the terminal is cleared, the officers are free to leave, so Jack heads home.

"What the hell happened?" asks Sharon, noting Jack's worn and tired face. "The news says a part of Brooklyn has no power. They showed videos of cars stuck all over the place, and they interviewed a bunch of people who complained that none of their electrical equipment is working."

Jack slumps onto the living room sectional. "We stopped them," he says with a yawn, "but one of them got away and set off an EMP weapon. That area of Brooklyn is gonna be fucked up for a while. Hey, I'm starving; is breakfast ready? I'm gonna eat something, then I'm gonna catch some Zs before I hafta get back to work."

Jack tilts his head back and closes his eyes as Didi walks in with Mark on her shoulder. When she sits down next to Jack, Mark reaches over and grabs his father's nose.

"Hello, little man," says Jack, opening his eyes with a tired smile. "Your daddy had a tough night. Be glad you're young."

CHAPTER TWENTY-FOUR

Jack's sleep didn't refresh him for the day ahead, but he's still determined to return to the office. So he changes out of his clothes and puts on a tan sports jacket, jeans, and his trademark boots. Then he kisses his sleeping son on the forehead and tiptoes out of the bedroom.

Sharon is watching her 'soaps' in the living room with the TV volume on low, so Jack sits down next to her. He knows that Sharon looks forward to watching her favorite programs during the week, so he's careful about breaking her concentration. But he needs to talk to her, so he says, "Hey, Mom." But Sharon is so glued to the screen that she doesn't seem to hear him. "Mom?" he says again, touching his mother-in-law's hand. "I'm heading down to the precinct. I don't know how long I'll be there, so Sonia's gonna bring Didi home."

Sharon nods, but her eyes are still glued to the screen.

"Okay, then," says Jack, shaking his head at his mother-in-law's intense concentration over the dialogue voiced by the television actors. Rising from the sofa, he continues, "I'm leaving now," and hopes that his mother-in-law understands.

On the way to work, Jack feels hungry, so he detours to Battery Park for something quick and to try to get inspiration from the Lady of the Harbor. Spotting a hot dog cart, he buys a loaded dog, then heads down to the water to eat it.

"You're welcome," he says to the birds flocking to a trail of sauerkraut falling in his wake.

At an empty bench, he sits down heavily and gazes at the statue, rising majestically on an island between New York and New Jersey. "What secrets are you hiding?" he mutters between bites of his dog. "I'm no closer to solving Catherine's murder now than I was before the Red Hook raid."

While people walk, run, or skate by, Jack notes how many of them are out today. "In New York, everyone comes out when there's even a hint of sun," he tells the birds that are looking for any bits of food he drops.

Jack swallows the last bite, downs the remaining soda, and looks at the statue again. "Still not talking?" he mutters glumly. "You're making things hard for me, Lady. But I'll get to the bottom of it." He tosses his garbage into a waste container, then makes his way back to his ride and heads to the First.

At the office, he knocks lightly on Lieutenant Conrad's door, then walks in and sits down, uninvited.

"I didn't expect you to come in today," says the lieutenant, looking up from his computer. "The rest of the crew won't be back till tomorrow."

"I know, but something's been bugging me. I need to find out who the hell drove that six-by out of Red Hook, and I need to know where the hell he went."

Conrad sighs, knowing that Jack isn't going to like what he has to say. "Well, I hate to tell you this, Stenhouse, but it's not our case anymore. The Feds took it over, so you may as well go home and take advantage of some extra playtime with your son. Relax, wind down, and come back in the morning. I'm sure the city will provide you with another dead body soon enough."

Jack purses his lips at the unwelcome news. "I'm gonna find that prick who was driving that truck, boss. I'm not leaving this case."

Conrad leans back in his chair, rests his elbows on the arm rests, and tents his fingers under his chin. "Stenhouse, I know how invested you are in this," he says kindly, hoping to avoid a meltdown. "But you're off the case, bud."

"Boss—"

"However," adds Conrad, leaning forward and lowering his voice conspiratorially. "Unofficially, I say give 'em hell. But remember, the department won't sanction your actions, so if this blows up in your face, I won't help you, and you'd be toast. So, if you still want to go ahead, you'll have to keep me informed — unofficially, of course."

With a grin and a nod, Jack leaves Conrad's office pleased but puzzled. He expected a roadblock from Conrad, not a free pass, so he wonders what's going on.

At his desk, he yawns repeatedly while thoughts of Catherine Stevens and the mystery driver run through his mind.

He's still tired from last night, so he heads to the breakroom for a coffee and a coke.

Holding the caffeine that he hopes will wake him up, he returns to his desk to find Jacob Assante sitting in his chair.

"Afternoon," says the special agent. "I have some information for you."

Jack sits on the edge of his desk and takes a sip of soda, then some coffee. "Go on," he says to encourage the FBI agent.

"You okay?" asks Jacob.

"Yeah, just tired from yesterday. You have something new?"

"Yup, some good news and some better news."

"Okay…"

"First, we tracked the truck through traffic cameras."

"Fantastic! Where is it now?"

"We followed it north from Red Hook to Rhode Island. But we lost it when it turned off I-95."

"Fuck'n shit!"

"I know. But the better news is that our agents found a cavern that the Guard's using, and I'm heading there now. Want to tag along?"

Jacob expects Jack to be excited, but he's not.

"Sounds promising," says Jack unenthusiastically, "but I want to go to DC to speak with Callahan again. I'm sure he knows where that truck went. Hey, do you know who was driving it?"

Jacob removes a thick file from a soft-sided case on the floor and hands it to Jack. "It was Sam Anderson."

Jack frowns and flips the file open while Jacob says, "There's a lot to read in there, so let me sum it up for you. Anderson was deployed in Iraq as a Marine Colonel. On a routine patrol outside of Bagdad's green zone, he caught a local deviate raping a young boy in a back alley, so he broke it up. However, he ended up killing the guy. That wouldn't have been too bad with a war and all, but it turns out that the guy was the brother of an Iraqi general."

"Uh, oh," comments Jack.

"Yeah. The general demanded an investigation, so Sam was arrested. However, our friends Senator Callahan and Serge Kaspin got involved somehow, and together, they managed to prevent Sam from getting court-martialed. He was demoted, though, busted down to captain and given a general discharge six months before his retirement. That caused a big hit to his pension, so Anderson was pretty bitter; he thought the military should have protected his ass. But Kaspin used that to his advantage. He hired Sam and put him in charge of all of Black Horizon's covert operations, and they ended up working together pretty closely. So when Kaspin went dark, Anderson did, too. They're obviously plotting something big with those EMPs — neither of them has any love for the government."

"Yeah, but how far would they go?"

"We're working on all scenarios, even a coup."

"Sheesh," says Jack, handing the file back to Assante. "Thanks for the summary. I wasn't looking forward to reading all that. It's pretty thick."

Jack finishes his soda, tosses the can into the recycle bin, and starts on the rest of his coffee. "Okay, I'll go upstate with you," he says after a few gulps. "You're driving."

Jacob shakes his head. "Uh, uh, buddy. That's at least a four-hour ride; we won't get there till after dark. It's better if we take a chopper from the Federal Building."

"A chopper? Righty-O, good buddy! I knew there was a reason I liked you, Assante!"

In South Kingstown, Rhode Island, a 6x6 all-terrain vehicle sits inside a multi-car garage at Serge Kaspin's mansion, while Sam Anderson talks urgently with a group of militiamen inside the home's media room.

"Thanks, honey," says Sam when a young woman offers him a drink. "Go find out what the holdup is, will ya?" he orders her. "It shouldn't take this long to cue up the video."

Just as the woman reaches the control room, Serge Kaspin suddenly appears on the 85-inch ultra-HD TV monitor fastened to the wall.

"Never mind!" Sam calls out as he takes a seat to listen to Serge's prerecorded voice.

"Gentlemen, I left instructions with Colonel Anderson to play this message if I get arrested or killed. So if you're watching this, our mission has been compromised, and it's only a matter of time before you will be discovered as well. Some of you may have already paid the ultimate sacrifice, but I know the rest of you will persevere. I've given Colonel Anderson instructions to continue to put Operation Hell Fire into action by any means possible. My own welfare is not as important as protecting our great republic, so the colonel will continue our mission in my stead. The next phase will call attention to our cause in a dramatic way — we will detonate a large EMP device in downtown Manhattan. If there are no further obstacles, this will occur in the next few days. Semper Fi, patriots!"

Later that afternoon, an FBI helicopter transporting Jack and Jacob flies over a forest of trees that are just starting to sprout green leaves.

"Looks pretty from up here!" remarks Jack over the loud engine noise.

The chopper follows a dirt road to an open field where several World War II military surplus Quonset huts mark a stark contrast to the contemporary towns surrounding them.

When the bird lands, Stenhouse and Assante join the swarm of FBI and ATF agents investigating every inch of the property.

"Find anything?" asks Jacob of a passing agent.

"Not much here," he replies. "But you might want to check out the cavern; that's pretty interesting. It goes about five hundred feet underground."

"Where is it?"

"Head into that bunch of trees. You'll know you're there when you hear the generator."

Inside the dense forest, the constant drone of a portable generator leads the duo right to the designated spot.

At the opening, Assante and Stenhouse duck down to enter the darkness. Then they begin their trek to middle earth. The lower they descend into the ground, the more they're struck by the hidden parts of nature's beauty.

"Wow, do you believe this?" exclaims Jacob.

The government's powerful LED lights are illuminating the moist cavern walls and turning them into brilliant oranges and yellows.

"It's fantastic!" agrees Jack.

Continuing past various geological features, they eventually reach a vast open area where several agents are taking photos.

"There's the ATF CSI team leader," says Jacob. "I'll be right back."

Jacob receives a status update, then returns to Jack.

"Here's what we know so far. This is where the bulk of the Patriot Guard went after they left the compound. And according to a few members they found trying to hide here, there were over one-hundred-fifty of them camped here at one time."

"Holy cow. There are that many people who are willing to rise up against the government?"

"Yeah, and there may be more than that. These guys are super dedicated; it took some heavy-duty explanations of the gravity of their predicament before they led agents to a cache of weapons and ammunition, including armor-piercing rounds and EMPs."

"Yikes. What are they planning to do with all that?"

"They want to stage a coup in DC and use the EMP weapons to cause chaos in the nation."

Jack gasps and stares up at the cave's ceiling. Then he focuses on Jacob. "We need to find those devices; Anderson must have them."

"But he has to know we're onto him by now. He can't be that committed to continuing with this, even though he knows we're gonna do everything we can to stop him."

"Well, that's what I'd do," replies Jack. "With all the planning they've done, do you really think he's gonna give up so easily?"

"No, I guess not," responds Jacob, looking critically at Jack. "You know, I sometimes get the feeling that you have the mind of a criminal, Stenhouse. Should I be worried?"

Jack laughs. "The only thing you should be worried about is not paying attention to what I'm saying. So, can we go to DC now?"

Jacob looks at his watch. "It's gonna be dark soon. We won't get there until late—"

But Jack is already halfway out of the cave. Without turning around, he raises an arm and yells back, "What's your point? The sooner we leave, the sooner we get there, and the sooner we stop that bastard!"

When Jack doesn't hear any movement behind him, he stops to see if Jacob is following. "Are you coming," he shouts, "or you just gonna stand there with your dick in your hand?"

"This is so great!" comments Jack as the FBI Learjet 40 lands at Dulles Airport. "I love flying over snarled traffic!" Turning to Jacob, he adds, "Thanks for your help, buddy. I'm grateful for your friendship and teamwork."

"It's nothing," responds Jacob dismissively. "The FBI has its perks. And besides, I decided to listen to what you were saying." With a low chuckle, he turns to look out of the window. "Ah, there's our ride."

Even though both men have been to DC many times before, they refrain from conversation so they can enjoy the sights on the thirty-minute trip to the J. Edgar Hoover Building. And as evidenced by the high levels of foot and auto traffic still active at this time of night, many others in the capital are also captivated by the famous monuments lit spectacularly against the dark sky.

However, not all of them share their enthusiasm.

While the men's SUV passes the Vietnam Memorial off Constitution Avenue, a lone protester strides up to the monument, thinking no one will notice him in the dim lighting.

When the activist thinks he's alone, he sprays an unflattering comment on a section of the wall, then steps back to admire his handiwork.

However, not a minute later, he wishes he hadn't done that.

No sooner has he put the cap back on his spray can than a retired Marine grabs him by the shirt collar and starts beating him to a pulp.

Shouting about honor and disrespecting the dead, the Marine continues his attempt at attitude adjustment until DC police arrive to stop him.

When the SUV deposits Stenhouse and Assante at the entrance to FBI headquarters, Jacob tells Jack to follow him. "Callahan is under house arrest with several charges filed against him, including material witness in the attack on Brooklyn. They called him in for us, and he's in an interrogation room now with his attorney, Maxwell Cauley. Oh, and you'll like this... Callahan is no longer the junior senator from New York."

Jack is stunned. "No shit! He resigned?"

"That's right," replies Jacob with a satisfactory grin.

In the interrogation room, Callahan taps his fingers on the table. "Hey, can you get me a drink of water?" he asks the guard.

When the guard steps out, Callahan complains to Cauley. "How much longer are they going to make us wait?"

Maxwell Cauley sighs and starts to recheck his watch. But he doesn't get far because the door suddenly swings open and Jack and Jacob stride into the room, taking seats facing the former senator and his attorney.

Attorney Cauley is miffed. "It's nine o'clock, and we've been here for over an hour and a half!" he protests. "What's so important that you made us come here at this time of night?"

Jack eyes the former senator. "Mr. Callahan, as you may know, Serge Kaspin is now history. But that hasn't stopped the Patriot Guard. We believe Captain Sam Anderson possesses several EMP devices, and we think he'll probably detonate at least one of them, based upon what happened in Brooklyn. So we want to know where he is."

Though Callahan is now under arrest and disgraced, he still doesn't feel the need to cooperate. Instead, the look he gives Jack is filled with his usual haughty self-importance and scorn.

"How the hell would I know?" he sneers. "Sam's his own man; he doesn't confide in me. And by the way, he's a colonel, not a captain."

Jack's hackles rise at the man's flippant remark, and his face turns beet red.

Jacob swears he can see steam coming out of Jack's ears, so he attempts to head off an explosion. "Mr. Callahan," he interjects, "Anderson was demoted three ranks after an incident in Iraq. Or maybe you didn't know that. And several Patriot Guard members have given us sworn testimony that you're involved in a plot to take over the government. So now would be a good time to cut the bullshit. Tell us where Anderson went after he detonated that device in Brooklyn. It *was* him, right?"

Callahan remains tight-lipped, and Jack doesn't like it. In one swift move, he leaps out of his seat and leans over the table, going nose-to-nose with the ex-senator. "Listen, you little shit," he growls in a low voice. "If Anderson detonates one of those devices in DC — or anywhere else — it'll be on you, and any deal you think you have will be toast!"

Attorney Cauley is alarmed by how angry Jack is. So to protect his client, he places a restraining hand on the detective's shoulder — and instantly regrets it.

At Cauley's touch, Jack bolts from his side of the table to where the attorney is sitting. Then, looming over the millennial, he warns him in no uncertain terms, "Cauley, I consider what you just did to be an assault on a police officer. So if you don't want me to arrest you right here and now, I suggest that you learn to keep your hands to yourself!"

Maxwell is worried that Jack will follow through, so he shuts his mouth and sinks into his chair.

With Cauley out of the way, Jack directs his attention back to Callahan. "Where's Anderson, you bastard? You better answer now, 'cause I'm not gonna ask again!"

Jacob is still concerned about Jack's temper, so he tries

to lessen the tension again. "All right, Jack," he says calmly. "I think you should—"

But Jack's tactic must have worked because Callahan finally realizes he no longer has the upper hand. Sighing deeply, he raises both hands in a gesture of surrender. "Okay, okay," he says, hoping to placate the furious detective. "I'm in trouble anyway, so what the hell. Anderson could be in Rhode Island. Kaspin conducted most of his business from an estate there, so that's where he may have gone. I don't think it's Kaspin's place, though. I think it belongs to a Ukrainian oil tycoon."

"It doesn't matter who owns it," says Jacob impatiently. "Where is it?"

"I'm not sure. I was only there once, for a party, and I arrived by helicopter. The pilot mentioned South Kingston, or South Kingstown. I don't remember which."

Jacob nods and makes a note on a pad of paper. "How many are involved with the militia? Are they at this estate as well?"

"They could be there, but I can't say for sure. There are hundreds of them; I think they're mostly special ops, ex-military. Serge had connections at the Pentagon, Congress, and the West Wing."

"Hold on," says Jacob. "He had connections in the *government*? Who's involved?"

"I'm only sure of one person — Congressman Gerald Butler. But you should definitely look at the joint chiefs and the president's staff."

Shaken, Jack and Jacob turn to each other in shock.

"Butler is speaker of the house," states Jack somberly. "Whiskey, tango, foxtrot?"

CHAPTER TWENTY-FIVE

After the talk with Callahan, Jack spent a restless night in his DC hotel room. So the next morning, when Assante asks to meet him at a nearby Starbucks, he looks forward to getting a good dose of caffeine.

"Man, it's cold," he shivers on the way.

The restaurant isn't far from Jack's hotel near FBI headquarters. But the sky is overcast, and the temperature is thirty degrees lower than the day before. There's also a chance of snow, and Jack isn't dressed for it. Yesterday, the two men left New York too quickly to consider the weather, so Jack is grateful for the hot liquid. While he searches for a table, he wraps his fingers around the cup to warm them up.

This place sure seems popular with the FBI crowd, he muses as a steady stream of people go in and out of the busy coffee shop. When he spots an empty table, he rushes over to claim it for himself and Jacob.

While Jack waits for the agent, he calls Didi with an urgent request. "Mornin'," he says when she picks up. "Listen, I need you to get out of the city as soon as possible. Make plane reservations for three; I don't care how much it costs. Go to your mom's place in Maryland."

"What the hell are you talking about?" retorts Didi. "I

can't just pick up and leave; I have a store to run! And your son has an appointment for a checkup!"

"It won't be for long," Jack replies reasonably.

Didi notices an underlying note of stress in her husband's voice. "Are you okay? What's going on? You don't tell me to do these kinds of things unless something bad's gonna happen."

"Yeah, I know. But all I can say is that the city may experience a major power outage soon. And if that happens, I'd feel better if none of you were there. I bought supplies, but the weather's turning nasty, and that old building will get cold real fast. Just go to Maryland; it'll be safer there. I'll join you when I can."

"I don't know, babe. I have so many things to do. There's a shipment—"

But Jack won't take no for an answer. "I'm serious, Dee. Sylvia can take care of the shop. Promise you'll go." Then Jack spots Assante ordering a drink at the counter. "Uh, gotta go," he says quickly. "Make the arrangements. I'll call again later."

When Assante joins Jack, he takes a sip of his drink, then leans close and lowers his voice. "I have some news. We picked up Congressman Butler earlier this morning."

"Really?"

"Yeah, it was easy. The guy's a scum ball. As soon as we started questioning him, he threw everyone under the bus."

"I'm not surprised," says Jack. "I never liked the guy. What did you get out of him?"

"He says the Patriot Guard has two training facilities, one in New Jersey and one in North Carolina. ATF and Homeland Security are on their way to both places as we speak."

"What about the place in Rhode Island?"

"I have agents researching properties there, so we should have something to go on soon." Then Jacob hands Jack a boarding pass. "Go back to New York," he says. "There's nothing more you can do here. I'll let you know when we find out where Anderson is. You can come with us when we go after him."

Jack fingers the airline ticket. "What about Butler and the others? What are you doing about those assholes?"

"We'll take care of them. Now, we think we got most of the Guard, but we still have to find Anderson. Look, I'll drive you to your hotel so you can check out. Then I'll drop you off at BWI."

Jack thinks to himself, *The FBI can fuck up a one-car funeral, so there's no way the Guard is out of commission. And there's no way they can take care of Butler and Serge's government cronies, either. I hate the Feds! But I'll make an exception for Jacob.*

Jack calls his wife again from the departure gate at Baltimore/Washington Airport. "Hey, did you get a flight out yet?"

"Yeah, we have a ten o'clock flight tomorrow morning. We're going to mom's house."

"Good choice. I'm coming home now. I'm at the airport, waiting for my flight. When I get back, I'm gonna have to go into the office to file some reports and catch up with other paperwork. And I also have to pick up the beast; I left it there yesterday."

"You gonna drive us to the airport?"

"Yeah. Kiss Mark for me, will ya?"

"You know I will. But wait, is that all?"

Didi expects Jack to respond, and when he doesn't, she's surprised. "Did you forget about me?" she asks impishly.

Jack knows what his wife's getting at, so he responds playfully, "How could I ever forget about you, Mrs. Stenhouse? I'll take care of you as soon as I get home."

Though Didi is pleased, she's still a little irked by his last-minute demand, so she baits him with a taunt. "Okay," she says, "but I'm not gonna wait all night. If you're not here by eleven, I'm gonna start without you, understand? Ta, ta, babe," she adds before abruptly ending the call.

Jack looks down at his now silent phone. *Uh, oh. I think I may be in trouble.*

That night, Jack gets a better night's sleep in his own bed. Especially after "taking care of his wife" like he said he would. So when he's the first one up the following day, he makes breakfast for everyone so the family can get to the airport early.

When the smell of cooking bacon begins to wake up the household, Sharon is the first to enter the kitchen. "Oooh, smells great," she says.

Jack looks up at his mother-in-law, then does a double-take and averts his eyes. Didi's mom is wearing a skimpy robe over a short nightgown, and the robe isn't tightly closed.

Living with Sharon these past few months has shown Jack where Didi gets many of her ideas. But he often wishes the older woman would be more discreet. She's not bad looking for her age, and that sometimes makes it hard for him.

Sharon pours herself a cup of coffee, unaware of the effect she's having. Then, she leans back on the counter, watching Jack at the stove.

"So what's the big hurry?" she asks her son-in-law. "Didi wouldn't give me any details. Is it a secret?"

"What are you talking about?" asks Jack, still not looking at Sharon.

"Why do we have to leave home?"

"Oh. There's no secret," says Jack, making sure to keep his eyes on flipping the pancakes. "There's a psychopath running around with an EMP weapon, and he needs to be stopped. Did you hear about what happened in Brooklyn?" Sharon nods, so Jack explains, "That was a small one. If he detonates anything larger, the tri-state area will be in deep shit. I'll feel much better if none of you were here while he's still on the loose."

"Oh, so that's what happened in Brooklyn. The news reports were pretty vague. But you say a larger weapon can shut down the whole city?"

"Fuck, yeah, and parts of New Jersey, all the way into upstate — depending on where it's detonated. It'll fry everything electronic — computers, phones, cars, trucks, airplanes — the entire power grid will go down. And if there's no power, there's no internet, so there won't be any banking, shopping, or anything else. None of the stores' alarm systems will work either, so there will probably be looting and all kinds of shit going on."

"Holy crap," comments Sharon just as Didi walks in with Mark.

"Can you take him, mom?" she asks, passing the infant to her mother. Then she tells Jack, "We're all packed. We should leave here no later than 7:30."

"Got it," he says. "Food's almost ready."

"You know," says Sharon, noting that Didi and Mark are already dressed. "I think I better get dressed, too. So take Mark back, okay?"

Didi holds out her arms for her son, and when he fusses at the changeover, she pats his backside to calm him down. "I guess we could all use a little vacation," she says, kissing Mark on the cheek.

Jack looks lovingly at his little family, more convinced than ever that he wants them out of town. "What did you tell Sonia?" he asks his wife.

"She knows the power may go down, so she's gonna take some cash out of the bank and get some extra supplies. She's in a newer building, so she's not too worried. I told her to post a sign at the store saying we'll be closed for the week, and I sent an email to our customer list to make sure everyone gets the message. You think you'll catch him soon?"

"We're gonna do our best," says Jack, turning off the stove. "Well, breakfast is ready. Let's eat."

Jack eats his fill, finishes his coffee, then checks the clock on the microwave. It's a little after seven, so while Sharon clears the table, he reaches over to Mark on Didi's lap.

"He's gonna be a big guy," he says, stroking his son's hair. Then he leans back in his seat when his cell phone rings.

"Morning," says Jacob. "We got a lead on Anderson, so we're heading to Rhode Island around nine. I'll meet you at the First."

"Perfect. I'll drive this time."

Jack looks at Didi with a satisfied smile. "We got him," he tells her. "Maybe all that will happen is that you get a nice little vacation."

When Jack pulls into the airport departure lane, he puts his blue light on the Road Runner's dash and flashes his badge at the traffic cop on duty. "Hey, I'm just gonna bring my family in, then leave," he tells him.

"Make it quick," retorts the cop. "Gotta keep things moving, bro."

Didi holds Mark while Jack carries the car seat and pulls Didi's luggage through the terminal doors, with Sharon trailing behind them with the rest of the baggage.

After everyone checks in, he kisses his wife and son and starts to leave, but Sharon won't let him get away too quickly. Just like her daughter, she holds her hands on her hips and pouts. "Hey, what am I, leftover cat food?" she frowns. "Where's my kiss?"

Jack rolls his eyes, but he dutifully kisses his mother-in-law's cheek. "Best looking cat food I've ever seen," he says. "Thanks for everything, mom. Love ya lots."

Jack waves as his family heads for TSA, then walks toward the exit without turning around for another look. He doesn't want his tears to show; he's going to miss his family more than he cares to admit.

But Didi does turn around. While shepherding her mother toward the TSA line, she sees Jack disappearing through the terminal doors. Didi knows her husband well. She understands why he's not sticking around any longer, and she's going to miss him just as much.

CHAPTER TWENTY-SIX

At the same time Jack is sending his family to Florida, Colonel Anderson is stopping to rest on a picturesque road near Serge Kaspin's Rhode Island estate. The former military man is in good shape and means to keep it that way. Whenever he can, he adds a five-mile jog to his daily routine of pushups, lunges, and planks.

Anderson drinks some water, then starts up again, increasing his pace. He's hungry now and wants to shower before downing a hearty breakfast. But his annoying cell phone interrupts that plan.

Grumbling at the shrill interruption, he answers, "Hello —" but gets no further.

"You've been burned," says the caller, who hangs up quickly.

Later that morning, Jacob looks absentmindedly at the passing scenery from the passenger seat of Jack's Road Runner. As promised, Jack is driving them both to the estate in Rhode Island where the FBI thinks Anderson is hiding. In front of them are trucks filled with members from an FBI SWAT team.

Neither of them has said much since they left the congestion of the New York area. So when a few strains from the Overture of Figaro break the silence, Jack is startled.

"What the fuck is that?" he asks, glancing sideways at Assante.

Jacob shrugs and picks up his phone. "It's my ringtone. Have a little class, will ya?"

As Jack exits onto Connecticut State Route 2, Jacob listens to the caller, getting angrier and angrier as the speaker goes on. Another minute later, he shouts "FUCK!" and pulls the phone away from his ear.

"What the hell?" asks Jack, with another sideways glance.

"NSA picked up a cell conversation that pinged near Kaspin's estate. Anderson was tipped off!"

Jack adds his own loud "FUCK!" then asks, "Do they know who made the call?"

"Yeah, Callahan."

"Double shit on a cracker!" exclaims Jack, infuriated by another obstacle.

He pounds the steering wheel over and over, then points to his glove box. "Fuck that man! Take out the two pouches in there, will ya?"

"Phone protection again?"

"Yeah. We can't afford to be without those things. Put

mine in one and yours in the other."

Former Marine Colonel Sam Anderson is unwavering in his commitment to Serge Kaspin's vision. Along with Kaspin, he believes the country he loves is in trouble, and he'll stop at nothing to get it back on the right track.

He hasn't heard from Serge since Brooklyn, but his dedication is so complete that he intends to go ahead with their plans whether Serge participates or not. He'd prefer to wait for his mentor, but since others are aware of what they're doing, he decides that now is the time to go into action.

The first thing Anderson does is mobilize the other members at the mansion. He calls them together in the media room to warn them to expect a visit by law enforcement. Then he tells them to break out the emergency supplies because he's going to leave the estate to execute the final stage of their plan.

After that, he gives his fellow patriots last-minute instructions, then picks up one of the compact EMP weapons. "Semper Fi, patriots!" he declares proudly. "I know the estate and our mission are in good hands!"

Amid a rousing chorus of "Semper Fi's" and "Good lucks," Anderson carries the weapon outside the house and places it near a clump of bushes.

Kneeling on the ground, he opens the box and adjusts the detonator. *This will make them sit up and take notice,* he thinks self-confidently. *"Maybe after they get a taste of this, they'll stop trying to ruin this country!"*

When the timer starts ticking down, he heads for the 6x6 truck, where the more destructive device is still secured inside the open bed.

While the militiamen and women in the house prepare for the onslaught Anderson warned them about, he starts up the truck and leaves the compound with a case of grenades on the seat next to him and the larger EMP weapon in the back.

By the time he reaches the end of the driveway, a rush of blue ionized air spreads over his vehicle and rushes across the landscape of southern Rhode Island.

There goes the first one, Anderson mutters with satisfaction.

Not far from the estate, Jack and the law enforcement team are shocked to see a wall of blue barreling toward them. Most of the team has no idea what it is, but Jack knows, so he steps on the brake and screeches to a halt.

When the damaging electromagnetic energy engulfs the Road Runner, the car shudders but doesn't turn off, unlike the newer vehicles of the rest of the team. All of those trucks suddenly stop right where they are — their sophisticated electronics are now damaged and unusable.

While the team tries to figure out what happened, a vehicle suddenly whizzes by, unaffected by the energy pulse.

"Hey, that's Anderson!" they shout, whipping out their firearms.

Though they take shots at the car and driver, the olive

drab cargo truck continues to rumble past them all, unscathed by their attempts to stop it.

"Dammit!" shouts Jack as the truck continues down the road. "I'm going after him! This beast still works!"

Turning the wheel, he backs the Road Runner away from the stalled vehicle in front of him and swings it around to pursue the reckless former colonel.

Jack follows the 6x6 to I-95. The blast didn't reach the interstate, so traffic here is moving along as usual. However, south of this area, the locals are in deep kimchee. They have no power. None of their expensive electronics or newer vehicles are working.

Jacob eyes the other cars around them on the busy interstate. "How the hell are you gonna stop him?" he asks.

"I'm not," replies Stenhouse. "Call your guys and set up a roadblock."

Jacob nods and makes the call. When it's arranged, he drops his phone into his lap. "Okay. Here's what's gonna happen," he announces. "ATF and Connecticut Highway Patrol are gonna block the highway near New Haven. They already sent up drones and have eyes on the truck. When they stop him, they'll take him back to the city."

Jack shakes his head in dismay. "New Haven's at least an hour away; that's too long to find out if there's a bomb in that truck. Look, I have an idea. I'm gonna pull my car alongside him. When I get in his blind spot, you jump into the truck bed."

Jacob's mouth drops open in shock. "What?! Are you crazy? How the hell am I gonna do that?!"

"You're gonna have to climb out," smirks Jack. "Get into the back seat. When I get close, lean out the window and jump into the truck."

Jacob is still dumbfounded. "Are you completely fucking nuts?"

"Just do it," snaps Jack, with his eyes glued to the truck. "Didn't you learn anything in the service?"

"Yeah, I learned a lot," snaps Jacob, "but I'm not in the service anymore!"

Jack momentarily takes his eyes off the truck to frown at Jacob. "Well, do you think if we ask Anderson nicely, he'll stop the truck so we can check it?"

The young special agent sighs deeply, knowing Jack's right. He gives it a moment of thought, then says, "Okay. Just get as close as you can. And keep the damn car steady!"

Traffic thins considerably after the Mystic Seaport Museum exit, so Jack guides his Road Runner to the truck's right side. "Get ready!" he shouts to Jacob at the open back seat window.

When the Road Runner is in position, Jacob swings one leg out of the window like a Nascar driver exiting his vehicle. Then he reaches out, grabs a bar on the side of the 6x6, and pulls himself into the open truck bed.

When Jack sees that Jacob is safe, he shouts, "Good man!" then slows his car down until he's well behind the truck.

Keeping low, Jacob opens the large case strapped down in the truck. "Fuck," he mutters under his breath. "I'm gonna need help." Reaching for his phone, he calls Stenhouse, but there's no answer. "Dammit! I bet he never took his cell out of the bag!"

Jacob scrolls through his contacts to find the number for the chief ATF agent. "This is FBI Special Agent Assante," he whispers when the agent answers. Speaking fast, he says, "I'm in the back of the 6x6, there's a large EMP device in the truck, and it's armed." When the agent replies, the outside noise makes it hard to hear, so he covers one ear. "What?" he asks. "Yeah, it's armed!!" he repeats. Then he listens and answers, "No!! I don't have access to Anderson! I'm in the back of the fucking truck!"

Though Jack is now some distance away, he can still see the truck barreling down the road and wonders why Jacob isn't calling him. Then he remembers that his phone is still shielded. "Crap!" he shouts and reaches over to open the bag holding his phone.

At the wheel of the 6x6, Anderson's knuckles turn white with tension. He's so focused on what he intends to do that he has no idea what's going on behind him. Briefly, thoughts of his companions at the house enter his mind, but they don't linger. He knows they're highly trained, so he presumes they'll be okay.

Suddenly, a line of flashing blue lights ahead captures his attention. "Fuckin' shit!" he shouts at the windshield. "They're not gonna stop me!"

Slowing down, the colonel takes a moment to analyze the situation, and his military mind comes to a quick decision. Turning his vehicle hard to the right, he rides the shoulder, increasing speed as he goes. The 6x6 is typically governed for under 50 mph; however, Anderson accelerates to at least 70 in the rough breakdown lane.

When the state troopers and ATF agents see the truck barreling toward them in the outside lane, they realize Anderson intends to run around or through their barrier, so they scatter in all directions. But they don't break out their weapons. They can't fire because they can't risk damaging the EMP before they can deactivate it.

At the truck's excessive speed, it doesn't take long before it's ramming the barriers like a runaway elephant. With barricades flying in all directions, it rocks back and forth, tossing Jacob around like a rag doll.

Next to go through is Jack, who follows the path Anderson made. As he snakes around the broken barricades, he shouts to the agents, "I won't let him get away!"

Breathing heavily, Anderson watches the blue lights fade in his rearview mirror. "Whoop whoop!" he shouts, thrilled to have eluded the cops. But he's still unaware of his tail, as Jack makes sure to keep several cars between them.

The demoted colonel continues east on I-95 until he reaches the Westchester County exit for Mamaroneck Avenue and decides to get off the highway. Exiting there, he drives down Barry Avenue into a residential community lined with tree-shaded homes from the fifties.

Still following, Jack mutters, "Where the hell is this guy going?"

The area is quaint, but Jack doesn't have time to take it in. He knows he can't risk being seen, so he keeps several cars between him and the 6x6 while continuing to keep sight of its bumper.

After traveling a while down the residential street, Jack decides that the situation is calm enough to check-in. But when he takes his eyes off the road for a minute to look for his phone, a garbage truck pulls into his path, and the appearance of the behemoth forces him to step on the brakes. Unfortunately, the sudden action causes the Road Runner to spin around in a circle, leaving it pointing in the opposite direction when it finally stops.

"Holy crap!" breathes Stenhouse. "Thank God no one was behind me!"

Recovering quickly, Jack turns the car around and speeds up. When he passes the garbage truck, he flashes his badge at the driver and yells obscenities. Then he starts looking for the 6x6.

But the incident was a boon for Anderson. It provided him with enough time to significantly increase the distance between them, and Jack has a tough time catching up.

A couple of miles later, Anderson becomes furious when the road ends at a sign for Mamaroneck Beach & Yacht Club. "Fuckin' shit!" he exclaims. But he continues on, passing the sign and driving into the club, around a large building and a couple of tennis courts, until he sees a small beach and boats tied up beyond it.

"That's exactly what I need," he utters, spotting a middle-aged couple preparing to cast off their 40-foot yacht's moorings. "If I can't drive the bomb into Manhattan, I'll leave it here and bring that box of grenades instead!"

Pleased with his plan, he skids the 6x6 to a stop and runs down to the dock.

When the truck stops, Jacob pops his head up. "What the fuck is he doing?" he mutters, leaping out to run after his target.

Anderson senses someone behind him, so after he jumps aboard the luxury craft, he turns around to see who it is. "Fuck!" he shouts, grabbing his sidearm and firing at the special agent.

"Whoa!" shouts Assante, ducking for cover as bullets whiz past his head.

Aboard the yacht, the owner and his wife run to the other side of the vessel when they hear the gunshots. "What the hell's going on?" they shout to their uninvited passenger.

But Anderson doesn't pay them a lick of attention.

When the gunshots continue, the husband decides not to stick around. "I don't know what's happening!" he yells to his wife. "Let's get out of here!"

Grabbing the woman's hand, the two of them jump into the murky waters of Long Island Sound and begin paddling toward the dock.

Hearing splashes, Anderson turns around. "Thanks, folks!" he waves at them. Then he runs to the cockpit, revs the motor, and points the craft toward open water.

Jacob saw the couple jump, so he stops to check on them.

"You guys okay?" he asks as they climb a ladder attached to the dock.

"Yeah," says the husband, turning around to give his wife a helping hand. "What the hell's going on?"

But Jacob doesn't answer because he's already rushing toward a small fishing boat that just docked.

"Sorry, bud! Gotta take your boat!" he says, showing his ID to the boat's startled owner.

"You can't take my boat!" exclaims the owner.

But Jacob is determined, so with his hand on his holstered firearm, he says, "I have no time to explain. You need to go ashore now."

Reluctantly, the owner complies, but he's not happy. "Don't wreck my boat, asshole!" he shouts as Jacob speeds off.

After Jack rounds the tennis courts, he finds the 6x6 where Anderson left it — with its door open and the engine running.

Squealing to a stop, he jumps out of his car with his gun drawn. "Police!" he shouts. "Leave the truck with your hands in the air!"

But the vehicle is empty.

Looking around, he sees a boat heading out to the Sound and squints in the bright sunlight to get a better look.

"Holy crap! That's Jacob!" he shouts, recognizing the familiar figure at the helm.

While ATF and FBI agents swarm the area, Jack calls Jacob. "What the hell are you doing?" he asks, raising his voice above the surrounding noise.

"Looks like we're going west, maybe to the city!" he responds, shouting just as loud as Jack. "I called the Coast Guard; they're gonna put eyes in the sky, and they're gonna pick you up! So get to Harbor Island Park, it's nearby, on Mamaroneck Avenue! There's a Coast Guard Auxiliary unit there that will take you aboard one of their ships. You can follow us in their boat!"

"Shit, shit, shit!" mutters Jack when the call ends. "This case just won't end!"

On the way to his car, he spots newly arrived bomb technicians inspecting the EMP in the truck bed. "What's the skinny?" he asks from a safe distance.

An officer shakes his head. "I don't know... It's pretty sophisticated!"

Jack thinks for a minute, then points at the beach. "You know, there's a whole ocean out there! Why don't you call up the shallow water sailors? They can dump it somewhere deep...easy-peasy! But that's your call, so I'll leave you guys to it!"

Returning to the beast, Jack fires it up, hits the horn twice, then uses all of his 400 horses to trail a police escort to a small park operated by the town of Mamaroneck.

CHAPTER TWENTY-SEVEN

At Harbor Island Park, Jack parks his baby near the harbormaster's office and jumps out. "Watch her for me, will ya?" he calls back to his escorts while he runs to the docks.

Waiting for him in the stern of a Coast Guard Response Boat-Medium — a workhorse of a boat designed for multiple missions — is a tall, well-muscled Coast Guard officer.

"Welcome aboard," says the Coastie.

"Thanks. I'm Detective Stenhouse, NYPD."

"Lieutenant Commander Ben Bennett," replies the officer. "Hang on tight, Detective; I'm gonna run you out there at wide-open throttle."

When the twin engines roar to life, the boat tries to leap out of the water. "Whoa, baby!" yells Jack, quickly buttoning up his pea coat against the forty-three-degree sea air stinging his face.

"You been doing this a while?" shouts Jack into the wind.

"Been with the USCG for fifteen years!" responds the officer proudly.

Up ahead, a fishing boat drifts along, dead in the water,

and it looks familiar to Jack. "Hey, that's Assante!" he shouts. "Commander! There's an FBI agent on that boat out there! We need to pick him up!"

Bennett nods and pulls alongside the "borrowed" fishing boat.

"Jack! I'm so glad to see you!" shouts Assante, climbing aboard. "I ran out of gas and lost sight of Anderson. I have no idea where he is now."

Bennett listens to the exchange, then keys his radio and pushes the throttle forward.

As the boat leaps over the waves, the Coast Guard officer talks to colleagues, then relays the latest information to his passengers. "He's in a blue and white Regal 3060, and he just passed Sands Point! NYPD Harbor Patrol is on their way to intercept him near Rikers Island."

While the boat bounces across the choppy waters of Long Island Sound, Stenhouse and Assante give Bennett thumbs up, each man hoping for a quick end to the chase.

After a particularly bumpy patch of rough water, Jacob yells to be heard above the engine noise. "How fast will this thing go?"

The tall sailor at the helm looks back at him with a smile. "It can go over 40 knots! If that guy's lucky, the Regal might reach 34! Don't worry; we'll catch him!"

Back at the beach club, ATF Lieutenant Ansel Blake gives his superior an update about his officers' evaluation of the bomb.

"Sir, we examined the device, and our guys say it's pretty complicated. They think it may take too long to figure out before the clock runs out. There's only ninety minutes left."

Wallace Clark, ATF Resident in Charge of the Manhattan field office, turns grim. "Well, damn," he says. Then he brightens. "Hey, you're at a marina, right? What about a water detonation? We can dump it in the ocean; the water should shield us from the energy pulse. Can you put it on a boat?"

"I don't know if we can move it safely," Blake replies. "There are a several triggers."

"All right," says Clark. I'll advise in a few."

The resident in charge hangs up his phone, then searches through his contact list for the number of an old Army buddy stationed at Brooklyn's Fort Hamilton.

"Colonel Alborn," announces a young corporal outside of Colonel Dustin Alborn's office, "there's a guy from ATF on Line One. He says he knows you from 'Nam."

"Who is it?"

"His name is Wallace Clark, sir."

Alborn smiles and picks up the receiver. "Wally, you ol' son of a bitch! How's it hangin'?"

"Low and to the right, Dusty. Hey, I need a favor."

"Yeah? Well, it's gonna cost you another steak dinner. You up for that?"

"This is serious, Dusty."

"Okay, what's up?"

"We raided an anti-American militia camp this morning, but they armed an EMP weapon."

"Well, that will fuck up the East coast. Disarm the fucker!"

"That's why I called. Unfortunately, we don't have the expertise, and it'll take too long to figure out."

"You can't do it? Where is it?

"In the back of a 6-by at Mamaroneck Yacht Club."

"Yeah? I was there once, nice place. So, what do you want from me?"

"You still have access to a Skycrane?"

"Yeah... Hey, buddy, what're you thinkin'? You wanna dump it in the ocean?"

"Yeah, truck and all. But I want to put it in a deep place. There's a canyon off the tip of Manhattan that'll work."

"Hmm. We'll have to fly it over highly populated areas."

"I know, but we have time."

"Umm... Okay. We can get the crane there, but I'll need authorization from higher up. Shouldn't be a problem, though. Send me the info you have, and I'll get the Sikorsky over to you. And Wally, this sounds more like a prime rib dinner than that shit hole you took me to last time."

When Sam Anderson reaches Rikers Island, he sees Bennett's Coast Guard response boat closing in on him from one side and three NYPD harbor patrol boats speeding at him from another. But the radical isn't worried. He doesn't give two shits about his safety. Instead, he pushes his throttle forward and starts a game of chicken on the water, aiming directly at one of the patrol boats.

As the five crafts close in on each other, the target of Anderson's wrath watches nervously as the extremist heads directly for him. "That crazy fucker's gonna ram us!" he yells and turns his boat hard to starboard.

Behind him, the other patrol boats see that quick move and make their own decisions, but they don't fare as well. Rather than following their colleague, one turns hard to port, and the other plows right into him.

Witnessing the crash, the men on Bennett's boat involuntarily duck from the explosive sound. "Holy shit!" they exclaim.

Lieutenant Commander Bennett edges his response boat near the limping NYPD vessels. "Fuckin' hell!" he shouts. "You guys okay?"

"Aye," respond several of the sailors as they massage bruised elbows and check each other for injuries.

"Didn't you see the other boats?" he asks, not expecting an answer. Then he sighs and tells them to go back to base. "Damage doesn't look too bad. Just take it slow."

When Bennett is on the way again, he mutters something under his breath that Jack can't make out. Then he triggers his radio. "We lost Anderson," he declares without explanation. "Set up a barricade on Harlem River, near Gracie Mansion. Don't let him get through!"

Jack overhears Bennett's order and snickers. "I don't think that's necessary," he tells the lieutenant. "I don't think he'll take the southern Harlem River to do what he wants. I'll bet anything that he's going north to hook up to the Hudson. You can have your boys block the Harlem River south of here if you want, but you better send some of them north as well."

"All right," says Bennett after a moment. "I'll send air support to the Hudson near lower Manhattan, and I'll have our guys monitor the Harlem River going north."

Bennett looks at Jack thoughtfully, then directs his boat into the Bronx Kill, a narrow strait between the southern Bronx and Randall's Island. "You know something I don't, Stenhouse?"

Jack shrugs. "Nah, just a hunch."

"A hunch, huh? Well, I sure hope you're right."

Anderson is going north on the Harlem River when a light on the yacht's instrument display panel suddenly catches his eye. "Dammit!" he yells. "This is no time to run out of gas!"

Turning around, he looks for anyone following and finds the coast clear. So he feels safe enough to slow the boat down for a while to save some gas.

However, up ahead, he sees a large freighter coming into view. "That thing is huge!" he mutters. "It almost fills the entire river!"

As the colonel watches, the slow-moving behemoth appears to be maneuvering to a recycling center on the opposite bank, crowding the way north. "Oh, that's perfect!" he laughs into the wind. "There's still enough room for me to slip past, but I know the Coast Guard is on their way, and when they reach this area, they're gonna be fucked!"

After Anderson passes the ship, he believes he's free from further interference on the water. So he takes his time coaxing his boat around a sharp bend in the Harlem River, then heads for a tree-lined cove at Inwood Hill Park, a mostly wooded and naturally hilly oasis at the northern tip of Manhattan.

The boat is operating on fumes by the time it reaches the cove, so he guides it silently the rest of the way to a dock in the mostly deserted park.

With the boat no longer useful, Anderson needs another

way to get around.

"Hmm, there's a pickup truck just sitting there," he mutters when he sees a man reading in his vehicle near an empty ballfield. "Sorry, guy, this isn't your lucky day."

Without tying the boat down, Anderson jumps out and runs to the pickup with his gun drawn. "Get out!" he demands of the hapless victim.

Shocked, the stranger complies without a fuss, but inexplicably, Anderson smashes his .45 on the side of the man's head for good measure. "Don't want you notifying the cops, do we?"

The colonel is delighted to find the keys in the ignition. "Time to get out of here," he mutters, and drives out of the park.

While an NYPD chopper begins to track Anderson's every move, Lieutenant Commander Ben Bennett, FBI Special Agent Jacob Assante, and NYPD Detective Jack Stenhouse curse their awkward situation. They're stuck on the Harlem River with no choice but to wait for the freighter to get out of the way.

The men pass the time with idle chatter, most of which involves boasting about past exploits. And after a time, they're hailed by a harbor patrol boat.

"The target is now on land," an officer reports as they pull alongside. "He commandeered a pickup, and an airborne unit is now following."

This news heartens Assante. "Don't lose him!" he urges. "He may lead us to other militiamen!"

Jack has a thought. "Can you guys get me back to Harbor Island Park?"

"Yeah," responds the officer, thinking quickly. "The fastest way is by chopper. We can send one to Inwood Park; it's just around the bend. The freighter's almost clear now, so you can put your boat up in the cove there."

"Thanks, and send another one for my FBI friend here."

Jacob frowns. "What the fuck?" he protests. "I'm coming with you!"

"Uh-uh," says Jack with a hand on Jacob's shoulder. "It'd be better if you followed Anderson from the air. I have a feeling he'll head back to the cave."

Colonel Anderson is no fool. He knows the police are probably surveilling him with airborne assets, so he urgently needs to find a way to evade them.

As he drives, he notes the road is weaving in and out under elevated train tracks. *This could be useful*, he surmises.

The next time he's under the El's shadow, he makes a sudden U-turn, thinking, *They'll probably assume I'm continuing north.*

Initially, he pats himself on the back, thinking he's being pretty clever. However, the very next minute, he becomes more practical. *Yeah, I may lose them for a while, but I should really switch cars. That's sure to confuse them!*

Determined to ditch the pickup, he begins to look for an easy mark, and a few blocks away, spots a driver parking a red Camaro in front of a restaurant. *Nice car*, he thinks. *I wouldn't mind driving that for the rest of the mission!*

Turning abruptly, he gets into the right lane and double-parks a few cars away. Then he jumps out of the truck with his gun pointed at the Camaro's driver. "Get out!" he orders, expecting to make a quick switch.

But the man in the car is a New Yorker, and he's not easily intimidated. "What the fuck?" the driver shouts, staying rooted to his seat.

So Anderson shoves the gun at the driver's head. "You gonna die for your car?" he asks, cocking the trigger menacingly.

That does it. "You can have it!" shouts the victim with his hands raised in surrender.

As soon as Anderson lowers the gun, the man flings the door open and runs onto the sidewalk, leaving the motor running.

While the colonel speeds off in his latest acquisition, the vehicle's owner curses and pumps his fists in the air helplessly. "Did you see that?" he demands of disinterested pedestrians going about their business all around him.

Miles away, Stenhouse and Assante finally arrive at Inwood Hill Park. They thank Lieutenant Commander Bennett for his help then start running toward their respective choppers.

But before they can board, an FBI agent waves them down. "Hold on!" he shouts. "We have news — some good and some bad!"

"Fuck! Why does there always have to be bad news?" mumbles Jack, annoyed by the possibility of further complications. "What's wrong now?" he asks, nearing the agent.

"We were tracking Anderson from the air, but we lost him when he passed under a section of elevated tracks along Broadway."

Jack throws his hands up in the air. "You guys can screw up a one-car funeral!" he barks. "Aren't you blocking all roads leading north? We gotta keep that asshole in the city!"

With a shrug, the FBI agent lets Jack's rudeness roll off his back like unwanted baggage. "You didn't let me tell you the good news," he retorts. "We got a report that a Camaro was hijacked in front of a restaurant in that area, and it has one of those security tracking devices. So we got the owner to activate it, and we're following him again."

Jack smiles uncomfortably, knowing he spoke too soon. "Halleluiah!" he says. "What color is the car?"

"It's a nice, bright red. Should be easy to spot."

Jacob doesn't wait to hear more. Turning around, he runs to his chopper, calling back over his shoulder, "I'll find the fucker!"

"Right!" responds Jack, nodding hopefully. "Let me know the minute you see him!"

Looking around, Jack spots several NYPD patrol cars parked along the roadway. "Hey! I'm gonna need your vehicle!" he shouts at the nearest officer.

Though Anderson has a significant lead on Stenhouse, high-flying drones and police helicopters keep track of him through the Camaro's location signal.

Following the beacon, the officers see Anderson turning onto West 230th Street, then Riverdale Avenue. They watch as he follows that road and stops at a red light in front of a stone tower within a small park.

While Anderson waits for the light to change, he drums his fingers on the steering wheel and looks curiously at the tower. *You never know what you'll find around here*, he muses. Then he notices a small sign for Route 9/A Henry Hudson Parkway South.

When the light turns green, he turns left.

Now going south on Henry Hudson Parkway, Colonel

Anderson contemplates crossing over into New Jersey when he begins to see signs for the George Washington Bridge. "I can cause just as much trouble in the Garden State as in New York," he ponders.

However, when he sees a line of cars getting into the turnoff lane, he discards that notion in a hurry. "Too much traffic," he mutters and continues going south. "Lower Manhattan is probably best."

To reinforce his decision, he tells himself that he'll have a better chance of evading capture in the Financial District because it's a crowded business area. He rationalizes that there are so many people around all the time that he's sure the cops wouldn't risk blocking streets or forcing an armed confrontation.

Guided by aerial law enforcement, Stenhouse enters Henry Hudson Parkway several miles behind Anderson. As he passes Fort Tryon Park, he turns up the radio of the NYPD patrol car to listen for police updates.

"This POS is no Road Runner, but it'll have to do," he mumbles while swerving through traffic.

Minutes after turning the radio on, a static-filled voice says, "Jack, this is Assante. He just passed the GW Bridge. We see you behind him on the Henry Hudson."

Jack speeds up and keys the mic. "When I find him, I'll get as close as I can. Don't try to stop him until he gets off the parkway. Oh, and can you let my team know what's going on?"

"They already know."

Jack weaves in and out of traffic, then spots two similar red vehicles, so he keys the mic again. "Hey, I got two red Camaros down here, right next to each other. Which one is Anderson?"

Jacob doesn't reply right away, which doesn't give Jack a warm and fuzzy feeling. "You guys don't fucking know, do yah?" he scowls.

From his seat high above, Jacob is looking down at the two red vehicles. "What are the odds of *that* happening?" he says into his mic. "We're not gonna know for sure until they separate!"

"You're kidding, right? You got a tag number on Anderson's ride?"

"Yeah, um…hold on… It's XJ120B9, New York plates."

"Well, thank God for that! When I find the one with that plate, I'll get in the same lane."

Unfortunately, before Jack can spot the correct tag, the two Camaros exit onto Canal Street, one directly behind the other.

"Damnit!" yells Jack, following in their tracks. "One of these cars better be the one we're looking for!"

The stretch of Canal Street off the exit is filled with heavy traffic. Everyone getting off there has to slow down to a crawl, so when Jack finds himself stuck behind several trucks and busses, he has to crane his neck to keep the two cars in view. Then he suddenly catches a glimpse of a flash of red turning at the next corner.

"One of them just made a right!" he tells Jacob. "Is that him?"

"Yeah!"

"Here we go!" yells Jack, flicking the switch on the blue light and blasting the siren.

Startled by the sudden activity, the vehicles in front of him move aside as best they can. But when Jack finally makes the same righthand turn, the red Camaro is nowhere in sight.

Jack slows down and yells into his mic, "Where the fuck did he go?"

"He pulled into the parking garage you just passed!" says Assante. "NYPD is responding!"

"Fuckin' shit!" shouts Jack, screeching to a halt in the middle of the road. Then, with a hard turn of his wheel, he spins the car around and moves in the opposite direction, causing oncoming vehicles to smash helplessly into one another.

Jack looks up at the carnage in his rearview mirror, but

he knows he can't do anything about it — he's focused on finding the garage.

When he spots the entrance, he skids in and stops in front of the attendant. "Where did the Camaro go?" he shouts.

"That crazy asshole shot at me!" responds the attendant, pointing at the upper levels.

"Raise the fuckin' gate!" screams Jack.

With tires squealing, Jack heads to the upper levels as NYPD vehicles follow, all of them spinning wildly, level after level.

At the fourth level, Jack spots the Camaro, but it's stopped in the middle of the lane. Cautiously, he pulls the squad car up to its rear, then slowly and carefully exits the car.

The vehicle looks abandoned, but Jack won't take a chance that Anderson is hiding inside. So with his Glock leading the way, he creeps up to the car.

"Shit!" he mutters when he peers inside. "Where'd the fucker go?"

While blue lights from the police vehicles dance around the cement cave, four NYPD officers, including Hector Gomez, approach Jack.

"Hector! Glad to see ya, buddy!" says Jack, facing the officers. "He's on foot now, so search the garage."

While the officers fan out, Anderson continues to drag a female body behind a Toyota SUV parked at the end of the next row. Shielded by other cars, he picks the woman's keys up from the floor and sneaks over to her BMW. Then he backs it out of its spot and squeals down the exit ramp.

The car makes so much noise that Jack and the officers turn to see what's going on.

"What the hell…?" asks one of the officers, listening to the squealing tires fading down the ramp.

Jack exclaims, "Holy shit! That must be Anderson! I only got a glimpse, but I'm pretty sure it's a BMW! Update the FBI! I'm gonna find that guy if it's the last thing I do!"

When Jack's patrol car whizzes past the garage attendant, Anderson is nowhere to be seen, so he doesn't know which way to go. "Hey," he says into his mic, "Did you guys see a BMW screaming out of the garage a minute ago?"

"No, why?"

"That was Anderson; he switched cars again! Can you help me out? I have no idea which way he went!"

"Shit! I guess it's your call, Jack. I'm looking down at the street, and there are Beemers north and south of you."

Jack sighs and turns south. "You guys stop the northbound one. Let me know if it's him."

At the first intersection, Jack hesitates, then turns right. Then at West Street, he makes another snap decision and turns left.

Fortunately, Jack's instincts were correct. Anderson is now only a few blocks ahead — he's weaving through traffic and blowing through red lights to get away from anyone who may be following.

But the colonel's erratic driving is causing problems for other drivers, and New York police soon start receiving reports of traffic accidents on West Street. When they respond, they find a BMW racing down the busy roadway and begin to pursue it.

While several police cruisers follow the Camaro, others race to the intersection where West Street ends at Battery Park.

The police hope to stop the maniac before he reaches the widely used public area; however, Anderson blows through the intersection and T-bones a Prius.

As airbags deploy in both cars, the Prius is slammed again by a police cruiser. Thankfully, none of the drivers are hurt. But the accident gives Anderson time to run into Battery Park.

With luck on his side, Jack reaches the scene just as Anderson disappears into a crowd of people.

Screeching his cruiser to a halt, he leaves his vehicle in the middle of the road to chase after the colonel.

The anarchist has a substantial lead, but Jack is determined to catch him. However, as he yells for people to get out of the way, he loses sight of his target in another crowd. "Fuckin' shit!" he yells, slowing down to catch his breath.

When Jack resumes the chase, Anderson is way ahead of him, bounding over bushes and undergrowth, knocking people aside left and right in a desperate bid to get away.

Eventually, Anderson reaches the ticketing area for the popular ferry ride to the Statue of Liberty. Here, a line of barricades separates the ticketing building from the wharf, but Anderson refuses to let that stop him. He merely jumps over them and runs down to the ferry, hoping to catch it before it leaves.

However, he's a little too late. There's already a growing amount of water between the ship and the dock.

Still, Anderson won't stop. Seized with adrenaline, he takes a mighty leap and lands squarely on the deck amid a group of shocked passengers.

"Fuck!" pants Jack when he also reaches the dock area, only to see the ferry steaming toward the Lady of the Harbor with his adversary on board.

Doubling over, he works to catch his breath, then spots a park ranger directing a new line of ferry passengers to the waiting area.

When he recovers, he walks over to the ranger and gets right up in the man's face. "How the *fuck* did you let that guy on board?" he screams at him.

But the much older park ranger doesn't bat an eye. Instead, he looks at Jack and retorts firmly, "Hold your water, bud! I retire in a week, and I am *not* gonna confront a guy with grenades and a forty-five! That's *your* fucking job, man!"

Disgusted, Jack walks off and pulls out his cell phone. "The fucker is on the ferry to the Statue of Liberty!" he shouts at Jacob. "And he's armed with grenades and a forty-five! Get the harbor patrol and the Coast Guard out there, and have a boat pick me up at the ferry dock!"

Just then, the unmistakable sounds of gunshots drift across the water. "Shit, shit, shit!" Jack shouts, raising his fists angrily to the sky.

Though Colonel Sam Anderson is on the Statue of Liberty ferry, he has no intention of touring the Lady of the Harbor.

He strides through the ship, waving his firearm at terrified and screaming tourists, pushing them aside until he reaches the top deck. When he's in the open air, he discharges his weapon skyward.

Hearing the gunshots, the men, women, and children below him cower and cry out in fear. But Anderson doesn't care. Brandishing his M1911 pistol, he rushes into the bridge and confronts the captain. "If you want to see your family tonight, do as I say and shut this ship down!" he orders.

This is Greg Arnold with WPIX channel 11, reporting to you with breaking news. An armed terrorist has just commandeered the Miss Independence *Statue of Liberty ferry and is holding all passengers and crew hostage. The ship is now a quarter of a mile offshore, and harbor patrol and Coast Guard cutters are rushing to encircle it. A spokesperson from the mayor's office has confirmed that the FBI will be negotiating with this unknown person to release everyone on board. I will stay on-site as this story unfolds, and I will continue to stream updates as we receive them. This is Greg Arnold with WPIX, always on the job for you."*

Anderson is now surveying the water and the sky from the helm of the *Miss Independence*, looking for signs of trouble.

There's nothing in front of him, but when he turns back toward the New York skyline, he notices dark specks in the sky. "What the hell is that?" he asks.

The ferry captain picks up a pair of binoculars. "That's odd; they're helicopters, and there's a truck hanging below one of them."

"What the fuck?" replies Anderson, grabbing the binoculars out of the captain's hands. Peering at the enlarged images, he identifies the choppers as two AH-64 Apaches and one Sikorsky S-64 Skycrane.

"What the hell are they doing?" he asks, frowning in thought. Then suddenly, he's struck by a revelation. "Fuck me!" he shouts. "They're bringing it out to sea!"

Angered by the realization that his EMP bomb is about to be rendered useless, Anderson turns around and cold-bloodedly shoots the ferry captain in the head.

"Someone had to die today," he tells the shocked crew."

With the engines shut down, the *Miss Independence* drifts in the currents of Upper New York Bay, but it's not alone in the water. A fleet of harbor patrol crafts and USCG cutters have surrounded it, and police helicopters and drones are keeping watch from above.

Once again, Jack finds himself in a go-fast boat with Jacob Assante, but this time, with harbor patrol.

Armed with *Miss Independence's* radio frequency, Assante contacts the ship. "Sam Anderson, this is FBI Special Agent Jacob Assante," he intones. "We need to talk."

Anderson hears the message from his position on the bridge, but he doesn't reply. Instead, he points at the dead captain and orders the cowering crew to throw him overboard. "And don't return here," he warns them.

Minutes later, Assante and Stenhouse are horrified to see a body hit the water.

Jack asserts, "That must have been the shot we heard."

"Yeah, but what's he gonna do next?" worries Jacob.

The next moment, the radio cackles with Anderson's voice. "That was the captain," he informs them. "Unfortunately for him, I had to kill him to make my point, and I'll kill many more if I have to. Keep those ships back. If any of them get closer, hundreds more will die. Got it?"

Assante opens his mic. "What do you want, Anderson?"

"What do I want? I want the Constitution of these United States restored to its rightful place in our nation! But no one is listening, so my group of committed patriots and I are taking things into our own hands! We're forcing people to notice what's really going on!"

The absurdity of Anderson's statements confounds Jacob. "So you're willing to kill people to bring democracy back? How does that help your cause?"

"Drastic measures always lead to action," the ex-colonel explains condescendingly. "Now, I don't plan to be one of the ones who dies today, so here's what you need to do. Send me a fully fueled seaplane, and tell your puny little navy to leave the area. When they're all gone, I'm gonna fly that plane out of here, and no one's gonna follow me. You have thirty minutes to comply, or you'll force me to send more bodies into the water for every minute the plane is late. 10-4?"

Anderson flicks the switch on his mic and lays it down to wait for a reply. As the seconds tick by with no response, it seems to him like a series of long, slow minutes.

Finally, the silence breaks.

"10-4," is the answer.

CHAPTER TWENTY-EIGHT

Army Captain Eddie Switt monitors his instrument panel while he flies the big Skycrane southward. "We still got five minutes," he tells his copilot. "Drop the load."

When the 6x6 cargo truck falls away, the cables holding it sway in relief, and Switt banks the Skycrane so they can watch it smacking into the Atlantic. When it disappears into the ten thousand feet of saltwater below, he radios Fort Hamilton.

"Mission accomplished. Returning to base."

Jack wonders how Jacob could agree to Anderson's terms. "You aren't seriously thinking about giving him a free ticket out of here?" he asks his friend and colleague.

Jacob responds with a grin. "Yes and no," he says. Then he radios a contact at his Manhattan office. "I need you to get me a seaplane that's already fueled and ready to fly. Call Sea Foam Tours in New Jersey; they've helped us before. And tell them that we'll need to do some work on the plane. I want our guys to rig up a switch that will shut the engines down remotely. And listen, this needs to be done yesterday. That plane has to be out of there in no less than twenty minutes."

Jack is still confused, so Jacob explains, "We'll give him a plane, but we're gonna shut it down after he gets airborne. He'll land her if he's a good pilot, and we'll get him. If not, well…"

Jack laughs, "Damn, you remind me so much of your sister!"

Then Jacob's phone rings, and he turns away to answer it. "Assante, are you out of your mind?" yells the assistant director in charge of the Manhattan field office. "We can't get that plane airborne in twenty minutes! It'll take at least two hours to do what you want!"

Jacob knows his request is unreasonable, but he's also sure that Anderson is unstable. "Sir, if you don't want a killing field out here, I sincerely hope you can find a way. However, I may be able to stall him. What's the absolute minimum amount of time they'll need?"

Jacob ends the call, sighs, and runs his fingers through his hair. "Fucking guys can't get that plane done quick enough," he tells Jack. Then he grabs the radio mic to speak to Anderson.

"Colonel Anderson, this is Agent Assante. We need more time to get that seaplane for you. There's only one available right now, and it's on its way back to the airport to refuel. So we're gonna need at least ninety minutes to get it out to you. However, I'm pulling all patrol boats away now, except for mine, as a gesture of good faith. Choppers, too."

Sam paces the bridge, thinking, while a thousand yards away, a SWAT counter-sniper hunkers down at the base of the

Statue of Liberty. The sniper watches Anderson moving across the small room at the top of the ferry while he waits to be called into action. He's confident that he can't be seen, so he calculates wind speed, distance, and other factors that he'll need to make a kill shot.

But the officer isn't unnoticeable. When a sudden flash of sunlight on the rifle scope catches Anderson's eye, the former soldier instinctively knows what it is.

"Really?" he mutters angrily, grabbing the radio mic and crouching down below the windows. "Tell your snipers to stand down," he orders Jacob, "or someone else is definitely gonna die today, and it's not gonna be me. I'll give you one hour, no more."

Then Anderson lowers himself to the floor and hits the switch for onboard communications. With his voice booming over every deck, he declares loudly, "If any of you knows how to swim in frigid water, you can leave now — have at it, and good luck. But if all goes well, this will be over in an hour. Meanwhile, I need a crew member up here on the bridge. One of you has twenty seconds to get here, or another person dies."

While the *Miss Independence* bobs in the water, her one hundred seventy-three passengers huddle together on the lower deck. Some of them are crying, and some of them are praying, but all of them are scared. And not one of them wants to swim to shore.

Across the harbor, FBI electronics experts are installing

the cutoff switch in a seaplane moored at Sea Foam Tours in New Jersey. They're working as fast as possible but can't be sure they'll get it done in time.

When there are ten minutes left, Anderson tells the crewman who volunteered to return to the bridge to get a lifeboat ready. "Launch one on the starboard side, and then get your ass back up here!" he barks. "You got five minutes!" Then he picks up the radio mic. "Okay, assholes, only ten minutes left to get my ride out here."

"You guys gonna make it?" asks Stenhouse.

"Hell if I know," says Jacob, clicking on his FBI contact's number.

At Sea Foam Tours, three FBI technicians are making final adjustments to the switch they attached to the ignition of a Viking Air CHC-6 Twin Otter when their superior comes to check on them.

"How's it going?" asks the agent in charge.

"We're almost finished, then we'll refuel her."

"Good."

The agent's phone vibrates just then, and he fishes it out of his pocket.

"Uh-huh," he replies to Jacob's question. "They're working fast."

Then Jacob says something else, and he frowns. "Assante, you're taking a big chance here," he cautions. "If he doesn't get her back on the water safely, we're gonna hafta buy these guys a new seaplane."

He listens again, then says, "Um... I'll ask."

Turning to the technicians, he says, "The agent needs to know when you'll be done."

When they reply, he tells Jacob, "She'll be airborne in ten to fifteen minutes."

Assante ends the call and picks up the radio mic. "Anderson, your ride is being refueled and should be airborne in ten minutes."

"You better be right," says the familiar voice dripping with anger. "Or someone else is gonna die."

When Anderson signs off, Jack says, "I've been watching you, and I don't know how you can be so calm with that bastard. I would have had a sniper take him out long ago."

Jacob rubs his tired eyes. "I'm doing what I think is best for the passengers and crew."

"I know," says Jack. "I sure hope the plane gets here soon. And I *really* hope Anderson doesn't take a hostage. I know I would."

When Jacob winces, Jack instantly regrets his comment. "Sorry, buddy. Sometimes my mouth gets the better of me."

"No matter," responds Jacob tiredly. "But I've been trying not to think of that."

The weather has gotten warmer, so Jack unbuttons his pea coat as he and Jacob walk the deck, waiting for word that the plane is airborne.

While their ship bobs lazily, the radio comes back to life, and they hear Anderson shout, "Times up, you fuckers! Where the hell's my plane? Which one of these people should I kill?"

Alarmed, Jacob runs to the radio and grabs the mic. "Calm down!" he says urgently. "Oh, look! The plane is up!"

Sam is pleased to see a white seaplane growing larger in the sky, but he's still pissed at the entire situation. "I should kill someone anyway," he fumes. "You guys are a minute late."

When the Twin Otter nears the ferry, it descends to the water, and the pilot maneuvers it to the other side of the ship.

"Why the hell did he go where we can't see it?" shouts Jack. "Now we don't know what's going on!"

"Fuck if I know," sighs Jacob. "But the drones should be keeping an eye on everything."

When the plane is close to the ship, Anderson grabs the crewman who volunteered to return to the bridge. "You're coming with me," he orders, pushing him in front of him down to the lower deck.

When the passengers and remaining crew see the mysterious man with his gun at the seaman's back, they shout over each other to find out what's going on. "Who are you? What the hell do you want? When are we getting out of here?" they ask.

But Anderson won't have it. "Shut up!" he screams, waving his gun at them for emphasis. Then he grabs a young woman and pushes the crewman away.

"No!" cries the woman as a young man tries to pull her back.

"Get away!" yells Anderson. Then he swings his forty-five into the man's head.

When the man goes down, Anderson points his firearm at the crewman. "Sorry, I like this lady better than you," he says matter-of-factly. Then he discharges the weapon into the crewman's shoulder.

"Oooh! Owwwhh! You fucking bastard!" screams the man, hitting the deck with blood streaming from his wound.

"The plane was late, so someone has to be an example," says Anderson, somehow expecting that statement to be a reasonable defense of his action. "Better hope you get off this ship before you bleed out." Then he wraps his arm around the young woman's throat. "We're going to a lifeboat," he tells her. "The rest of you, stay here!"

After they climb into one of the rigid crafts, Sam hits a button to activate a motor that lowers them from the ferry. The cables holding it release at two feet above the surface, then the boat freefalls the rest of the way.

On the water, Anderson hands the woman an oar and points his gun at her. "Start rowing," he orders.

"Where... Where are we going?" she asks nervously.

"Shut up and do what I tell you!"

With Anderson off the ship, the seamen run to the bridge. "He left the ship!" one of them shouts into the radio to whoever is listening. "But he took a woman hostage! And we need a doctor! He pistol-whipped a passenger and shot a crewman! He's bleeding pretty badly!"

"Can you pilot the ship?" asks Jacob.

"Uh... Yeah, I think so," he replies, to affirmative nods from the other crew. "We'll do our best."

"Then get the hell out of there!" shouts Jacob. "Return to Battery Park; EMTs will meet you there!"

When the crewman signs off, Jacob calls in the EMT request, then he and Stenhouse watch anxiously as the ship moves away.

Soon, the lifeboat becomes visible.

"There they are!" shouts Jack.

"I see them! They're near the seaplane!"

The minute the lifeboat reaches the plane, Anderson ties it to a strut and orders the pilot out. Then he and the woman climb in, and Anderson begins to familiarize himself with the setup. Then he starts the engines and taxies across the water.

At takeoff velocity, the Twin Otter bounces a few times, then climbs as its pontoons throw clinging seawater to the wind.

"He's up!" shouts Assante into his phone. "Shut it down!"

At Sea Foam Tours, an agent hits the cutoff switch, and the plane's engines turn off.

"What the fuck!" yells Anderson, scanning dials while struggling to keep the craft in the air.

But the Twin Otter continues to descend, so he pulls hard on the yoke to keep the nose up.

"Oh, my God! What's happening?" shouts the woman.

"Engines are gone! Get ready for a water landing!"

A few seconds later, the seaplane hits the water with a massive thud, and as it struggles to stabilize itself, it continues to move forward. So Anderson uses the momentum to guide it to a ramp at a dock on the far side of Liberty Island.

As the cutter shuttling Assante and Stenhouse speeds toward the dock, Jacob updates everyone tuned to his radio frequency. "He has a hostage! Let us go in first!"

While fellow officers, choppers, and patrol boats converge on the island, Jack and Jacob scramble out of the cutter to confront Anderson, who is standing his ground fifty feet away from the dock.

"Stay the fuck back!" he screams, holding the hostage in front of him like a shield, with one arm tight around the woman's throat and the other pointing a gun at her head.

Jack aims his Glock. "Let her go, Sam!" he yells. "I'm not gonna let you hurt her! I have a straight line to your head, so if she dies, you die!"

Anderson was expecting this and isn't worried. "This isn't over!" he shouts. "The country's going down in flames, but no one seems to care!"

Then he tightens his hold on the woman and slowly backs away.

As Anderson retreats, Stenhouse curses inwardly. The woman's head is now blocking most of Sam's, making it harder for him to take the shot.

Jack shouts, "Let her go, asshole, or I'm gonna hafta blow your brains out!"

But Anderson merely grins and pulls back on the hammer of his 1911.

When Jack sees Anderson's thumb move, he knows the

hostage is in grave danger. So he inhales sharply and squeezes his trigger, instantly causing Anderson's head to jerk back and his arm to fall from the woman's throat.

When Anderson hits the ground, Jacob rushes to pull the young woman away.

"Nice shot!" he tells Jack when she's at a safe distance. "You took him down without killing him!"

But Jack isn't happy. "Nice shot, my ass," he scoffs, picking up Anderson's weapon. "I was aiming for his eye and missed. Must be getting old."

As law enforcement converges on the scene, FBI agents lead the woman to an ambulance, and EMTs examine Sam, leaving Jack and Jacob by themselves.

"Good job!" praise passing officers as they go about their duties.

While Jack and Jacob acknowledge the good wishes, Jack tiredly pinches the bridge of his nose. "Are you as exhausted as I am?" he asks Jacob.

"Yeah, but we still hafta fill out paperwork before we can go home."

"I know. But you wanna grab a beer before we hafta do that shit?"

"Sounds good," responds Jacob while looking down at his vibrating phone. "Crap. I'm gonna hafta answer this. I'll meet you on the boat."

Jack nods and heads for the cutter while saying, "Bet

that's your boss with congratulations!"

But a few yards away, he turns around when he hears Jacob gasp.

"What happened?" he asks, running back to see the agent's face turning pale and his eyes going wide.

"A bomb went off near the Washington Monument! At least twenty people are dead, and there are multiple injuries! Jack — it was the New Patriot Guard!"

CHAPTER TWENTY-NINE

A couple of months later, a beautiful spring evening finds Sharon babysitting while Jack and Didi enjoy a night out with Allison and Vincent Giancarlo and John Burley and Sylvia Stone.

As the couples walk down Mott Street, their conversation turns to John's and Sylvia's recent engagement.

"You're a lucky woman," says Didi. "Can I see your ring again?"

Sylvia stops and holds out her left hand, happy to comply.

"It's gorgeous," admires Allison. "What is it, two-carats?"

"Yes," smiles Sylvia. "He's so good to me," she declares, looking lovingly at John.

John smiles back while he shifts uncomfortably from one foot to the other. Unfortunately, his wounds from the shooting haven't fully healed yet, so he's still not in the best of shape.

"How're you doin', hon?" asks Sylvia, noting John's discomfort. "I knew it wasn't a good idea for you to walk all this way."

"I'll be okay," John replies, brushing off his fiancé's concern. "It's good to get out of the house, but I'll feel better when we get there."

"You're actually walking pretty well," comments Jack. "Are you still set against getting those fragments removed?"

"Yeah, it's too risky," John replies. "I'm gonna take it day-by-day for now."

Looking on, Didi urges the group forward. "Let's get to the restaurant so this guy can sit down," she says.

As their walk resumes, Jack turns to Allison with a friendly warning. "You should know that I'm gonna toast you and Hector tonight, so get ready to drink!"

"Who's gonna drink more…you or me?" she teases.

Jack laughs and says, "Everyone's happy that you're joining the terrorism unit, but I'm really gonna miss you in Homicide!"

"Oh, you'll see me around," Allison replies. "And of course, you still have Hector. Now that he made detective, you can take out your frustrations on him instead of me!"

Jack laughs again. "You know I will! I was hoping he could join us tonight; it's too bad he's on duty. You think he'll mind if we get drunk without him?"

Listening, the friends chuckle at the thought. Then Jack points at Burley. "Hey, John-boy, you know you're buying the first round, right? We're gonna start this evening off by toasting your fiancé! Poor thing! She doesn't know what she's getting into!"

The friends stop at the restaurant door, and Allison pulls her husband aside. "I'm getting second thoughts, Vin," she whispers in his ear. "I don't know if I can do this."

Vincent squeezes her hand supportively. "You'll do fine," he assures her. "You're not alone; all of us are with you. Maybe try to think of him as just your uncle."

Allison sighs, then bravely leads everyone into the establishment. Once she's inside, the chatter of Italian speakers mixed with the aromas of familiar cooking helps quiet her sense of foreboding.

"The place is almost full," remarks Jack. "I wonder if there's a table big enough for us.

Just then, a voice calls out, "Mia famiglia!" and Allison braces herself for an awkward situation.

But the man coming toward them shows nothing but happiness. "I am so glad you have come!" Vito Lucchese gushes, kissing Allison lightly on each cheek. "And you have brought your handsome husband! But where are your children?"

"Maybe next time," responds Allison, pulling away from Vito's embrace.

The mobster lets her go and says, "My dear, you know you are welcome here anytime. Provided you come as my niece, of course."

Looking around, Vito spots his son and beckons him over. "*Michele*, it is your *cugina*, Allison, and her husband and friends! Make them feel welcome!"

While Michael prepares a table, Vito wipes tears from his eyes. "I am so happy you are here," he says, patting Allison's arm. Then he leans close. "This one is on the house. But next time, you must pay, capeesh?"

Vito pats Allison's arm again, then turns to Jack. "Detective Stenhouse, it is also good to see you. You are also welcome here anytime, but you cannot come without your beautiful wife. Diedre, you make me feel young again!"

Didi grins at the compliment, then Vito turns his attention to John. "Sergeant Burley, I am pleased to see that you are recovering well. And who is this lovely woman on your arm?"

"Um, this is my fiancé. Sylvia."

"Your fiancé? Well, permit me to give your future bride my congratulations!"

Vito kisses Sylvia on both cheeks, then takes her and Didi by the hand. "Come with me," he says, leading the women away. "I recommend the eggplant parmigiana. It is *deliziosa*!"

Jack smiles at the older man's charm, but Burley is less than impressed. Every twinge reminds him of what he and others like him are capable of.

While Jack and his friends enjoy a delicious meal and great conversation in New York City, Speaker of the House Gerald Butler prepares for bed in an out-of-the-way hotel in Columbia, Maryland.

Due to the congressman's connections with Serge Kaspin and the New Patriot Guard, authorities sequestered him there while they wait for further action against him.

However, the powerful man isn't used to being treated this way. At least once a day, he complains to the federal marshal assigned to him, but his diatribes go in one ear and out the other.

This evening, the marshal is watching television when he hears a loud thump through the door connecting his room to Butler's. Gun in hand, he rushes into the next room to find Butler's head half blown away and the room splattered with blood, bone, and brains.

The marshal inspects the congressman's body while across the street, a man dressed in a black jumpsuit lays a weapon on a desk in a darkened office building, then makes a phone call. "One down, one to go," he intones. "Semper Fi."

In New York, Vito surprises everyone by pulling a chair up to their table. "Are you enjoying yourselves?" he asks, pleased to see empty liquor glasses at each plate.

But no one responds, so Didi speaks up. "We're having a wonderful time, Vito. Sorry we're still here; I know it's late. I hope it's okay with your staff."

"*Non è importante*," replies Vito, waving away her apology. "It is my pleasure."

Then Jack's cell phone rings, so he excuses himself to take it outside.

"This is Stenhouse," he says on the way to the door. Then he listens while Jacob imparts unwelcome news. "*Shit!*" he shouts and rushes the rest of the way out of the restaurant.

www.ingramcontent.com/pod-product-compliance
Lightning Source LLC
Chambersburg PA
CBHW021531250626
47154CB00006BA/2063